Because you're worth it

Banks Brothers Series: Book Two

Rebecca Braden

Because you're worth it

Banks Brothers Series, Book 2

Copyright © 2026 Rebecca Braden.

Content Warning

This Novel contains descriptions of assault, past attempted sexual assault, past domestic violence, and past childhood neglect and abuse.

Please read at your own discretion.

One

Briggs

When I step into the elevator, I hit the third-floor button. Birdie had my new niece last night, and I figured I'd better see the munchkin. The little one was an overachiever, arriving three weeks early. Harley is fucking ecstatic to have a sister. I'm just glad Beau is here now to raise them.

Not that I minded when Birdie needed us with Harley. She's one of my best friends, and I knew she'd end up being my sister-in-law one day.

I wander the halls until I make my way to room 308. I knock before cracking the door open. Peeking in, I see Beau's big ass holding the tiny human, a massive grin on his face. Birdie looks absolutely exhausted, lying in bed with tired eyes.

"Uncle Bigs. Look at my sister." Harley whispers, scrambles off the bed, and comes up to me. She grabs my hand and walks me to her dad. It breaks my heart that she's graduated to calling me 'uncle' instead of 'unkey'.

When I stand beside Beau, I look at the baby. Is it bad that I don't feel the urge to have my own kids one day when I look at her? I'd like to get married, but I don't want children. I decided that years ago. I prefer adoption… maybe. I've always thought there are already enough kids who could use good parents, so why create more?

"What did you name her?" I ask as I take her from my brother. My lip curves up as I look at her perfect, sleeping face. She is adorable.

"Blue Riley Banks," Birdie answers from the bed.

I can't help but chuckle at the name. She called her Blueberry while she was pregnant, so I guess half of the nickname stuck.

She looks just like Harley did when she was born.

"When are you going to settle down and have a few? You've always been good with kids," Birdie asks sleepily.

"Ah, you know me, sis. I'm in the 'thinking about the next stage' phase, but I'm sitting idle there for a bit."

"Good for you. Take time to consider what you want. I'm sure it'll come to you when the time's right. It usually does when you're not looking for it," Beau chimes in.

I know that's probably not how things work, but I really don't feel like debating it right now. When the baby pouts and starts crying, I hand her over to Beau, who finds it amusing.

Honestly, I'm just not in the mood today. I can't quite figure out what's bothering me. I'm feeling irritable, and everything is agitating me. All I want is a drink.

"Sorry, guys, I have to head out. I wanted to stop by and see her first," I tell them. I bend down, hug Harley, then step over and kiss Birdie's head. "You did well, sis. I'll come by and see her again once you guys get home."

"Okay. Thank you for coming," Birdie says, her eyes growing heavy as she yawns and closes her eyes.

"It took a lot out of her. I'll let you know once we're home," Beau whispers. I clap him on the shoulder and head back down to the parking lot.

Back in my car, I drive to the shitty bar across town that usually has only a few people. I still plan to have a drink, but not with anyone.

When I enter the musty, dim building, I count four older guys at the other end of the bar. I've been coming here lately, so I don't have to worry about running into anyone I know. The place is usually forgotten.

I take a seat and watch the guy behind the bar slide me a whisky on the rocks. Yeah, I've been visiting this place too much lately.

I stay pretty busy at the tattoo shop and doing murals for different businesses, but damn, it gets lonely sometimes. Guess that's why I was always chasing tail, but it got to be exhausting. I won't date the woman in this town. Hell, I went to school with half of them, and I know how stuck-up they can be.

All my friends are moving on in life. Birdie just had her second child, Astor is engaged to Noah, and Anna is focused on her bakery. Jamie has Tink. And me? I'm drinking alone on a Saturday before noon in a dingy bar, trying to drown my thoughts while everyone else seems to be moving on. Meanwhile, I'm still trying to piece my life together. I'm almost 30, and the tattoo shop is my only accomplishment.

"Is this seat taken?" I hear a raspy, feminine voice beside me. Glancing over, I see a tall woman wearing her hoodie over her head, concealing her face.

"Have at it," I tell her and sip my drink.

She takes the seat next to me, and the scent of sweet lilacs fills my senses as she moves. It's an arousing aroma.

"Whiskey and two shots of tequila." She tells the bartender.

I catch long, tanned fingers with a ring of some sort on each one in the corner of my eye. Damn it, I want to look at her, but I don't want to be that guy.

When the bartender brings her the drinks, she slides a shot over to me.

"You look like you could use it. Seems you might be overthinking something." I see her silhouette shrug. "Or underthinking. I like that I'm not the only one sitting here drinking on a Saturday."

She holds her glass and waits. Here's the opening I need to get a look at her. I turn my eyes to soak in her delicate features in the dim light: beautiful, full lips, a perfect, straight nose, and high cheekbones. The light reflects off her silken, shimmering, tanned face. There's blonde hair sticking out of her hood, but it doesn't look real. It's a bit too shiny, and it doesn't match the curved black eyebrows.

My gaze flicks to her blue, almond-shaped eyes, surrounded by thick black lashes. I see the ring that tells me she's wearing contacts.

Huh, wonder why she's wearing a disguise? She's hot, but I'd like to see her without the getup. I can tell this woman has a strong Native American heritage—another indication she's trying to hide her true looks with a wig and contacts.

"Did you get a good look, Hercules? Shouldn't your beautiful self be in Olympus?" Her raspy voice is the most alluring thing I've ever heard.

With a chuckle, I tilt my head and look at her again. "Shouldn't your gorgeous self be ruling the underworld, Persephone?"

"Oh, I like that one. To long days, gods, and magnificent people," she says, raising her shot glass.

We clink our glasses and toss them back. Sweet burn. I haven't had tequila in a while, and I'll stop at one. Tequila makes me feel invincible.

"I haven't seen you around here before," I tell her. Might as well make conversation with the hot goddess.

"Well, damn, look at you, Captain Obvious. Good thing you're pretty." When I glance at her, she raises a brow and smirks. "I'm just fucking with you, Playboy. I just got into town yesterday. Figured I'd come smash some down before I have to go back to sober city."

I can't help but laugh. It feels good to relax and converse with someone who isn't trying to get me into bed.

"Sober City, huh. Heavy drinker?" I ask, lifting a brow at her glass.

"No, I'm taking a vacation to forget about life for a day. Sober City is where I live. What about you, cowboy? You must come here a lot to say you haven't seen me here before." She says, and, well, she has a point.

I shake my head and introduce myself. "My name is Briggs. I only have one drink when I come. I'm not much for getting loaded anymore."

She nods in understanding. "Gotcha. So, what put you in such a somber mood, Eeyore?"

I watch as she takes a large drink without a hiss at the flavor. This chick isn't anything like what I'm used to. What should I say? Sure, I was feeling down earlier, but this woman just rode in on a white horse and lifted me.

"Let me guess," she says, studying me.

I watch her tap her perfectly manicured finger to her lips.

"Your body is too sexy, and your dick is too big. I get it, man. It's tough out there for guys like us," she says, grinning broadly. She winks at me and takes another drink.

I give her an amused look before I can't help the burst of laughter that escapes me. I haven't smiled this much in months. "You know, you keep mentioning my looks. I'm starting to think you're flirting with me."

"Eh, just trying to make you feel more secure about yourself, Dobby."

Holy shit, this woman is an anomaly compared to what I'm used to. Scrubbing my hands over my face, I try to wipe the smile off before I look at her again.

"You are something else. Aren't you? Do you have a name, sweetheart? I told you mine." I drawl.

I didn't miss that she skipped giving me her name, but I will find out who she is. Her eyes flicker when she hears the nickname. She likes it.

A smile finally breaks across her face. "You can call me Ny, and I'm giving you my best. You'd better make sure that frown stays upside down. I don't flirt with just anyone. Are you feeling better?" The look in her eyes makes me feel like she might actually care if I am.

Staring into her fake blue-filled irises, I feel my lips tilt up. "Yeah, I am. Thank you."

She bows her head, then sips her drink. We sit in silence for a few minutes before she turns on her stool to look at me.

"Would you be up for an adventure, Casanova?" she asks, looking back at me with a wicked grin.

"What did you have in mind?"

I'm intrigued. How do we go from drinking in a bar at 12 in the afternoon to an adventure?

"Mm. You'll have to trust me. When was the last time you let loose and said fuck it all?"

"Never. But I will today."

"Do you trust me?" Her eyes sparkle with excitement.

"Yeah, I do," I answer. It's weird because I'm not lying. I'm not sure what it is about her, but I would walk through hell with her if she asked me to.

"I'll make sure you have the time of your life. Do you work tomorrow? Any pets I should know about?" she asks, standing.

"Not until Tuesday, and no pets."

"Okay, I can follow you to drop off your car. Remember, you said you would trust me."

"I did say that." I chuckle. I hope she isn't planning to kill me.

After paying the bartender, we leave, and she follows me to drop off my car. Once I park mine at home, I get into her Bronco. My heart pounds against the ribbed prison bars. I don't know what she has planned, but it's exciting as hell not knowing where the day might go. Does the 'don't trust a stranger' rule apply at my age? Too late now.

Her hood is down now, but she's still wearing the blond wig and contacts. Her features are beautiful, even if I don't know her hair or eye color yet.

Forty minutes later, we're parking at the airport. Confusion swirls through me. Is there ever anything adventurous happening at an airport?

We both get out, and she takes my hand. "Come on, pretty boy, we only have 30 minutes to make it."

With my hand in hers, we rush through the airport. When we check in, Ny has me turn so I don't know what she's doing. Hurrying through security, she grabs my hand again, and we rush to a terminal just before it closes.

"Wait, we made it." She holds up two tickets and then hands them to the attendant when we come to a stop. Holy shit, we're actually fucking flying somewhere.

"Just in time. Ms…" The attendant begins, but Ny interrupts her before she can finish. "Ny. Thank you."

The attendant eyeballs her, then me, before nodding.

Upon boarding, the attendant directs us to the first-class section. Who is this woman? After we take our seats, she orders each of us a couple of whiskeys.

She lifts her glass, then looks at me. "To our adventure."

I chuckle, clinking her glass with mine.

As I take a sip, I look at her over the rim of my glass and ask, "Can I ask why the disguise?"

"If you keep trusting me, you'll find out. For now, enjoy the mystery," she says, lifting her drink and looking back at me.

My eyes study hers. I can't help but feel I would follow this woman off a fucking cliff if she asked me to. I've never been around anyone who makes me feel as comfortable as she does.

"Okay, mystery and adventure," I say, dropping the subject.

Happy with my response, she drinks the last of the whiskey and orders us another.

She turns to me and asks. "How does it feel so far?"

"What?"

"To be free. Even if just for today. How does it feel to only have to worry about what you're doing right now, with zero pressure?" She clarifies.

"Amazing. It's been a while since I've let loose and stopped thinking. How much do I owe you for the tickets?"

"Pfft. I am a gentleman. I know how to spoil a lady, Goldilocks," she says in a playful tone.

I bark out a laugh and shake my head. "Have you ever done this before? You know. Taken off and flown to a random place with a stranger?"

"Nope, this is my first time. I've always wanted to, but I couldn't find a willing victim until you. It's exhilarating, isn't it?" she says eagerly, bouncing in her seat.

"It is,"

It's official. I may have lost my mind and fallen in love with a stranger at the same time. The sad part is no one will even know I'm out of state.

Four hours later, we're both buzzing and feeling the vibes when we deplane in fucking Vegas. We're in Vegas. Being here has been on my bucket list since I turned 21. She flew us to the party capital.

Ny gets us a ride and keeps typing on her phone while making more jokes. My jaw hits the ground when we pull up to what I can only assume is a hotel I could never afford. She retakes my hand and leads me in.

Fuck, maybe she is Persephone.

My skin is buzzing from the whiskey, and my heart is racing from her touching me. She might be the Queen of swoon-worthy dates. Wait. Is this a date? Fucking better be if I'm in another state with her.

"Ny, it's good to see you. I have the penthouse suite ready for you, and I also put your other items in there. Jared and Sam will be here at six-thirty to escort you and your guest through town." The concierge says as we approach the counter.

"Thanks, Miles." I choke when I see her hand him a black card to pay. Shit, she's loaded. They don't give those to regular people. Miles hands her a few things, then she waves and leads me to the elevator.

Between the disguise and this fancy-ass hotel, I can only assume the guys he mentioned are bodyguards, and I'm freaking out a little. I don't want to get knocked off for running off with a mob princess.

Inside the small box, she taps her phone to the pad, and the doors close. I have a hella buzz and feel pretty brazen right now.

I step up behind her, gently grabbing and squeezing her hip. When I inhale her lilac scent, it hits me, making my knees weak. Her body responds to me as if it knows mine.

I lean in and whisper into her ear. "Who are you, Sunrise?"

Still feeling the alcohol's influence, I brush my lips against her neck just under her ear.

She arches into me for a moment. "Soon. You said you'd trust me." She scoots back, pressing her round ass into me. I stifle my groan and tighten my hold on her hip. "Last promise. Once you find out, nothing changes. We still enjoy ourselves as we are. We're two strangers letting go and living in the now. Deal?" she says breathlessly, her hips moving as if they have a mind of their own.

"Mm, I guess I can wait a little longer. Deal." Taking a small step back, I leave my hand on her hip.

When we exit the elevator, I look around at the ample open space. The sleek black furniture and glass tables with fancy-ass lamps. The double doors to the bedroom and an eye-bulging balcony overlooking the casinos, with a hot tub and a pool.

I died. That's the only explanation for what happened. I'm dead. Glancing around, I see a rack with men's and women's clothes on it.

"Pick something nice, princess. We have dinner and cocktails first." Looking at her, I see her smirk and grab a dress. Yup, dead. This is my afterlife—Sin City with a hot chick.

Glancing at the options, I check the size and am surprised to find she has the right one. After grabbing an all-black suit, I head to the other room to change.

Two

Journey

I take a final look in the mirror before leaving. My makeup highlights a smoky eye and bold red lips. Miles always knows what I need. The blonde hair and blue eyes are gone. My waist-length black hair and amber eyes are in their place. The hoodie and baggy pants now lie on the floor, replaced by a high-thigh, black, deep-V-neck dress that showcases my slender body. I slip on the strappy heels and roll my neck. Good thing Briggs is tall; these heels will put me at 6'3".

The God in the next room will know who I am as soon as I step out. I hope he doesn't change his behavior once he knows it's me. I am the daughter of the King and Queen of Elite Fighting Champion, a multi-billion-dollar industry, and everyone knows it.

But I'm more than that. I'm a supermodel and designer, and maybe a bit of an actress. I've been in a few movies over the past nine years. I wanted to do it all, but I've found that design is what I'm most passionate about.

Five years ago, I launched my own brand, and it's been fucking great so far. I'm currently working to expand my collection. Yup, I'm a busy bitch. I do it to prove I don't need my parents' money and can work hard to earn my own. I keep doing more to prove I'm better than I used to be.

A year ago, I went through a breakup with EFC former champion Van Wallen. He's a bad guy who used psychological and physical warfare against me. I finally had enough and broke it off. We dated for eight months, and sex was never part of it. He knew I wanted to wait for marriage, and he preferred to fuck with my head. I later found out he was banging anyone willing. Van tried to destroy me so he could control me. I'm pretty sure he only wanted me for my money.

Thankfully, I snapped out of it and got away. I'd rather chew off my own arms than be near him again. He's made public statements and has had people follow me since the breakup. Thank you, childhood trauma, for making me mentally vulnerable in the first place.

I've been working on my confidence around men. So I took a spontaneous day trip across the US with a stranger for a night on the town. YOLO. Briggs is a stud and seems like a sweet guy. I've never swooned over a man, but buckle up, buttercups, because I'm about to.

When I open the door, I step out and drool over the manly, mouth-watering God.

Briggs stands there in fitted black slacks and a black dress shirt, the top two buttons undone, his tattoos visible on his neck and chest, his hand in his pocket. His shoulder-length blond hair is down and flipped to the side.

Holy hotness.

Good gods, I think my panties just evaporated. The shirt hugs his rippled stomach, and his thick, inked arms bulge beneath the

12

sleeves. Oh, he is all man, and I want him. I'm pretty sure he has an invincible Super Soaker because I'm drenched right now.

Features? He has all the manly features. His firm, chiseled jaw and boxer nose tell me he's been in a few scuffles. He looks like a bad boy but has a soft-hearted vibe.

Then, oh, I meet his blue-green gaze, which reminds me of the Caribbean, and I'm a goner. His wide lips and breathtaking smile almost stop my heart. And his voice. Girl, don't get me started. He has a voice made for erotic audiobooks.

"Damn, GQ. You look like you're ready to take a trip to hell with me. I knew you were going to be pretty, all dressed up." I say, then wait for him to notice who I am.

When his gaze meets mine, I feel something deep in my soul that sucks the air from my lungs and makes my heart skip. I watch his heated gaze drink me in, and I know he's hooked when I see him bite his bottom lip.

Not taking his eyes off me, a broad smile crosses his face, and he chuckles lightly. "Holy shit. I'm in Vegas with Journey Preston. Now I'm completely convinced I died. You're even more gorgeous than in the pictures and movies."

I giggle, walk up to him, and tuck his hair behind his ear. "Surprised?" Damn, he's still taller than me in my heels.

Love that.

"Hell, yeah. I started to think you were a mob boss's daughter or something. Not that I would mind. But I like my hands and dick attached to me." He says with a beautiful twinkle in his eye.

I burst out laughing at his confession. "Come on, stud. Let me be your guide through the underworld."

He laughs as I loop my arm through his, and we head to the elevator. As we ride down to the lobby, he stands behind me and rests a hand on my hip. The intoxicating scent of mahogany and teakwood has overwhelmed my senses. I am all too aware of this man. I can't help but tilt my lips. Briggs isn't letting this weird him out, which is exactly what I wanted.

I'm looking for a night out with a nice man who isn't interested in my status or what I can do for him. As we step out of the elevator, I see Jared and Sam waiting for us. They're the bodyguards I've used every time I'm here.

"It's good to see you, Ny. Costello's first?"

"Yes, thank you, Jared." I thank him and take Briggs' hand.

He walks with me to the large sedan, and like a gentleman, Briggs blocks my view when I get into the vehicle.

The drive from the hotel is quick. Hercules exits the car first and takes my hand to help me out. It feels good to be with a man who's a good guy. I've never had this before. The media thinks my ex is, but he's a monster.

I keep my slim hand in his large mitt, and we walk into the restaurant. I have to admit, we look hella good together. Briggs looks like a fucking model, too. Huh, I don't even know what he does for work.

As we enter the elegant restaurant, people pause and stare for a moment. The young hostess smiles brightly as she approaches.

"Ms. Preston. We have your table ready. Right this way."

Briggs keeps his hand on mine as we follow the hostess. I should be more concerned about being out in public with him, but today is our day to be free.

I look around the familiar room. The chandeliers emit a gentle light, filling the space with a warm glow. The tables are spaced generously apart, offering more privacy. In the corner, a small dance floor sits beside a piano.

At the table, he pulls out my seat and scoots my chair in when I sit. Damn, he's smooth. Are all small-town men like this? I should have picked one up sooner. Nah, I got the one I want now.

The server takes our drink order while Briggs looks over the menu. I get the same thing every time I've been here, so I don't bother looking.

"I'll be honest, I've never been to a place this nice." He tells me.

"Don't worry, baby. I like to spoil my arm candy. I shall lavish you with nice dinners and shiny gifts." I joke.

"Wow, laying it on thick, aren't ya?" Briggs says with amusement.

"Hey, I'm making sure someone's panties are dropping tonight. They might be yours; they might be mine, or they might be Cupcake the strippers. Either way, it'll happen." I say, wiggling my brows.

Unable to control himself, he laughs, then covers his mouth. "You are unlike anyone I've ever met. It may be my panties if you keep it up."

"Challenge accepted. Drink up. Loaded is part of this adventure." I say, giving him a mischievous grin.

He lifts his glass and finishes its contents in one gulp. After placing our food and drink orders, we continue flirting, going back and forth. I have a strong feeling my panties will be the first to drop.

When the server brings out our plates, we eat in silence. Once we've finished, I tilt my chin up and look at him.

"What did you think?"

"It was better than I expected."

"Are you ready for the next stop?" I swallow the last of my drink and stand.

"Don't we need the check?"

Giggling, I take his hand, and he stands. "No. They already billed me, and the tip is always included."

He releases my hand, then places his on the small of my back and leans in. "I can pay."

I turn into him when we stop and run my finger under his collar. My burning gaze meets his Caribbean irises. "So, can I. Have you ever had a woman take you out before?"

"No."

"Look at that. I'm taking another one of your firsts." I lean in and kiss his cheek. Twisting in his arm, we exit the building and get into the car.

"Echo," I tell Jerad.

I nod, and Jerad drives us across town to the exclusive nightclub. I'm sure Briggs has never been to one. As we pull up to the black building, Briggs gives me a questioning look. Guess it does look like I'm taking him to an underworld party.

Sam and Jerad walk past the line and approach the doorman, staying with us this time.

"You're good to go in, Ny," he tells us.

As soon as you step inside, the space is dimly lit, with spotlights highlighting the semi-naked women swinging from the ceiling. There are podiums with half-naked men and women dancing on them. The room is filled with black tables, chairs, and leather couches. The female bartenders and servers are dressed in lingerie from my brand, while the men wear tight boxer briefs. Yeah, it's a sexy fucking club.

Briggs tightens his grip on my hand as we make our way to the VIP section. The next bouncer nods at me and unclips the rope.

When the waitress comes to our section, I order tequila shots and whiskey. Man, I feel like I'm in one of those billionaire-boss romance novels. I'm slaying the shit out of this day, winning and dining with the handsome man next to me. Can you say boss-bitch goals?

"Is this your first time at a nightclub?" I ask him.

When the server returns, we both take two shots. I can feel my skin tingling as the buzz takes over. Briggs scoots to the side and leans in close. I can smell the sweet scent of whiskey on his breath.

"It is. How about we finish our drinks and dance, Sunrise?" he whispers, tucking my hair behind my ear.

I inch closer to him, and our breaths mingle with liquor. "I'd like that."

We lock eyes and take the drink in one swift swig.

He takes my hand and guides us onto the dance floor. I feel the bass thrumming under our feet. The buzz I had has moved into the next stage of drunkenness. The lights seem dimmer, but I can still make out his strong features and muscular body. Turning so my back is to his chest, I press my body against his and start swaying my hips.

Briggs moves in rhythm with me. His large hands roam my stomach and the tops of my thighs as we sway together. He moves his hand to my collarbone and the base of my throat, and his arm rests between my breasts. My lips part at the sensual touch. Is this what it's like to be touched by a real man? Holy wet panties.

When I face him, I feel his knee slip between my legs, and my hips spin as I grind against his thigh. I sense he's aware of my heat. Groaning, he cups my ass with one hand, pulling me closer, while his other hand presses between my shoulder blades. I wrap my arms around his strong neck, and we move together seamlessly. It feels as if our bodies were meant to be one.

I'm not sure how long we dance before someone bumps into Briggs, interrupting the moment. Laughing, I grab his hand and lead him back to the table.

Three shots later, we're both dancing and laughing at our table.

"Let's go get tacos," I yell over the thrumming music.

Briggs throws both arms in the air and yells, "Tacos." Lifting me, he slings me over his shoulder and carries me out, his hand over my ass to cover it. I chortle and giggle the entire way out.

As I wobble toward the taco truck, I notice the fountain I've always dreamed of running through.

"Fountain," I yell. Kicking off my heels, I take off running. Jerad stops me before I can jump into it.

"You'll get arrested."

"Damn. Good thinking, Velma."

Laughing, he passes me off to Briggs. Spotting another bar, we go in and take more shots. Stopping at the food truck, we get our food.

My body thrums as we walk the strip, eating and laughing. My bodyguards do a great job of keeping people at a distance.

"Why are tacos so good when you're drunk?"

"I don't know, but they fucking are," Briggs says, shoving half a taco in his mouth.

Finished with our food, we stopped at another place to refuel our drunken high. The night starts to blur as we walk and drive. I can't remember what we're doing or why we're signing shit.

Back on the strip, we stop at shop after shop that are still open—riding out the complete drunken haze. I take him into the casino, where we play a few games, and Briggs wins money. I don't know how much, but he wins. Oh, maybe that's what we were signing. Silver sparkles dance across my eyes. Words are mumbled and slurred—lights speed and flash by in fast-forward.

We stumble into the hotel, laughing and dancing as we head to the elevator. Then the doors open on our floor, and blurred lights greet us. Unable to keep my balance, Briggs helps me to the bed, where we both pass out from our drunken adventure.

Three

Briggs

My eyes peel open halfway, and my head pounds from the inevitable hangover I knew I'd have today. I haven't drunk that much in years, but fuck, was it fun. Journey knows how to show someone a good time.

The end of the night is a bit hazy, though. Guess I need to face the music. I open my eyes all the way, lift my head, and see Journey's clothes-covered body draped over mine. Pew, safe. We were both too drunk to make that decision.

Then the screeching sound of a phone pierces my ears, making my head pulse. Groaning, I start searching for my phone. When I pull it out, I see a ton of messages, but the ringing isn't mine.

"Sunrise. Your phone's ringing." I wake her.

"Oh, god, why?" She groans, rolls off me, grunting, reaches over, and grabs it. "Hello," she says in a sleepy voice.

"Journey Leann Preston. Turn the fucking TV onto CGT." A woman's sharp tone says on the other end of the line.

"Why, Mom? Can't it wait until later?" Ny murmurs.

"No, honey, it can't. Turn it on now."

With a groan, Journey grabs the remote and turns on the TV in the room. She flips through channels until she lands on the station.

"This just in. Journey Preston spent the night out in Vegas and has tied the knot with a mystery man." Both of us shoot up like rockets and focus on the TV. "Journey was spotted entering the Horror Chapel at 4 am with her boyfriend, only to come out 20 minutes later with rings on their fingers and smiles on their faces. Photographer Addie Johnson captured this photo before the newlyweds were escorted back to their vehicle. I think it's safe to say she's well over Van Wallen."

I'm not breathing. My lungs no longer work. The picture shows us kissing. Ny is holding my face with a big-ass diamond ring and a wedding band on her finger. My eyes flick to my hand. When I see the silver ring, my chest tightens as panic seeps in. Fuck me, this is why you don't go to Vegas with a hot-as-hell woman with an adventurous side. I watch in shock as the pictures keep coming. Someone documented half our night together.

"Oh god. Oh god. It's not real. Those things aren't real." She tells her mom and stands up. Ny crouches on the floor and digs through her purse, pulling out shit. She puts her mom on speakerphone while uncrumpling papers. "Mom. Those chapels are fake, right?"

"No. And you two drunken idiots were spotted leaving the clerk's office. You're married, Journey."

"No. No. No. I'm sorry. I'm so sorry. I didn't mean to. Mom, I'm sorry." Her eyes meet mine, tears welling in hers. "Briggs, I can fix it. We can get an annulment. I fucked up."

Shit, she's about to have a full-on panic attack. I quickly get to my feet, kneel in front of her, take her into my arms, and hug her, hoping to stop the attack. "Relax," I whisper into her hair, kissing her shoulder. I rub a circle on her back to help calm her.

Ny's thin arms come around my waist as she inhales and calms. We can't stress it right now. She's right. We can undo this. Shit, I married a fucking lingerie model, designer, and actress. She has her own lingerie line and has appeared in multiple movies. Now that my panic has passed, I feel a little smug. Suck on that, Van Wallen. I know her ex has made her life hell in the media.

"Ny, I'm going to let you two talk. Come straight to the house when you get home. Both of you. I love you, honeycomb."

"I love you, Mom. Tell Dad I'm sorry," Ny tells her mother.

"I will. I'll see you soon."

When the line goes silent, Journey looks at me with tears in her eyes. "I don't know what to say. I'll fix it."

My fingers run through her hair to reassure her. "Hey, it's okay. Who wouldn't want Journey Preston as their wife?" I tell her. Ny giggles, but her voice breaks into a small sob.

"Whatever happens, I'm okay with it. Are you okay?" I ask her.

"Yeah, I think the wowing went too far, and I don't think either of us dropped our panties." We both chuckle and try to make the best of it. "Everything is hazy. I'm trying to remember how we even ended up doing it."

"Check our phones for pictures and videos. When I'm drunk, I take a lot of pictures," I tell her, digging my phone out. After swiping away all the messages and ending my mom's call, I pull up my photos. As I look through them, I realize we had a hell of a night together.

I chuckle when I land on one where Journey jumps into a fountain. Then another shows her running from the chubby cop, with an animated look on her face.

"What?" Glancing at my phone, she laughs when I show her the photo. "Hell yeah. I did it anyway."

Journey sits next to me, and we both forget our hangovers as we look through the pictures.

"How much did we eat? It's no wonder we could keep drinking."

"Oop, I'm holding you while you throw up in this one, and there you are, holding your arms up afterward, like a champion."

"We had a good time, didn't we?" Sighing, she rests her head on my shoulder.

"Are you kidding? Last night was the best night of my life. I'd do it all again with you."

Ny thumbs through her phone as we look at the images she took. My heart skips a beat when I see the picture of me standing behind her, her ring finger out, looking back at me. My hand is on her chest, showing off my band, and I'm looking at her. The picture is beautiful. I want this picture.

"Can you send that one to me?" I ask her.

"Yeah," she giggles, looking at me. "What's your number?"

We both laugh as I rattle off the number. A minute later, I have the picture.

Back on my phone, the last thing on it is a video. I'm not sure who recorded it, but I'm glad they did.

I'm on one knee, her hand in mine. "Ny. You have given me the best night of firsts. I want to steal your heart now. Even if we wake up tomorrow and ask, 'What the fuck,' I will still want to be your husband. I can't wait to see what other adventures you can come up with. Let this be one of them. Will you marry me, Journey?" I slur a little in the video.

"You know this is crazy, right?" She wobbles, laughs, and cups my cheeks.

"I know," I slur.

"Alright, Dream Machine. Fuck it. Let's get hitched. I always wanted to marry a God. No backsies." Her words come out slightly slurred.

I cross my heart, then stand and pull her into my arms. "She said yes," I yell to the crowd, and they clap as the video ends.

"Well, guess now we know how it happened." I lean against the wall and huff.

Ny scoots closer to me and rests her head on my arm. "Yeah, guess we'd better get ready to face everyone. Or we could take some Tylenol and go swimming."

"I like that idea. They can wait until we're ready."

With a light laugh, she gets to her feet and holds out her hand. I take it, then rise and pull her into a hug. The scent of sweet lilacs fills my nose as I breathe in. I know I should be weirded out, but her body feels meant for mine. I'm not a rash kind of guy, even when I'm drunk. If we get an annulment, I still want to date this woman.

With her hand in mine, we enter the kitchen, take the medication, and change into swimsuits. When she walks out of the room, my body warms, and a spark flickers in me when I see her perfectly toned stomach. My eyes keep roaming, landing on her hip bones and the gap between her thighs. Her tanned skin and black hair do something to me. She is definitely Native American. Journey resembles a live-action Disney adaptation of Pocahontas. Christ, she's fucking sexy.

I'm mesmerized as I stare at her face. She's the most beautiful woman I've ever met. For now, I can say she's my wife.

As I follow her outside, I watch her round ass. She dips a foot into the water and inhales with contentment.

"I love heated pools. I don't have to worry about freezing my tiny tits off."

I shake my head with a smile and jump in close to where she's standing, splashing water on her. The water is the perfect temperature.

Ny doesn't waste any time, jumping on top of me. I hold her and bring us both to the surface. She turns in my arms, dunks me, and tries to swim off. Grabbing her foot, I pull her under with me.

Once we're done goofing off, we lie back on the pool stairs. The Vegas sun is beating down on us, but it feels amazing.

"What's your job?" she asks, and I realize we know nothing about each other.

"I'm a tattoo artist."

"Damn, I didn't think you could get hotter," she says in that sexy-as-sin voice. She fans herself dramatically, then winks at me. "Do you date much? How old are you?"

"I'm 28 and no. When I was younger, I thought I was a Playboy. As I've grown older, I've come to realize I want something more." It's an honest answer.

"This is where it sucks for me. You probably already know, but I'll tell you anyway. I'm 26, and it's been a little over a year since I've dated."

"Same."

"Really? But you're like the whole package. You're stunning, you have a good career, and you know how to treat a woman. That's the best quality a man could have for me," she says, tipping her head skyward and closing her eyes.

I can tell this woman has been hurt many times, not just as an adult. The way she apologized to her mom spoke volumes to me. There's undeniable trauma she tries to hide.

"Guess we'd better start getting ready."

I let out a sigh because I'm not ready for this to end yet. "Yeah. I had an amazing time, sunrise."

Her gaze softens when she meets mine. "I did too, Hercules. Can I ask why you call me that? I like it. I'm just curious."

"Because you were the rising sun when I was headed to a dark place. You renewed my mind and made it bright again. You're full of contagious optimism and energy. It felt fitting."

"That's inspiring. You're a beautiful person, Briggs. Inside and out." She smiles at me.

"So are you, Ny." Her sparkling eyes meet mine briefly before she gets out of the water. I want to kiss this woman. I hate that I did last night and can't remember it.

Inside, I grab my clothes from the day before. In the bathroom, I swipe through all the messages, asking all the questions, and then I see a few bank notifications.

When I open the app, I almost have a fucking heart attack seeing 1.5M in my bank account. Scrolling through, I see a casino deposit of 1.65, then a purchase of 150k at a diamond place.

I really am dead. I died. Quickly changing my clothes, I rush out of the bathroom and see Journey with two disposable cups.

"I got you coffee, but I don't know how you like it." Glancing at her hand, I exhale when I see she's still wearing the rings. The very expensive rings. But is that what I'm worried about?

"Do you remember us going to the casinos?"

"Oh, yeah. You won. How much was it? I don't remember."

I look around and see a stack of papers on the coffee table. Picking them up, I flip through them. There are copies of our marriage license and the jackpot paperwork.

"2.2 million was the jackpot. After taxes, they wired 1.65 million to my account." I barely whisper. Is there a word for what I'm feeling right now? I'm sure there is, but I can't think of it right now. Then my brain rejoins me and starts naming shit. Shocked. Stunned. Flabbergasted. Surprised.

"That's great, Briggs. I guess I didn't completely fuck up bringing you here. You won. You should have come here sooner, you lucky bastard. Don't worry, I won't take any of it in the divorce," she jokes. Hearing the word divorce leaves a sour taste in my stomach. I don't like that.

I've never been this lucky in my life. My life is good, but last night I won millions and married the hottest woman on the planet.

I look at her, the sunlight catching the massive rock on her finger and sparking in my eye. I have to. I have to do it.

In two strides, I pull her into my arms and bring my lips to hers. Ny has the softest mouth I've ever kissed. She parts her plush lips and kisses me back. Our mouths open for each other, and our tongues meet. My taste buds explode with the sweet flavor of her, making me groan. I've never experienced anything like this from kissing a woman.

Her warm mouth tastes like berries and sin. Our tongues explore each other in slow, soft movements. Sparks ignite through my body. Cupping her neck, I pull her closer. Journey moans and arches into me, still holding both drinks. My heart pounds uncontrollably against my chest as our tongues explore. I'm already addicted to the feeling of her against me.

Our lips part, and I kiss her once more before pressing my brow to hers. Our breaths mingle as we ride the high of what was the best kiss I've ever fucking had.

"Damn," I murmur.

"Yeah, damn. I've never felt sparks from a kiss before," she whispers, then licks her lips.

"Me neither."

I swear, when our gazes lock, her eyes swirl with gold. She is a goddess. I reach around her slim waist and circle her lower back. She can't be real. This can't be real.

"Are you ready to go, princeling?" she asks, still breathless from the heated moment.

Letting out a half laugh, I step away and grab all the papers.

"I'm ready, sweetheart."

"You can put the papers in my pack," she says, twisting slightly and gesturing to her backpack. After I slip the papers into it, I take one of the coffees. "And I like all the sweet names. They're cute and endearing."

"Noted. I'll be sure to keep using them."

"Yeah, you planning on sticking around, Hercules?"

"I'm still convinced I'm dead, and now you're stuck here with me."

Inside the elevator, we make our way down to the car waiting for us. "Eh, it's not so bad here. I have one condition, though."

"And what is the condition?"

"We have to haunt people. I mean, I want to scare the shit out of some folks."

"Deal. Anything else?" I asked as we got into the car.

"Nah, you're pretty good company. Guess I don't need to haunt people." She thinks for a moment, then shakes her head. "That's a lie. I need to do it."

Chuckling, I listen as she goes on about who she wants to start with and why. I can't believe how drastically my life has changed in the past 24 hours. Yesterday, I was pondering my life and starting to think I was never going anywhere. Now I'm married to a model.

"My parents live in Nashville. It's an hour and a half from the airport. You don't have to go. I can handle it," Journey says as we walk to the terminal.

"I want to."

After boarding the plane, we start our four-hour flight. Journey tucks her legs up in the chair beside me. I reach over and wrap my arm around her knees. She must be comfortable with me because she loops her arm through mine and hugs it as she rests her head on my shoulder.

Four

Journey

"Do you want to stop at your place first?" I ask Briggs as we get into my Bronco.

"No. I'm pretty sure my mother is camped out there right now," Briggs says as we get into the car.

I knit my brows and look at him. "You haven't called her?"

"Not yet, but I will. Honestly, after I checked my account, I forgot to. Then we had the flight."

That makes sense. I would have short-circuited, too. I remember hitting my first million in sales, a milestone that showed my growth and resilience, which I value deeply.

I text my mom to let her know we're on our way, then put the car in drive and head toward my parents. Most people know that my brother and I are adopted. I shouldn't have to explain that when he meets my family. I have tanned skin and black hair, and my brother has fair skin, freckles, and fiery red hair.

"I have two dogs I have to bring back with us today. They're big, sweet, and protective. I wanted to warn you in case you don't like them," I tell him as I merge onto the highway.

"I do. Thank you for the heads-up. What are their names?"

"Charm and Ebony. Charm is black with a small white spot on her chest, and Ebony is all black. They're Caine Corso's."

"Cute. Are your parents chill, or are we looking at a nuclear explosion when we show up?"

Laughing, I shake my head. "They're amazing and usually soft. Don't get me wrong, they're stern when they need to be, but I try to make sure they don't have to be. I don't like upsetting people I care about. I know it happens, but I don't like it. What about yours?" I ask, then get off at my exit.

"Usually, they're chill, but I'm the first one to run off and marry a stranger. My brother and his wife got married without telling anyone. If anything, my mom's going to be more pissed that she hasn't been able to help plan a wedding than she will be about the actual married part." He chuckles.

"Well, there's always the next time." I try to hold my fake smile. I always planned to save myself and get married only once, and I managed to fuck up half of that in one night.

"Eh," Briggs shrugs.

I glance at him, and he gives me a subtle sideways grin. I'm not going to approach that one. Turning left, I head to the gate shelter and come to a stop. The guard waves and opens the iron gates for me. Briggs leans forward and watches the mansion come into view.

He whistles when we pull into the roundabout with a fountain in the center, and his jaw slackens. After I park, I turn to look at him.

"Everything will be okay," I tell myself more than him.

"I agree. Come on, I have some parents to wow with my godliness," he says with a bright smile.

I open the door with a laugh and step out of the vehicle. As soon as I'm beside Briggs, my short, curvy mom rushes out the door. She's so cute, with her brown skin and eyes, wearing a bright floral shirt and white pants. I always loved her braided hair. When I was younger, she would do mine to match hers. My tall, muscular dad steps out behind her, smiling. He has a peachy skin tone and brown hair, with green eyes—dressed in his usual slacks and button-down. I love my mixed family.

"Well, I'll be damned. Sully, she married a god," my mom says to my dad, then embraces me and moves toward Briggs. "You're a big guy. I'm Audrey, and that's Sul. Well, hug your mother-in-law." On tiptoes, she wraps her arms around him. Chuckling, he hugs her back ever so lightly.

"He's no god. A prick is what he is." Glancing up, I see my brother step beside my dad. I watch confusion cross Briggs' face. Hell, I'm confused, too. Jamie is usually nicer.

"Jamie? The hell are you doing here?" Briggs asks after my mom, who's still hugging him and, borderline, feeling him up, finally lets him go.

"That's my sister, asshole. I hope you enjoy being married. There's no divorcing her," Jamie says, narrowing his eyes at Briggs.

"Uh, how is she your sister?" Briggs asks.

"We're adopted, idiot," Jamie says, shaking his head.

"Jamie, leave the boy alone. I take it this is your friend and business partner, Briggs, you've told us about?" Dad asks, then takes me into his arms for a gentle hug. He's always been careful with me. "How are you doing, babycake?" he whispers to me.

"I'm okay, Dad. I'm sorry," I say.

Dad draws back and takes my face in his hands. "There's nothing to be sorry for. We raised you both to be free spirits. Mom went and got everything we needed to make pizza together. We'll do that and talk."

"Dad, they got drunk and had a Vegas wedding. I'm allowed to give him shit. I thought we were best friends, man." Jamie walks up to Briggs, gives him a bro hug, then punches his arm, making him grunt. "That's also why I never told you about her." He laughs.

"Yup, I get it," Briggs says, rubbing his neck.

"Yeah, yeah. We all know the story. Well, some of it." Dad says, guiding us into the house.

Briggs steps next to me and whispers. "Did he say we're making pizzas?"

Giggling, I glance at his warm eyes. "Yeah. Anytime one of us needs to talk, we pick a meal we can all make together and talk through what we need while cooking. Mom says it helps us bond and listen to each other's feelings better."

"I like that."

When we step into the large foyer with stairs on both sides, my big-ass dogs come barreling toward me, waggling their butts. Charm likes to smile, so her teeth are on full display. I kneel and pet them both—Briggs squats and pets Ebony, who is trying to jump all over him. I watch in awe as the encounter unfolds. I got them to feel safer, and they're both pretty good judges of character.

"She likes you. She doesn't usually jump." Once Charm notices, she trots over and starts licking him. Damn.

"They're beautiful." He says, helping me to my feet.

"Thanks. They're my babies."

The four of us walk into the extra-large kitchen, where Mom has everything out. I wonder where Jamie's girlfriend, Tink, is tonight.

"Tiny, did you at least take the pretty boy to the taco truck?" Jamie asks.

"I did, along with what seems like every other food truck we could find. I'm going to have to spend extra time in the gym this week." I laugh.

"Why do you call her Tiny?" Briggs asks with genuine curiosity.

"Ny was a little thing as a kid. She shot up at 14, but I've always called her that." Jamie shrugs.

"Alright, everyone, come on. I have the dough separated," Mom says, getting our attention.

When we start, I watch Briggs try and fail to spread the dough on his pan. Smiling, I step next to him. "Like this." Taking his hands, I show him how to work it out. "There you go. You got it, Hercules." We both chuckle at his nickname, which seems to be sticking.

"Since we're all here, can I ask what prompted this? I'm not upset, honey. Only curious." Mom starts.

"Um, getting married wasn't part of the plan. I wanted a night where I could feel free. I met Briggs at a bar in Cedar Creek, and he looked like he needed the same thing." My cheeks start to flush and burn. "I don't know… when he agreed to say fuck it all with me," I shrug, but I don't look up at anyone. "It was a feeling. That's all I know. We ended up having too much fun and drinking too much." Sighing, I grab the ladle and swirl the sauce onto the dough.

"Ok, what else?" Dad asks now.

"He didn't know it was me at the bar. I had a wig on, contacts in, and was wearing baggy clothes. I was just a normal person, trying to get someone to go on an adventure with me. He said yes when I asked. Not because of who I was or what I could do for him, but because he wanted to."

"She's right. I needed it. I had just left my brother and sister-in-law at the hospital. Then my brain spiraled." Briggs reaches over and palms the small of my back. It's the simplest gesture, but it instantly calms me. "Sunrise helped me forget the depressing 'what am I doing with my life' feeling."

"Damn it. That's sweet. He called her Sunrise. Have you two figured out what the plan is now?" Mom asks, adding toppings to her pizza. "I'm asking because it's not going to look good that you got drunk and married a stranger, then dissolved the marriage a week later. We support you either way. But you know Van will have a field day with this one, honey."

"There's also the clause in your trust. It states that if the marriage is ended in the first three years, the trust will cease." Dad says.

Shit. I forgot about that part. It's fine. I never wanted the money anyway. And of course, Van's going to run his mouth.

"I'll deal with the fallout. That's the only thing I can do. As for the trust, I've made good money; I'll be okay without it," I say with a shrug.

"I don't know, Tiny. This looks bad. Van will spin this into you having a mental breakdown. We know what he did, but they don't." Jamie growls. My entire body stiffens. Van is a mean son of a bitch, and I hate that it took me so long to walk away from him.

"I won't fucking let him get to her. As of right now, she's still my wife, and that's all anyone needs to know." Briggs' tone is firm. He turns to me, his eyes wide. "Not that I own you. You can do whatever you want. I mean, I won't let another man get close to you. Shit, that doesn't sound right either." He runs a hand down his face and groans. "I mean, I won't let anyone hurt you. I'd make sure you're safe and taken care of."

"Man, I didn't know you could be so soft. Pussy." Jamie jokes.

"Shut up, dickhole."

I look at my parents and see them both cover their grins with their wine glasses.

"Seems you're left with two options. End the marriage, and we'll handle everything that comes after. You can guarantee the media is watching you now. They'll know as soon as it's over, and Van will speak out when it does." He sighs and refills his glass. "That man has been trying to make you look unhinged because he can't stand that you left him after he showed his true colors. Babycake, I can't watch you go through that again."

Briggs looks over at me with an angry, questioning expression, but not at me. I know he's thinking about what my father just said. I can feel his fierce need to protect. He steps closer to me and rests his hand at the base of my ass.

"If you stay married and the two of you try to make it work, or at least show that you're a happily married couple, then they'll see you're not what he tried to make you out to be, and you'll keep your trust. I know you don't care about the money, but I put that clause in there for a reason, honey," Dad says, sipping his wine. "I'll support you either way. You know that. But I would like for you both to give it a try."

"That's not fair to Briggs. I can't ask a stranger to stay married to me because I'm worried about an ex-boyfriend or a trust fund. It's just money, and you could change that clause," I tell my dad with a cheeky smile.

Dad chuckles and looks at me. "I could, but I won't. Tell you what. Give it a year. If you come to me and say the marriage absolutely won't work, I'll consider changing it, but I want to see that you've actually tried." Dad shrugs. He's going to push for this.

"I'll do it," Briggs says, bringing his arm around to the side of my hip. "We live together, date, be happy, and see if this works for us, right?" Briggs asks my dad, who tilts his head and shrugs. "The decision is easy. We can stay married if she agrees, and it's what she wants."

"I don't want to be an obligation." Huffing out a breath, I finish adding the toppings to the pizza. "Done," I say, sliding the pizza to my mom. I turn on my heels and walk out of the room before anyone can say anything.

I really messed this up. Briggs seems like such a good guy, and if I stay married to him just for protection from some asshole, I'll never know whether he likes me or if it's just a pretense.

When I whistle, the girls come running and follow me out the back door. At the pool, I roll my loose jeans up, sit on the edge, and stick my feet in the water.

How can I be confident enough to walk a runway in underwear but not when it comes to relationships and love? Lying back on the warm stones, I watch the dogs play in the yard. It's better to get an annulment. Then maybe I can try dating the God that is Briggs Banks.

"What are you thinking about, Tiny?" Jamie asks, sitting beside me.

"I like him, Jamie. Like, I really like him. If we stay married because of Van and money, I'll never know if he genuinely feels anything. Last night, I was a different person. I was cool and cocky. He brought that out in me," I say, folding my hands over my stomach.

"Then keep channeling that from him. Show him why he should feel lucky to have someone like you. What else? I know you," Jamie says, nudging me with his elbow.

"The anxiety and panic attacks I still have sometimes. I can walk a runway and pose half-nude for photos without a problem, but little things like fish or too many men around me at once can send me into a spiral. Van made me feel crazy. I don't want to feel that way again. What if Briggs sees it and does the same thing?"

"The things we went through as kids will always stick with us in some way. Even more so for you, Tiny. What Van did to you reset the progress you made. I've known Briggs for a long time. He's nothing like Van or any other man you've encountered. I don't want to tell you he's a good guy because you're my baby sister and he's my best friend, but he is."

"What do you think I should do?"

Jamie takes a deep breath and turns to me. "I think you should give Van the biggest fuck-you by showing him you're happy and safe with Briggs. And if you want Briggs, Journey, grab him by the balls and make him your bitch. Show him the woman you are. You're amazing, little sis. He's lucky to have you, and you deserve true happiness."

Laughing, I rise to my feet with Jamie beside me. I hug him lightly, then step back, meeting his dark green eyes. "Thanks for being my brother."

"Not being your brother was never an option. Keep your confidence, Tiny. Take back what Van stole from you."

As I walk back into the house, the dogs follow me. When I enter the kitchen, my heart skips a beat, and my chest warms when I see Briggs laughing with my parents. Van would never take the time to get to know them like this.

"Better, Honeycomb?" My mom's beautiful, warm eyes meet mine.

"Yeah, Mom. Better. I've decided to give Hottie McFly here a chance to wow me and keep me as his wife. I hope you have your

A-game ready, husband." Sauntering over, I stand next to the hunk and tuck his hair behind his ear.

"Oh, shit. You're going to have your hands full, Bigsby."

"I've never been one to back down from a challenge, wife." Briggs's heated gaze meets mine. His soul-piercing Caribbean irises make my breath hitch as he steps closer. "When do I move in?"

"You're off tomorrow, if I remember correctly."

"That I am. Tomorrow it is."

"Briggs, I'd like to meet your parents. Would you mind inviting them to dinner with us in Cedar Creek in a couple of weeks?" Mom asks as she and Dad take the pizzas out of the oven.

"Yes, ma'am. I'll have Journey text you once I talk to them."

"Just Audrey and I will send you my number so you have it. Time to eat."

Before we step away to eat, Briggs stops me. "You're not an obligation. You're a gem worth protecting," he whispers.

My breath catches at the seriousness and determination in his eyes. I'm not sure how to respond, so I do the grown-up thing and kiss his hot, plush lips. Fire burns through me as our mouths meet. I could kiss him for the rest of my life.

As we sit around the table, we joke and have a good time. After dinner, we load the dogs into the car and say goodbye to my family.

Five

Briggs

I knew my mother would be camped out at my apartment. As soon as we turned onto my street, I saw my dad's truck parked on the curb, along with my brother's truck. I doubt Beau is here, since they have a new baby and all, but I'm banking on Bay sitting inside with Bax.

I'm not sure what Journey thinks of this marriage, but I plan to keep her as my wife. She's mine. I told her she wasn't an obligation, and I meant it. Now I need to show her.

"Next round of family, I presume," Journey says as she parks in the driveway next to my car.

"Yup," I say, watching the front door open. Mom stands in the doorway, arms crossed over her chest, with Bay behind her, grinning.

"Is it okay to bring them in?"

"Of course. Maybe they'll see my brother's evil and bite one of them," I say, giving her a toothy grin.

She laughs and opens the door. "Don't say that." She grabs the leashes. The dogs jump out and stay on her side. Taking her hand on the other side, we make our way into my tiny-ass apartment. To my surprise, Beau's big ass is sitting on the couch next to my dad. Journey's grip on my hand tightens with all the people, or maybe all the men around her. I release her hand and move it to the small of her back, rubbing circles. I've learned it calms her down a little.

When Journey lets out a low whistle, I watch both dogs lie down at her feet. My jaw drops when I see it. She just commanded them with a whistle.

I recover from the shock and meet my mother's angry stare. Damn, this might turn out differently than it did for her parents. Mom stops pacing in the middle of the living room. I watch her gaze settle on our hands, and her breath leaves her.

"Shit. I was going to ask if it was true, but I just got my answer. Do you two know how many photos I've seen of you out on the town in Vegas? When did you even have time to go there? You were at the hospital yesterday morning." She says it like it's the worst news she's ever heard.

"Ah, that was my doing. I asked if Briggs was up for an adventure, and boom, four hours later, Vegas." Journey does jazz hands with a smile, then drops them. My mom looks at her, stunned. Journey purses her lips, then speaks again. "Not funny. The moral of this story might be never to trust a stranger." She giggles uncomfortably, then steps into me. I bring my arm around her and palm her hip.

"Damn it, I'm trying to be mad, but I can't do that when she's being cute." Mom looks Ny up and down, smiling gently. It's like she can see what I see inside her.

"She is cute," Bay smirks at me.

Anger hits me like a jackhammer when Bay makes that comment. "My wife, little dick," I growl at him. I don't miss the amusement on his face; the little bastard is trying to aggravate me, and it's working. Glancing at the others, I see them raise their brows and stare at me.

Journey smiles, then lets go of the leashes. Charm and Ebony get to their feet and start sniffing everyone. Dad doesn't waste any time petting them. He's always liked dogs. I wonder why we didn't have any growing up?

"Journey, this is Ivey, my mom, and that's Bryce, my dad. And those are my three brothers."

"It's nice to meet both of you, and hello, three brothers. Sugar Booger here seems to have misplaced the other half of his manners." Ny says, with a giggle.

As soon as she says it, everyone starts laughing.

"Did she just call you Sugar Booger?" My mom chuckles with the others.

"Yeah, she has something new almost every time." I shake my head and point to my brothers. "Beau, Baxter, and Baylor."

"Briggs just found out my brother is Jamie."

They each stare at her like she's a fucking alien. Yeah, she looks nothing like her family.

"Which part are you questioning? How is he my brother, or how did Briggs not know I was his sister?" she asks them.

"They're questioning both things, honey, but won't say it," Mom says.

"Jamie and I ended up in the same foster home when I was nine. He instantly became my big brother and protector. We bonded and became inseparable. It was always Jamie and me against the world." I can hear the pride and affection in her voice.

"Our parents loved it and adopted us together. Jamie still has that protective streak when it comes to me. One of his former friends said something after my first lingerie fashion show when I was eighteen, and Jamie lost his shit. Let's just say they are no longer friends, and the guy needed plastic surgery to fix his nose. Now he doesn't mention that I'm his sister."

"That's a beautiful story about how you bonded and were adopted together," my mom says gently.

"Remind me not to piss Jamie off. I like my nose in its original condition," Baylor jokes.

Journey chuckles and shifts her weight. It just occurs to me that we're still standing in my house. I wrap my arms around her waist and pull her closer so she can rest her weight on me.

"I have to ask. What made you two do this?" Mom asks, looking at us.

"Which part? The up-and-flying halfway across the US was due to a shit day and an attractive, witty woman asking me to have an adventure with her. Getting married was mostly the alcohol's fault. However, the events leading up to the proposal and the eventual nuptials ultimately sealed the deal. It felt right," I say to my mom.

"Briggs thought he died, and we were in his afterlife. Still feel that way, McDreamy?" she asks, and Dad barks out another laugh.

"No. Not anymore."

"So much for haunting people," Journey says, tilting her head and looking at me with a smile. My eyes meet her golden amber irises. Her beauty has my heart sputtering out of control.

"Is there a plan moving forward?" Dad asks this time.

"We talked about an annulment, but landed on Hercules trying to wow me instead. I knocked his socks off with my impressive dating skills. Now it's his turn to show me why I should let him keep me as his first wife," I say, laughing with Journey at the last comment.

Dad lets out another hearty laugh. "I like her, Briggs. Don't fuck it up, son."

Mom chuckles. "You two are going to try to make the marriage work, is what you're saying?" she asks, pleased with our answer.

"We are. I have to show Ny she'll be my only wife. I'm moving in with her tomorrow," I tell my mom, then look at Ny, who's beaming at me with twinkling eyes.

"Do you need to use the truck?" Dad asks.

This is going to be embarrassing. Glancing at Journey, I see her shrug. "The house is already furnished, but if you prefer your things, we can do that, except for my bed. I'm not giving that up. Those two take up a lot of space, and we'll need the Alaskan king." She points to the two dogs still soaking up attention. Shit, she's talking about us sleeping in the same bed.

Chuckling, I rub her bicep. "This is a furnished apartment. I only have clothes and shit like that. I hate buying furniture. It was easier to rent a place with it already."

"Well, I'm out. I only came to spy for Birdie." Beau rises to his feet. "It was nice to meet you, Journey. Welcome to the family." She thanks him, and he walks out the door.

"I'm out too. You may have met your match with her, Briggs," Baxter says, walking out.

"Ugh, I have to go. He's my ride," Baylor sighs. "Nice meeting you, Journey. Guess I have to take all your posters down now."

"I'm going to kick your ass, Baylor," I growl at him while Journey laughs at his joke. He dodges my punch as he walks past us.

Dad gives each dog another pat before standing. "Ivey, dear, we should let the kids get some rest. Journey, it was a pleasure meeting you."

"You too," she says politely.

"Before I forget, Journey's parents want to have dinner with us and you two soon," I tell my mom.

"We'd like that. Let me know when and where, and we'll be there. Journey, I look forward to getting to know you better," Mom says, then gives her a light hug. Ny tenses slightly but plays it off.

"Same," she says.

With everyone finally out of the apartment, Journey and I are left alone at last. It's been an insane day. Ny strolls over and flops onto the couch.

"What a day. Next time, we're staying gone for the whole two days."

Smiling, I sit beside her. "There's going to be a next time?"

"Hell yeah, and next time we won't have to worry about accidentally getting married."

"That's true, honeybottom," I say, tilting my head back.

"I like the cute names," she tells me again, leaning back. I can tell she's not used to hearing them from anyone. She turns her head and looks at me with her almond eyes. "You sure you're up for this? I can handle it if you're not."

Smiling at her, I take in her delicate features. "I'm positive."

Ny lifts her hand, looks at the ring on it, and beams as she admires it. It's a big-ass diamond. I'll give myself that. It looks good on her finger. "Does it feel weird for you?" she asks, then gestures to my finger, reminding me I have a ring on.

I glance down and twirl it around my finger. "Not really. Kind of forgot it was there."

Journey reaches over, and her delicate finger traces the skull on my throat. I tilt my chin up, giving her better access. I can feel my skin warming under her touch and my cock stirring against its barrier. My heart picks up as she traces the design. "Did it hurt? I know they all probably do, but does it hurt more on the throat?"

"Yeah. My neck and sternum were the worst two for me."

"Did you know the crow holds a lot of meaning?" I know she's referring to the crow that covers the top half of my chest. I got it because it looked badass with the geometric design I wanted, and crows are my favorite birds.

"I didn't, but I'll be sure to look it up."

"My parents started learning about our cultures with us after we did a DNA test online."

"That's great that they did that for you both. I can see how much they love you guys."

Ny lifts her knees to her chest and turns toward me. "I should probably go home soon."

Staring at her glowing features, I can see she doesn't want to go home alone, and I don't want her to either. It's fucking insane to feel attached to someone in 24 hours.

"Stay. You can shower, and I'll give you something to wear. It's midnight. There's no sense in going home this late just to come back in the morning."

"Ok. I suppose it's no different from what it will be tomorrow. I'm going to take the dogs for a walk before we settle in for the night."

"I'll go with you." I get to my feet and hold out a hand for her. She stares at me, stunned, for a few moments. Good god, what did her ex do to her? It's a walk with the dogs, not a murder spree. "Are you ok, sweetness?" I ask, trying to snap her out of it.

With a shake of her head, she takes my hand. "Yeah, sorry. I spaced out," she says when I tug her into me. My eyes meet the pulsing vein in her neck. Her heart is racing. Oh, sweet girl, I will show you how a man should treat his woman.

"Sunrise, I truly am going to wow you. I'll hold the leases, and you can hold my hand." I bend down, gather the leases in one hand, and hold out the other. The biggest smile spreads across her face, and her chilled fingers lace with mine.

Journey opens the door, and we step outside. The night sky is crowded with stars, lit up, and a warm breeze blows. The smell of summer is thick tonight.

"It's nice out here. I like how quiet it is."

"Yeah. It's usually pretty peaceful," I chuckle.

As we walk, Ny surveys her surroundings. The neighborhood is quiet at this hour. The only sounds are our footsteps on the concrete and the crickets' chirping. Dim streetlights illuminate the sidewalk, guiding us back to my apartment.

After we walk the dogs, I show her where the shower is and grab her some clothes. When she closes the door, I go into the living room to get the couch ready for me to sleep on. I don't want her to think we have to share a bed. We did last night, but that was because we passed out.

Glancing down, I see both dogs already asleep on the floor. Ny got them so they could protect her. I'll be with her now, and she'll be safe.

Not once in my life did I picture myself married like this. I'll have to stay on point. Journey is a boss at getting someone to fall for her. Now I need to make sure she falls for me, too—no pressure, or anything.

I roll my tense shoulders and exhale. When I hear the water shut off, I go into my room and grab something to change into.

A feeling I've never felt before hits me as Sunrise walks out of the bathroom. Seeing her in my clothes sends a bolt of possessiveness through me. It's primal and powerful. No woman has ever worn my clothes or slept in my bed. I never wanted anyone to do either, but I want that with Journey more than anything.

She's breathtaking. Striding toward her, I stop when we're chest to chest. I cup her cheek lightly, then bring my lips to her forehead and kiss her gently. My gaze meets her dazzling amber eyes. Her lips part slightly, as if she's about to say something, but she doesn't. I brush my thumb along her jaw, then step into the bathroom.

Turning on the cold water, I strip and step in. I need to control the bald-headed yogurt slinger that thinks it's game time. I have to remember this is just an arrangement for her. For now.

I wash quickly, step out, dry off, and get dressed. After brushing my teeth and hair, I step out and notice the bedroom door is still open. Stepping into the doorway, I see Ny sitting at the foot of the bed, typing on her phone. When she senses my presence, she turns and smiles at me.

"Social media. You should check yours, stud muffin." Ny gets off the bed and follows me to the living room. She sits on the couch and pats the spot beside her. I open the app and am flooded with a fucking ton of posts and DMs. But the only ones I care about are the ones she posted of us and her status change. Grinning, I do the same. After finding my second-favorite photo, I post it with a hashtag. *#TiedTheKnot #ForeverInVegas #JourneyPrestonIsMyWife*

"Are you ready for bed?" she asks me sleepily and gets up.

"Yeah." As I rise to my feet, I stand there awkwardly. "Good night, Sunrise."

"Oh, right. You're sleeping here. Ah, good night, Hercules." She pecks my cheek, then rushes past me into the room.

Shit, she thought I was sleeping in there with her. Turning to go after her, I hear the door click. Huffing out a breath, I lie down on the couch. I'm an idiot. Flinging my arm over my face, I groan at my stupidity. Closing my eyes, I let sleep take over.

Six

Journey

I take a deep breath and stare at the white ceiling. I've had 8 hours of sleep over the past 2 days. I should not be awake right now. I've never been good at sleeping in new places. That's why I chose the hotel we went to. I've been going to that one with my parents and brother for years. Mom and Dad hated leaving us with nannies or sitters, so they took us everywhere, and we did a hybrid schooling approach. Mom would coordinate with the teachers and get our lessons for the days we would be out of town. She made sure she was always with us, regardless of the circumstances.

Leaning forward, I pick up my phone and glance at the time—almost seven. I don't know whether Briggs is a morning person or if he'll hear me sneak out for coffee. Screw it. I can't lie here anymore. I throw off the covers, stand up, and stretch. Then I reach into my pack for my toothbrush, clothes, and hair tie to braid my hair. Slowly, I turn the knob, open the door silently, and creep like a weirdo to the bathroom.

I shut the door behind me and stare at my exhausted face in the mirror. With a groan, I splash cold water on my face and try to revive myself. Teeth brushed, and hair braided, I slip on the crop top and baggy jeans. I really need a change of clothes. New plan. If he's asleep, I'll stop at the store for boxes and something different to wear, then get coffee and a quick breakfast.

The door is silent as I open it again and sneak into the living room. Briggs is on his back, his arm over his eyes, snoring lightly on the couch. He's sexy. I've seen some beautiful men, but Briggs tops them all. His sweet protectiveness melts my heart. He's nothing like anyone I've ever met, but I have to consider that this isn't as serious for him, especially since he chose the couch over sleeping in the bed with me.

My low whistle has both girls getting up and trotting over to me. Purse in hand, I unlock the door and open it silently. My ears perk up when I hear him still snoring lightly. I twist the bottom lock and shut the door. I wait a moment for the dogs, then load them into the car and drive to the store.

In the car, I pull up my friend Winters' number. She's been calling since yesterday. It rings once, then she picks up.

"You dirty bitch. I can't believe you left me on 'read' and made me wait. Send me a picture of the husband. Oh my god, that sounds weird."

I chuckle at her rambling. "Sorry, we had to meet the parents yesterday. It's weird hearing it."

"I'm so fucking proud of you. You went out and had a crazy night. Are you staying married? Wait, did you bang him?"

"No, I didn't bang him. We decided to give it a try. I'll text a picture when I stop. He's gorgeous, and his name is Briggs. It was so much fun. He brings out my wild side." I giggle like a child.

"Oh, good. I'm so happy for you. Hey, the boys and I were talking. We thought we'd come visit for the Fourth of July and see if we want to move there with you."

Excitement barrels through me. I miss Winter and the twins. "Yes. Please. Yes. I have a guest suite you're welcome to use until you find a place to live. I would love for you and them to stay with us. Briggs is super chill, and the boys would love him."

Winter chuckles into the phone. "Ok, hot tits. We'll be there for the fourth. Sorry, I have to go so I can take these two knuckleheads to a dentist appointment."

"Ok. Talk soon, and I'll text a pic. Love ya"

"You'd better. Love ya, too."

When I hang up, I feel a surge of joy. Winter was only 16 when she had her twins. She blames it on being young and dumb. She's a wonderful mother, and I look forward to Briggs meeting her.

After I park, I pull out the window sign with a note that the AC is on for the dogs and to please not break my windows. Inside, I grab a ton of boxes, underwear, a crop top, ripped shorts, and sandals. I know my house is close, but I'm trying to make this quick. After checking out, I stop in the bathroom to change, then load the boxes and grab coffee and breakfast sandwiches from a drive-thru.

I park in his driveway, realizing I have to lock the door and that I'll now have to wake him to let me in. With the door open, I let the dogs out, grab the coffee and food, and walk to the front door. Before I can knock, the door flies open, and I'm greeted by Briggs, fully clothed, with keys in hand. A look of worry and panic etches his face.

Without a word, he steps out, takes me into his arms, and exhales a shaky breath.

"Everything okay?" I ask him. What the hell happened while I was gone to make him so worried?

"It is now. I woke up, and you were gone." He murmurs into my hair.

"I'm sorry. I couldn't sleep this morning, so I went to get some boxes and breakfast. I didn't want to wake you," I say, rubbing his defined sides.

"You can wake me anytime. I want you to," he says, keeping his face buried in my hair and holding me a little longer.

My heart beats faster as a surge of emotions swirls within me. No man has ever worried about me like he just did. It's going to be hard not to let my heart get attached to him. I'll admit it. I'm a clinger, and I'm already at stage two with him.

"I'll wake you next time. I'm sorry I worried you." I reach up, place my palm to his face, and feel him relax under my touch.

He draws back, takes the drinks from me, and kisses my forehead. "You don't have to be sorry with me, sweetheart. I panicked. I thought maybe you changed your mind."

This man is going to set my heart on fire. "Not yet, big sexy."

Chuckling, he leads me into the apartment. I set the bag on the counter and pull out its contents.

"I wasn't sure what you liked, so I got four different sandwiches. There's also cream and sugar for the coffee. I'll learn your preferences. One of mine is important. No fish of any kind. Ever."

"Got it. No fish. Ever. I don't like it either," he says, leaning against the counter and grabbing a sandwich.

"Really?"

"I hate the taste. Actually, it's pretty much all seafood I dislike. Don't tell my family, but I don't like fishing or the process that follows, either. I only went with my dad and brothers because I had to. Now, when I go, I don't fish. I help watch my niece and have a few drinks, but that's it."

My eyes light up when he tells me that. Van would order the shit on purpose, then not eat it because he knew it would send me into a spiral.

"I know it's a trivial little thing, but you have no idea how much of a relief that is," I tell him, biting into a sandwich.

Briggs furrows his brows and looks at me with his brilliant Caribbean eyes. "If there's anything you don't like, whether it's food or anything else, all you have to do is tell me. I won't do or cook anything you don't like. And if I do something you like, I want you to tell me that, too, so I can make sure to keep doing it."

I stare at him, my mouth opening and closing. If I'm going to show him this could be more than an arrangement, I need to be honest. I need him to see the real me—even the more vulnerable side.

"I like that you can tell when I start to feel anxious, and you rub my back. It calms me down. And I like the forehead kisses because they're sweet." I admit, showing a twinge of vulnerability.

"Okay. I like it when you call me funny names," he says, smiling with food-packed cheeks.

"Is that right, John Smith?" I smirk, and he laughs before rubbing my back.

"That's fitting since I'm in the presence of Pocahontas." He smiles brightly at me.

"I think we have our first couple's costume," I tell him.

"They have a costume contest at Hideaway each year. I bet we'll win."

"Hell yeah, we will. We're a good-looking couple. Those other bitches can suck it." We both burst out laughing. "One last thing before we start packing."

"What's that, Sunrise?"

"Monogamous?" I ask, looking down at my feet. I need to know whether he plans to fuck other women, so I can't shield my heart. Just the thought makes me cringe.

He hooks a finger under my chin, lifts my gaze to his serious one, and steps in front of me. He places his other hand on my hip, and my heart quickens as he squeezes lightly. "It's just you and me in this relationship and marriage. There will be no others. Just us. Agreed?" My breath hitches at the seriousness in his husky voice.

"Agreed. You and me." My voice comes out raspier than usual. Briggs brings his lips to mine and brushes them lightly. He has the softest lips I've ever felt on a man. I want more of him.

He presses his forehead to mine, inhales, then kisses it. "This is how we make it work. We talk and share how we're feeling. What we like and what we don't like."

"I'm starting to think we're still in the afterlife. We need to try haunting someone to test the theory." I smile at him. There's no way this man is real.

"Who's the first victim?" he asks, moving away to dispose of the trash.

"Jamie. He doesn't believe in ghosts. Who would you pick?"

"Baylor. He fucked with me last night. I need to get him back," Briggs says. He takes my hand, and we walk outside to get the boxes from the car.

"Done. You said you have a niece. How old is she?" As I open the car door, I grab the bag of tape.

"Harley is five, and Blue is two days old."

"And they're which brothers?"

"Beau and his wife Birdie."

"Got it."

Back inside, we stand there and stare for a moment.

"Where should we start, Sparky?" I ask, then begin popping the boxes out and taping the bottoms. I watch Briggs rub his neck and look around the space. A sense of insecurity hits me. What if he isn't ready to live with me? He needs to know he doesn't have to.

"Hey, we don't have to do this if you don't want to."

"What?" He gives me a confused look, then registers my discomfort. "Oh, no. I was thinking. I want to. We can start in the bedroom. It's crazy that all I have are clothes and drawings."

"Why is it sad?" I ask, then head into the bedroom with several boxes in tow. "I think it shows you're not a material kind of person." Shrugging, I set a box on the bed and open the closet. "Does it make you sad that this is all you have?"

He opens his dresser drawer and thinks for a minute. "No. I have the shop with Jamie and my family. I was hardly ever here. I didn't see the point in spending money on stuff I would hardly ever use, so I saved it instead."

"See? It's not sad. You have what's important to you."

Briggs chuckles and adds the last of the clothes from the dresser. "And what's important to you?"

I glance away and pick a shirt off the hanger to begin folding it. "Love and family." Shrugging, I fold the last of the hanging shirts and put them in the box. Once everything is cleared out, I pull the hangers down and box them.

Briggs comes over and starts taping the boxes. Moving from room to room, we pack everything up and load my car as full as possible.

Briggs follows me on his motorcycle, and I can't help but feel excited when I see him on it. Yup, I'm definitely going to get on that with him soon. I've never ridden on the back of a bike, but I'd like to.

As we pull up the curvy drive, the large modern home comes into view. I chose a modern house with a shit ton of windows. The front maintains its privacy while allowing thoughtful glimpses into the gallery, office, and living areas within. A contrasting horizontal plane highlights the entryway.

The living room is spacious, with dark gray, almost black walls. An oversized brownish-orange leather sectional sits in front of the massive windows. Accenting dark wooden tables complements the space. A massive bohemian design rug highlights the furniture and wall decor throughout the space. The dining room is adorned with the same bohemian decor and wooden furniture.

I open the garage doors, pull in, and park, with Briggs pulling up beside me. When he gets off the bike, he gives me a wow look. Laughing, I open the trunk, grab a couple of boxes, and open the door to the mudroom off the kitchen. As soon as I walk in, the scent of amber and roses hits my senses. I love the smell.

The open kitchen features a large island with concrete countertops, dark wood cabinets, and stainless-steel appliances. The walls are dark blue, and large globe lights hang above the island. My favorite feature in this space is the backsplash. It's a dark orange with designs. I love the colors. Full-height windows provide open access to outdoor living from public areas while also offering a more protected main suite.

Outside, there is a sunken fire pit, a full kitchen, and a heated pool with a spa. A full three-bedroom guest suite also graces the first level. A courtyard creates natural separation between the main house and the guest area, and a four-car garage sits on the side of the house.

The second level has four bedrooms and a game room, all gathered around a generous balcony with an exterior staircase leading down into the home's courtyard.

"Damn. Your place is fucking gorgeous," Briggs says, looking around in awe.

Chuckling, I head to the master. I'm going to push it and not give him the option to pick another room yet. We'll see how he reacts to this first. "I do believe it's our place now, princess."

In this room, I had three walls painted a dark green, and the wall behind the bed has dark floral wallpaper. Sheer black fabric is draped across the ceiling and hangs from all four corners of the bed, creating a canopy vibe, paired with a dark, berry-colored comforter and several dark decorative pillows. Vibrant plants accent the entire space, giving it a botanical vibe. There are two large dark wooden dressers and a TV mounted on the wall in front of the bed. Shit, this room is really girly, and the en-suite bathroom matches the same vibe.

I set the boxes on the large bed. When I turn around, I see Briggs' shocked face, which quickly clears. I give him a slight grin before heading back to the car. Briggs stays quiet as we get more boxes from the car. Now I feel like I should ask if he's okay with the living arrangement.

In the room, I set the boxes down, and he still seems deep in thought. "Is this okay? There are four other rooms upstairs, or the guest suite, if you prefer separate living arrangements. I was trying to be bold, but now I'm less confident about it."

Briggs sets the box down and strolls up to me. He moves the hair from my eyes and looks at me. He reaches his other hand around and rubs circles on my lower back. "This is perfect. I want to make sure it's what you want, not because you feel like we have to."

I place my hand on his hip and inhale his intoxicating scent. "Slow your roll, Don Juan. All we'll be doing is sleeping in here together."

He barks out a laugh and tickles my side, making me squeal and squirm. "Come on, Sweetheart, let's get the rest of my things."

"Okay, okay," I say, wiping away the tears from laughing so hard.

After a second trip to Briggs's apartment, we're finally done and unloading the last of his boxes. I step into the large walk-in closet and begin rearranging my clothes. With the space now clear, I remove the clothes from the second dresser.

Each of us grabs a box and starts hanging his clothes back up and putting his shoes on the shelves. Once all his clothes are put away, I open a box of his drawings. Sitting on the floor, I look through each one. Briggs is a fantastic artist.

"You never wanted to frame any of these?" I ask as I keep looking.

He sits beside me and looks through them, too. "Didn't really think about it. These are the ones I do in my free time."

"Would you mind if I framed and hung them in the house? They're beautiful. They should be where people can see them." My eyes land on a sketch of a Viking woman. It's fucking stunning. "Gorgeous."

"You can put them up if you want to."

"Yeah? Thank you. It'll make it feel like our house." I beam at him, and he chuckles. "Maybe we should do that."

"Do what?"

"Make it feel more like our space."

His face lights up, and he smiles gently. "I like that idea." He pulls out his phone and pulls up his favorite photo of us. "I think we should get this one blown up, printed, and hung."

I have to stop myself from crying when he shows me the picture. "We should."

I exhale and gently rest my head on his shoulder. My heart warms even more when he kisses the top of my head. At this moment, all I feel is peace, something I haven't felt in a long time.

Seven

Briggs

Inside my tattoo shop, I inhale the familiar, sterile scent. It's one of the best smells, in my opinion. Anyone who enjoys getting inked will tell you the same. It sends a thrill down your spine and gets your adrenaline flowing. By the time you're in the chair, you feel like you could lift a 15-ton vehicle.

The graffiti wall, which I finished a couple of weeks ago, features the shop name Ink Anonymous. Pride fills me every time I look at it. It looks badass. The place is open, with a short wall dividing each station. Chairs sit, waiting for their willing victims. Toolboxes of ink and supplies wait to assist in the pleasurable torment. Each station has an array of artwork. I love the thrill of being the artist leading the torture.

It's been two weeks since I met Journey and married her the same day. We haven't seen each other much, with me at the shop and her on video calls discussing her new line, which she's about to release. Then, a few days ago, Journey had to leave for a photo shoot. She asked me to go, but I already had appointments scheduled for the week.

After I slept on the couch, she made sure not to give me that option again. I prefer being in bed with her anyway. I find comfort I've never known when I hold her at night. Every morning, we wake up still tangled with each other. I find myself panicking when I wake up, and she isn't there.

I haven't been able to relax since she left. I've been living alone for years and have never been attached to a woman. I shouldn't be this dependent on her presence this soon. I need to get a grip on myself.

As I stride past Jamie's booth, he peeks up at me and grins. "How's married life? You'd better be treating my sister right. I still can't believe you're my brother-in-law."

A smile curves my lips as I twirl the ring on my finger and walk to my booth. I still can't believe it either. I like being married to Journey. She's funny and witty, but she also struggles with self-doubt and anxiety. I can tell she's trying to be more confident around me and in our relationship.

"It's good. We're still getting used to each other, and I'm adjusting to people constantly taking pictures and asking questions. I have to leave by four today. I want to pick her up from the airport." I tell him, then set my backpack on the chair in my stall.

"Yeah, they do that. I'm not sure how Tiny does it. Where was she this time?" he says, strolling over and leaning on the half wall.

"Arizona. She said she doesn't have anything else lined up. She wants to focus on her designs, so we'll have more time together."

"Does that mean she'll be around here often?" He grins at me.

I chuckle and shake my head. "Of course. She's my wife." I say 'wife' a lot because Jamie still isn't used to me being with his sister. I've been secretly dying to know the whole story, but I won't ask either of them. They'll tell me if they want me to know.

He wrinkles his nose and shakes his head. "Still weird. Anyway, they're selling the space connected to ours. I want to buy it to add room for apprentice artists. What are your thoughts?"

"I like it. Let me know how much my half is."

"Just like that, huh?" He raises a brow at me.

I narrow my eyes at him. "I won money in Vegas and have been saving for years. I would never take advantage of Journey if that's what you're implying."

"Just had to be sure. I'll let you know the price for each of us." He says with both hands up. I can understand his protectiveness of his sister, but he knows me better than that.

Now that I know who his parents are, I'm thankful he's let me partner with him. He could have bought and opened this shop on his own, but he didn't.

"Sounds good," I tell him, then drop the subject. I had over a hundred thousand saved before my winnings, and we could use the expansion.

When the door opens, we look over and see four women walk in.

"Guess it's time to work. I'll get it." Jamie pushes off the wall and walks over to them.

I reach into my pack and pull out a photo of Journey and me that she took before she left. We're gazing into each other's eyes and smiling. Our foreheads are pressed together, and my hand cups her slender neck. I had it printed this morning. Standing, I pin it to the wall above my desk. I am not the sentimental type, well, I wasn't until Ny.

"Briggs, you got time for a couple before you have to pick up your wife, who's famous, from the airport?" Jamie calls out.

Glancing up, I see two of the women's faces turn bright red. I stifle a laugh because I know those women are saying something he doesn't like, so he pulls the Journey card.

"How big?" I call out, but don't get up.

"Two and a half inches. About an hour each." He says.

Checking my phone, I see it's noon, and there's a message from Journey. I have time for a couple of quick pieces. "Yeah, do they know what they want?"

"Working on them now. I'll get yours ready."

When I open my messages, an image of Ny pops up, making a goofy face.

Sunrise:

> Waiting at the airport sucks. I showed you mine. Now you show me yours, Honeybuns.

Laughing, I make a face and send it to her.

Me:

> Done. See you soon, Sweetheart.

> Sexy, silly, lovable, and
> mine. Take my heart. It's
> yours. See you soon,
> Hercules.

Whenever she calls me hers and asks me to take her heart, my heart feels like it's dipping, and my lungs tighten up. I just stare at the message, absorbing the shock of it all.

As I wrap up my messages, I keep a smile on my face and start prepping for the first client. Once I'm set up, Jamie calls two of them back and hands me the stencil.

I stand as the woman approaches my booth. "Where do you want it?" I ask, standing.

"Shoulder," she says, then gasps. "Shit, he wasn't kidding. Is Journey Preston your wife?" she asks, pointing at the picture.

"She is," I answer, circling the spot on her shoulder. I confirm it's where she wants it. When she acknowledges, I place it and get to work. Once she's in the chair, I sit on my stool, dip the machine, and start the lines.

"Oh my God. That's why he looked familiar. He's Briggs, the Vegas mystery man," the woman in Jamie's booth says.

"I love Journeys' designs. Did you know she had her first major runway debut at 16 and launched her lingerie line at 21? She made ten million in her first year." She giggles, then keeps yammering on. "Sorry, you know all this already. I find her inspiring. She's a genius, too. Shit, sorry. I'm geeking out."

Geeking out isn't the right word. I knew all this because it's public knowledge and because Journey told me. By the time I finish the tattoo, this chick is still talking about whatever she can.

Once I finish with the second woman, Tink and Alice are here, talking to customers. I walk over to Jamie's booth and lean against the wall.

"We're going to have to hire someone for the front," I tell him, then head to my station to start my last tattoo of the day.

"Agreed. I'll post the job. It's never been this busy before, and it's all thanks to you, lover boy. Good thing we're expanding." Jamie grins.

I roll my eyes as I walk to my booth, put on my gloves, and get to work. I should have known this would happen after I posted pictures and tagged Journey. She has over 25 million followers. Why the fuck does she want to stay married to a loser like me?

I have nothing to offer a woman like her. Then I remember. I can offer her what she values most. I can care for her, be patient with her, keep her safe, laugh with her, and understand when she's feeling a certain way. That's what she wants and needs. I have a feeling that's why she wants to stay married. She wants a husband, but she's still scared.

By 3:45, I'm finished and rushing to get out the door and jump into my car. It's Saturday, and we're having dinner with our parents tonight. Neither of us is looking forward to it. Hopefully, it all goes well. I don't see why it wouldn't, but you never know, I guess.

Eventually, she'll have to meet Birdie, Astor, and Anna. The Fourth of July is in two weeks, and my parents always throw a huge party. I presume she'll meet them then. At the airport, I park, make my way to her gate, and wait.

When I see her face come into view, everything around me stops, and all I can focus on is her. When our eyes meet, speckles of gold light up and glitter in her irises. I watch her breath catch as a beautiful smile stretches across her face, surprised by my presence. Journey is a fucking wet dream.

As we move through the crowd, we make our way toward each other. Before she can reach me, some motherfucker grabs her arm. Her eyes widen with panic, then she turns to look at the guy. Fury blinds me as I make my way to her.

I scowl at the guy, grab his wrist, and tighten my grip until it feels like it might break his bones. He lets go. Pulling Ny into me, I hold her tightly with one arm. She exhales with relief, wraps her arms around my waist, and clutches my shirt. I can feel the fear radiating from her. I've learned Journey doesn't like to be touched, especially by men. Ny has to trust you so she won't be uncomfortable. Even her father is careful how he approaches her. It makes me feel good to know I'm one of the few people she lets this close and feels safe with.

When I release the cocksucker, I place a hand on Ny's lower back and circle it to calm her. "Keep your hands off her. What the hell made you think it was okay to touch her?" I growl at him, trying to contain the pulsing rage inside.

"Who are you, her bodyguard? I wanted to ask for a picture and an autograph," the guy says, glaring at me. Glancing around, I see people taking pictures and watching the exchange, but I don't give a fuck. No one touches what's mine.

"I'm her fucking husband, dickhead. Grabbing someone isn't how you ask. She isn't taking a picture or signing shit after what you just did. Now back the fuck off, or I will make you." My husky voice comes out thick with anger. I want to smash this guy's face in. I shield her behind me and step toward him.

The guy holds his hands up and steps back. "Okay. I'm leaving."

I watch him go before turning into her slender arms, now wrapped firmly around me. My hands frame her slender face, and I stare into her amber eyes, flecked with gold.

"Are you okay, Sunrise?"

Her sparkling eyes ping-pong between mine before she tilts her head up slightly and brings her mouth to mine. Our lips part, and our tongues meet in slow, passionate desire. My chest feels like it's going to explode from my pounding heart. Holy hell. I could spend the rest of my life kissing only her and be satisfied.

We have to make this quick. I'm already starting to pitch a tent, and people are already taking pictures of us. Breaking the kiss, I inhale her lilac perfume, then kiss her forehead. I leave my arm around Ny and move her slightly in front of me as we start walking to get her luggage.

With her bag in one hand, I keep the other firmly planted around her and tucked into my side. I will not let some prick touch her again.

In the car, we start driving to the house. Journey needs to change, and I need to let the dogs out.

"I was happy to see you waiting there for me," she says, trying to brighten the mood.

"I will always be there waiting when I'm not able to go with you, Sunrise."

"Thank you for handling that guy. They don't usually grab like that."

"You don't have to thank me. You're mine. I protect what's mine, and I'm the only one who touches you." Was that a bold statement? Probably, but she needs to know I'm serious about her and us.

She looks at me, blinking quickly with her mouth open. Then a sly grin spreads across her bright face. "Damn. Even Caveman looks good on you. Okay. I can dig it. You're not going to piss on me to mark your territory, are you?" Journey scrunches her face and looks at me, making me bust out laughing.

"I can make no such promise, but I will try to refrain from doing so," I joke with her.

Ny starts laughing and looks at me flirtatiously. "I'd prefer the kissing and holding me possessively."

"Now those are two things I absolutely plan to do."

"That's what I wanted to hear. Keep it up, and I might consider dropping my panties for you, Big Spoon."

I almost swallow my tongue when I process what she said. Sex hasn't been something we've discussed, just innocent flirting, light touches, and a couple of kisses.

"Is that so?" I rasp, swallowing a gulp of air.

"You're giving off the 'touch her and die' vibe. Chicks love that shit. So. Yeah. Maybe." She glances at me and winks teasingly.

"Hm, I'll keep that in mind." I'm now all too aware of the goddess sitting next to me.

I haven't done much dating. Random hookups were my style when I was younger, and I haven't been with a woman in over a year. I want it all with Journey—the whole relationship.

Journey gives me a big smile, reaches over, and takes my hand in hers. Lacing our fingers together, she exhales with contentment and rests our hands on her upper thigh.

Damn it. The tent is rising again. I shift in my seat and tighten my grip on the steering wheel. Ny giggles beside me. Groaning, I shake my head at her, which only makes her laugh more. Yup, she sees it. That's confirmed when she whistles. Fuck, this is embarrassing.

"Don't be embarrassed, big guy. I like that I can do that to you with just a touch," she says in that sweet, raspy voice.

Glancing over at her, I see her give me a mischievous smirk before looking down and biting her lip. Shit, it's not going down. I release her hand and shift again to better conceal it.

"You know it's not really fair," I huff.

Journey covers her mouth to muffle her giggles. "Oh, I know. I could have a massive lady boner right now, and you wouldn't know."

I groan at her response, wondering if she's as turned on as I am. The rest of the drive is quiet as she listens to music and bobs her head. After parking in the garage, Journey jumps out and heads for the dogs while I get her luggage. Inside, I see her kneeling, giving all her love to Charm and Ebony.

She stands up and smiles at me. "I'm going to change, and we can go." When she skips to the bedroom, I chuckle. I open the back door and let the dogs out while I wait for her. I should probably change quickly.

I let the dogs in, go to the room, and dig through the closet. I change into a black button-down, roll up the sleeves, and put on a pair of light blue jeans. The Urban Butcher is fancy for Cedar Creek. Not as fancy as the restaurant in Vegas, but still decent.

When I step out of the closet, Ny exits the bathroom wearing a dark green strapless jumpsuit that hugs her upper body perfectly, paired with black stilettos. I'd like to know how the fuck a collarbone is sexy. Journey's black hair is in a chunky French braid, keeping it out of her face. There's a silver ring on every finger, like the night we first met. She goes from looking like Pocahontas to resembling Jasmine in her outfit and hairstyle. I am one lucky bastard to have her.

Journey sways her hips as she walks up to me. She fixes the collar of my shirt and runs her palms down my chest.

"All jokes aside, you look incredibly sexy tonight, Hercules."

"Sweetheart, you take my breath away with your beauty." I watch her face light up as the gold in her amber eyes twinkles.

"Thank you. Can I ask something?"

"Anything." Stepping up to her, I place my hands on her hips. Journey wraps her arms around my neck and smiles at me.

"Can we please take the motorcycle tonight?"

Chuckling, I bring one hand to the base of her ass. "Yeah, we can take it."

"Yes. I'm so excited." She kisses my cheek, grabs her clutch, and heads to the garage. Shaking my head, I follow behind her.

Eight

Journey

I stand here impatiently, barely paying attention to Briggs as he explains what to do while I'm on the bike. It's hard to stay focused with him looking fine as fuck in his tight shirt that shows off every rippled muscle and the ink on his neck, chest, arms, and hands. Tattoos cover 90% of his body, and damn, it turns me on—and holy sexy forearms. I don't think I'll ever want another man, especially after he turned into a growly, overprotective animal and almost mauled someone earlier. No one has ever treated me like this, and I'm starting to love it.

Briggs puts his helmet on me and chuckles. I'm still reeling from his godliness. I need to clear my head and try to remember what he said.

"I'll get you a smaller one, but this will have to do for tonight."

"Deal. Are we ready?" I chirp, bouncing on my toes.

"Yup," he exclaimed, got on the bike, and I did as he instructed. I placed my hand on his shoulder, steadied myself, and brought my leg over to straddle behind him. I placed my feet where he told me to, then brought my arms around his waist and held on.

When he starts the bike, I giggle at the vibration between my legs. Briggs revs the engine a few times before he takes off. Going down the drive is slow, but I already love how the warm wind feels on my face. I trust Briggs wholeheartedly. I'm not nervous or worried. It's nice to have that with a man.

On the main road, he accelerates, and the adrenaline I've been holding back finally releases. My heart races with the thrill of the ride. As we lean into the curves together, I take in the stunning view of everything passing by, unfiltered by a car window. It's liberating. No wonder people enjoy this so much.

Trees blur past; buildings look like I can reach out and touch them. The smell of fresh air and pizza fills my nose as we pass Mario's pizzeria. Downtown is bustling with kids outside the ice cream shop, and parents gathered in groups, talking. People are laughing and joking as they enter the stores. It's like something from a movie. It's so wholesome and homey here.

Between the vibration and Briggs' hot body pressed against me, I can't help but get aroused. Thank goodness no one can see.

In an alley, we park behind the building. I remember Briggs' words as I dismount and wait for him. I make sure I'm extra careful to avoid the hot muffler.

"What did you think?" he asks, helping me take off the helmet.

"I loved it. We should do this more often. You see everything around you differently than you do in a car. I loved the way the wind felt on my face." I gushed, still thrumming from the adrenaline.

"That's what I like about it, too." Briggs grabs my clutch and hands it to me, then takes my free hand. We casually stroll around the restaurant and walk into the building.

The place is quiet and dimly lit. The tables are spaced perfectly apart, and white tablecloths cover them. There's a bar in the back where a few people in business-casual attire are sitting, sipping their cocktails. I see several open tables, but I don't see our parents.

Briggs steps up to the hostess stand and waits for her. I watch his body tense as a few people pull out their phones and point them at us. He's adjusting, slowly. I squeeze his hand to reassure him.

"Just the two tonight?" she asks him, then looks at me with big eyes.

"No, we have reservations for Preston," he tells her.

"Right this way. Mr. Preston requested the rooftop seating."

Briggs places his hand on the small of my back as we make our way up the stairs to the seating area. When our parents come into view, I see them already laughing together.

"That's good, right?" I murmur to him.

"Let's hope so," he mumbles, before kissing my temple.

When we stop at the table, Mom and Ivey's faces light up when they see us.

"There you two are. Sit." Mom says, waving her hand at the open seats.

Briggs and I look at each other, then take our seats beside our mothers and order our drinks. Before we start talking, we take a moment to look over the menu and place our dinner order. Once the server walks away, Ivey restarts the conversation.

"I was just inviting Audrey and Sul to the Fourth of July party," Ivey tells us.

"They go all out every year. It's a ton of fun," Briggs tells my Mom, resting his hand on my knee. I'm starting to think that his touching me helps him calm down, too. Funny how two strangers can do that for each other.

"Oh, um, would it be okay if my friend Winter and her twins came? Sorry, everything's been crazy, and I forgot they'd be here that weekend. The boys are 10 and well-behaved." I ask.

"Absolutely. The more the merrier." Ivey smiles at me.

"I'm looking forward to it. We usually have a little thing with the eight of us before we go downtown to watch fireworks." Mom says, then looks at Briggs and me with a grin. "So, kids, how are you enjoying married life?"

"We didn't get much time together this week. Briggs worked, and then I had to go to Arizona. But the time we did get was really good."

When I look at Briggs, he winks at me, making the butterflies in my stomach flutter and my face flush.

"I saw the photos of Briggs stopping a man at the airport today. Followed by a steamy kiss." My mom jokes, and Dad grunts beside her. I cover my mouth and stifle a snicker.

"He shouldn't have touched her. I won't let anyone touch my wife. Especially not the way he did." Briggs grunts. When I turn to look at him and see his jaw working, he looks at me, and his intense demeanor softens. With a tilt of my lip, I run my fingers through the bottom of his hair. Looking back at our parents, I notice our moms smiling warmly at us.

"I'll admit I looked you up after you two got married. You're quite accomplished for your age."

"I try to work hard, but I owe most of my success to my parents. They helped get me where I am." I tell Ivey.

"Journey's being modest. She's done all the work on her own. All I did was take her to a fashion show, and after that, she knew what she wanted to do. Tilly West was the first designer she walked the runway for." Mom responds.

"Oh, you know Tilly? Our son Beau is married to her daughter. What a small world," Ivey says.

"No shit? We've known Tilly and Freddie as long as I can remember. Bryce will have to join Sul and Freddie for the fights sometime." My mom suggests.

With them absorbed in their conversation, I scoot over and whisper to Briggs. "I think we could sneak out and they would never know." I wiggle my eyebrows and grin at him.

He moves closer to me, smelling ever so manly, making moisture gather between my thighs. "You go first, then I'll follow."

Damn, even his breath smells delicious.

When I stand up, my mom turns her head. "Don't even think about it. Sit, little miss."

Damn it. I groan, and Briggs chuckles.

"It was worth a shot," he breaths.

My body shifts, and I scoot closer to him, resting my head on his shoulder. Briggs kisses the top of my head, takes my hand, and starts playing with my fingers.

"I apologize again for not mentioning Winter and the boys. They're going to stay in the guest suite if that's okay?" I say to Briggs.

"Of course it is. You don't have to apologize, sweetheart. She's your friend. I don't mind at all."

"You're pretty great, McSteamy. You'll like them," I whisper, and he chuckles.

"I'm sure I will, sweetness."

I breathe in as I watch our parents converse. I'm not sure why Mom made us stay here; they're still talking about getting together with Tilly and Freddie.

When I hear another's laughter, my eyes scan the room, taking in everyone sitting up here. They're all either deep in conversation or having a good time. It makes me smile until I see her as her feet hit the landing. My entire body stiffens as I sit up straight. My heart pounds in my ears, and my vision blurs. It feels and sounds like someone is drumming on my organs.

It can't be. Why didn't I get a letter? Then I remember I've moved three times in the past year. When her black-brown eyes meet mine, a wicked grin spreads across her face. She's aged but still looks young. If I didn't know her, I would never guess she's almost sixty. My looks and her Native American heritage are the only things I inherited from that woman. I grip Briggs' hand tighter, and he wraps his other arm around me, pulling me closer.

"What's wrong, Sunrise?" he whispered, confused.

My eyes don't leave hers as she saunters toward our table, and Van comes into view behind her. My breathing quickens as they draw closer.

"Audrey," Briggs says, twisting me in the seat to face him.

I lock my gaze on his Caribbean orbs. He takes my hand, brings it to his chest, and holds it there. "You're okay. I won't let anything happen to you," he tells me, then places a hand at the nape of my neck.

Nodding, I don't take my eyes off his as the fear and panic subside under his touch.

"Of course, that asshole would do something like this." I hear my mom growl, and her chair scrapes the floor. "Stay away from her." She spits.

"Keep looking at me, sweetness," Briggs says calmly.

"Journey, what are the odds we'd run into you here? I believe you know my dinner guest," Van says with pure spite.

"Zero. That's how many. Don't talk to my wife. Don't even look at her," Briggs snarls at Van, never taking his eyes off me.

"A bit barbaric, aren't you?" Van laughs at Briggs, who I know is using all his control to focus on me rather than rip Van's head off.

"Aren't you going to say hello to your mother, Lila?" Sheila says in a sickly-sweet voice.

I inhale sharply and move closer to Briggs when she uses the nickname.

"I got you," he declares, holding me even closer.

"Her name is Journey, and you fucking know it. Leave. Now. They should never have let you out of prison," my mother snapped.

"Good behavior. Now, Journey. How about you turn around so mommy can have a look at you?" Sheila coos, her voice laced with poison.

I close my eyes and control my breathing. Briggs holds my hand and moves his other hand to circle my back. Of course, this would have to happen while we're with Briggs's parents. Breathe and find your strength, Ny. I keep telling myself. Channel the confidence. I know what to say to set her off.

When I open my eyes, I meet my husband's brilliant gaze. I lean in and kiss him faintly, then stand. Briggs follows suit and holds me to him. I turn half my body into his arm and meet Sheila's glare.

"Sheila, I see prison has done you no favors. I heard about Joseph. It must have broken your heart to learn of his untimely death," I say, trying to keep my voice steady and my tears from falling. A pinch of satisfaction runs through me as I see the anger flash across her face.

"Yes, it was a shame. I still mourn him. We should never have been there or have been separated in the first place," she spat at me.

"The real shame is that you still haven't joined him in the pits of hell. If we're lucky, you'll see him soon. I'm sure he's saved you a place next to him. Do you want to know what I did when I found out?" I tilt my head, looking at the disdain on her face. I want everyone to see what this woman is.

I move my other arm behind Briggs, clutch his shirt tightly, and hold on to the strength I need to get past this. He's my poise and anchor.

"What did you do?" she snarls.

"I went to the store and bought the biggest fucking cake they had, and I celebrated his death for days until the entire thing was gone. Then I visited the prisoner who killed him and thanked him. I put money on his commissary every week to show my appreciation." I say sweetly with a forced grin.

"You little bitch. I should have killed you. If I had, he would still be here. But no, Joseph wouldn't let me kill his Lila," she says with such hatred. As she steps toward me, Briggs steps forward.

"I'd be really careful with your next move. I'm not above laying your ass out," Briggs says in a low, threatening voice.

"I see the monster is still in there," I tell her, then flick my glare to Van. "You can't hurt me anymore. I won't let you, and neither will he." I move my hand down Briggs' tense chest, take his hand, and we start to walk away.

"Don't forget what happened the last time you walked away from me, Ny," Van's voice comes out harsh and dripping with venom. My body tenses, and I gasp at the memory of that night. My grip on control is slipping.

"That's it. I'm done. I told you not to talk to her." Briggs turns and walks toward Van. I hold his hand firmly and don't let go. I want to beg him to stop. I need him with me. I'm stronger with him.

"Briggs, this isn't the time. Your wife needs you. Go home and take care of her. Sul and I can handle this." Bryce's calm, deep voice says.

"This isn't over. Stay the fuck away from her. Both of you."
Briggs bellowed, then turned me gently in his arms and held me
firmly against his chest. "You'll always be safe with me, Sugar
Butt. I promise." He whispers, then leads me down the stairs. I'm
not sure why he would want to stay with me after this mess of a
night.

I'm going to have to tell him about that part of my life when
we get home. Now that I know this is how Van plans to get to
me, he'll have others break me while he watches.

The ride home helped ease the anxiety wreaking havoc on me.
I love the wind on my face, the night sky, and watching life
around us speed by.

At home, I head to the restroom and take a long shower. Once
I turn off the water, I step out and go through my nightly ritual.
Then I slip on nothing but one of Briggs' t-shirts. I glance in the
mirror again and take a deep breath. I've been waiting until I was
married, and if this is my last chance, I'm going to take it. I want
my husband to have me. I want Briggs.

The bedroom door creaks as I open it and make my way into
the kitchen. I see Briggs making something. I hop onto the island
and sit there, watching his back in a tight cotton shirt. His hair is
wet, and he's in joggers. He's a stunning man. I wish I could
keep him, but I think I'll wake from the dream we've been living
in soon.

His sigh makes me hang my head. I jump off the island and
take a few steps. Behind him, I press my chest to his back, wrap
my arms around his waist, and rest my forehead at the base of his
neck. I can't ask him to stay in this.

Briggs places his hand over mine, laces our fingers, brings my
palm to his soft lips, and kisses it lightly. He's the sweetest man
I've ever met. I breathe in his mahogany and teakwood scent,
then kiss the nape of his neck, making his body shudder.

I try to pull away, but he keeps holding on. This is something I can handle. Holding Briggs feels right. He's safe and comfortable, and for the first time in years, I let the tears fall.

Nine

Briggs

When Journey starts sobbing into my back, my heart breaks for her. She's strong, but even the strongest people have their limits. Seeing that woman must have pushed her to hers. I don't know the story yet, but seeing her bio mother had her entire body locking up.

Not able to handle her silent sobs anymore, I turn into Journey's arms. Her tear-filled, speckled eyes meet mine. Her gaze goes straight to my soul. I reach out and wipe away the tears. I've learned that my physical touch helps her.

"What do you need, sweetheart?" I whisper to her.

"You." She breathes. Her slender fingers grab the hem of my shirt, and she starts to lift it.

Who am I to deny this gorgeous woman what she needs? I don't take my eyes off hers as she lifts my shirt over my head. Her warm fingers trail like a feather along the ripples of my stomach to my V-line, and my breath catches at the touch.

My heart picks up, and the soldier buried under the tent begins to rise. Ney leans forward, kissing my chest lightly with her full, soft lips, and my mouth parts.

My hand falls to her silken leg, and I let it glide up the back of her thigh to her bare, round ass. Holy hell, she isn't wearing panties, and she has one of my shirts on. Goosebumps spread across her skin at the touch.

We take our time, exploring each other's bodies. It takes all my control to move at this pace, but I will for Ney. I want to learn every inch of her. Journey takes my hands and slowly lifts her shirt, allowing me to remove her clothing. It's the most sensual romantic experience I've had.

The air is sucked from my lungs when I see her beautiful, glowing, bare, tanned flesh. My eyes roam, taking in the view before me. She has teardrop breasts and a strip of black curls between her thighs that makes my mouth water. She's fucking perfect, just as I knew she would be. I bring my hand up and let my finger graze beneath her breast. They're neither too big nor too small; they're simply beautiful.

Her breath hitches as I cup and thumb her taut, brown nipple while my other hand grips her ass. Her hooded, lust-filled gaze meets mine through her thick black lashes.

Gorgeous

Fuck me. She is my wife. Mine. Journey's lips part as she loses control, and she crushes her mouth to mine in an urgent, dominant kiss. Our tongues wrestle and twist together.

Journey's slim fingers slip inside the waistband of my joggers, and she pushes them down, freeing the soldier that's ready and standing at full attention. She grips my shaft tightly, then begins slow, calculated strokes while I kick my pants off. I let her delicate hand stroke and tease me. She glances down, bites her lip, then meets my gaze again. My lips capture hers again as she pumps her hand faster. Fuck, I'm about to cum in her hand like an amateur.

I groan, grasping her ass with both hands and lifting her. I do not want to cum with her the first time like that. She releases me, and her long, velvet legs wrap around my waist. In a few steps, I set her on the edge of the island, so much for taking it slow. If this is what she wants, I won't tell her no.

Breaking our kiss, I lick and nip down her neck and collarbone, then take her firm nipple into my mouth. Journey moans as her fingers tangle in my long hair. Her head tips back as I suck and twirl my tongue, teasing the most perfect nipples I've ever had in my mouth.

I reach between us, my fingers slipping between her folds to her warm, drenched center. Mm, my girl is ready.

"Oh God," she moans, tightening her grip on my hair. I release her breast with a pop and kiss up her collarbone and neck again, leaving no inch of skin untouched.

"Wrong god. It's Hercules," I tell her, making her giggle and moan as I work her swollen bud.

My heart pounds faster at the feel of her. Pulling her closer to the edge of the island, I slip one of my large fingers into her tight pussy. And I do mean tight. Slowly, I pump my finger and massage her bud with my thumb, making her moan louder and roll her hips.

"Lay back, baby," I rasp.

Her bright eyes meet mine, and her lips part as she lies back on her elbows.

My tongue trails down her chest and stomach, stopping only at the sweet juncture between her thighs. I kneel before her, inhaling deeply, breathing in her sweet, succulent sex. Fuck, even her pussy smells sweet.

Slowly slipping my finger from her, I spread her open and stare at her glistening wetness. Gently, I swipe my tongue over her swollen clit. God, she tastes like honey. I flick and suck, then slip two fingers halfway into her and massage her canal.

My eyes meet hers as she watches me eat the delectable dessert before me. Her hips roll and jerk as I tease her.

I'm going to have to go slow with her once I take her. She's tight, and I'm a big guy.

"Briggs, love," Journey moans. My heart kicks up at the word love. "I want you. Please." She begs, clawing at my shoulders.

She doesn't need to beg. I'll give her what she wants. I flatten my tongue and give her one last swipe, then slip my fingers from her and get to my feet. I bring my fingers to my mouth and suck her juices from them. Her eyes spark and light up as she watches me.

Journey sits up, and our lips meet again. Our tongues dance, and her legs wrap tightly around my waist.

My fingers find their way into her hair while my other hand grips her ass firmly. I line myself up with her, not breaking our kiss, and start to push inside her, agonizingly slow, but my girl has other plans. With one swift movement, she takes me to the hilt, making me groan loudly. Dear sweet mother of Mary, it's the tightest fucking thing I've ever felt.

Her body stills and trembles. Her breathing picks up, and she digs her claws into me. My entire being freezes. I may have heard that cry only once, but I know what it is. Virgin. Journey was a virgin. An overwhelming wave of emotion implodes inside me. I already cared for her, but now? Now there's so much more. The need to protect, possess, claim, and love her courses through me, taking over my entire being. My lungs stutter as I look into her hazy eyes.

"Baby. Why didn't you tell me?" I ask in a hushed tone. Fuck, I knew she was tight, but I never could have imagined that was why.

Her fingers brush my cheek. "I wanted it to be with my husband. No one has ever made me feel the way you do, Briggs. I want this. I want you." She says, trailing her fingers along my bottom lip. Then she starts to rock up and down my pulsing cock.

"I want you too, sweetheart. I want all of you," I groan, holding her slender body and letting her take control and set the pace she's comfortable with.

"Holy hell, Sunrise," I gasp as she snaps her hips. My hips move in harmony with hers, thrusting and rolling.

"You have me, Hercules." She moans, tilts her head, and arches her breast into me.

Fuck, she feels good. Too good. I'm not going to last. Being inside her is a rhapsody and an exultation. Sex has never felt this good. It's her. She's everything to me.

When my gaze locks with hers, my breath catches as I see the trust and admiration on her face. Ney holds me with one arm and raises the other, gripping my neck as we move faster.

Journey's eyes flutter shut, and her head tilts. I roll my hips, moving in and out of her warmth as my pace picks up to match hers. Fuck, I'm going to cum.

I can feel her pussy clenching around me, and I know she's close. When my stomach tightens, I know I can't hold out much longer.

"Oh God, Briggs," she cries out, urging me to pump faster. I watch the orgasm begin to consume her entire being. Thank fuck, I'm about to explode.

"Let go, Sunrise," I grind out, moving faster, watching her taut breast bounce.

Journey screams out my name again, responding to my command, and unravels before me. My own climax takes over as I feel her pulsing around me.

"Journey, baby." A groan rips from me when I say her name. I lock my lips with hers in an urgent, sloppy kiss and hold her tightly as I push in once more, burying myself to the hilt inside her. My stomach tenses, and my balls tighten as I cum. Hard. Harder than I ever have. The meteor shower explodes behind my eyes. I've never cum like that in my life.

Our bodies rock and jerk as we ride the high of consummation that solidified our marriage. Drawing back, I press my forehead to hers and run my hand up and down her moist spine as we try to catch our breath.

"Is it always that good?" she asks me breathlessly.

"Sweetheart, that was the best it's ever been. I have a feeling it will only get better for us." I respond, trying to catch my own breath.

With both hands, I brush the wet hair from her face and stare at her beauty. Water begins to glisten in her glowing eyes. Shit, I did something wrong. "Baby, did I hurt you? I'm sorry. I'll be more careful next time." I panic.

She shakes her head and wipes the hair from my face. "No, love. You didn't hurt me. It's only been two weeks, and I've never been happier."

Smiling at her, I scoop her off the island, leaving us connected. I lead us to the bathroom and turn on the shower.

"This is the happiest I've ever been, too, Ney." I can't bring myself to call her Ny after the way Van said that name tonight. When we step into the shower, she unwraps her legs from me. After I slip out of her, I reach down to remove the condom and freeze when I realize we didn't use one. Panic rips through me. Never in my life have I forgotten to fucking wear one.

"Ah, Baby. I fucked up. Shit, Sunrise, I'm so sorry."

"What? What's wrong?" She starts to panic, looking down at us, trying to figure out what the hell I'm talking about.

"Condom." I rasp, rubbing my sternum. Shit, I'm about to have a panic attack. My chest tightens.

"Hey, it's okay." She places her hands on my chest and rubs the spot with me. Calm starts to fill me through her touch. Huh, is this how she feels when I rub her back?

"Relax. I'm clean, obviously, and I trust you are too—Briggs, sugar bear. I can't have kids. I haven't been able to since I was twenty-two. There's no possibility of it if that's what you're worried about," she says calmly.

The relief that washes over me makes my knees want to buckle. She can't have children. That confession reminds me how much we still have to learn from one another.

"I'm sorry. I panicked. I should have been paying attention. I should have been more careful with you." I breathe rapidly, pull her into me underwater.

Journey giggles a little and strokes my sides. "Aw, my sweet baby just freaked out about the possibility of getting someone pregnant. Guess you're not as perfect as I thought."

I lean back, raise an eyebrow at her, then tickle her sides. "It's a real fear."

Ney laughs and squirms in my arms. "Don't worry, snookums, I still like you."

After releasing her, I quickly wash us off and turn off the water. We step out and towel off. I slip on my boxer briefs while Journey puts on some booty shorts with nothing else. I love how her long hair cascades behind her. She's sexy as sin. I watch her glorious body sway as she saunters into the kitchen.

This woman is going to kill me. I move quickly, following behind her.

"Is this our food from the restaurant?" she points to the food.

"Yeah. Our moms dropped it off while you were in the shower earlier." I walk up behind her, turn her slightly, and kiss her forehead. I can't help but catch another glimpse of her breasts before she picks up the plate.

"I love them. I'm starving." She walks over and sits at the kitchen table with the plate. Like a lost puppy, I follow her again. Charm and Ebony come in from wherever they were hiding and lie at our feet. It's wild to think these are my dogs now, too.

"Can I ask why you can't have children?"

Journey takes a bite, then swallows before she answers. My eyes roam over her flawless body, her long hair now covering her bare breasts.

"I had uterine fibroids. I was a rare case because I was so young. We tried all other treatments for years without success, so I had a partial hysterectomy. Can I ask why getting someone pregnant scared you so much?" She raises a brow at me.

"I decided a long time ago that I didn't want kids. When I was younger, I remember coming home from school one day and seeing my mom crying on the couch while watching the news."

After taking a bite, I swallow before continuing. "I sat beside her and held her hand. It was the worst case of abuse and neglect Autumn Falls had ever seen. Later that night, I heard one of my dad's cop friends tell him it was a little girl and how bad it was. The bruises, starvation, and being locked up." I shake my head at the memories.

"I remember thinking how sad it was that that child had parents who would do that to them. The older I got, the more I thought about it. It was seared into my brain. That girl deserved parents like mine. She deserved to be loved."

Sighing, I shift the food on my plate. "So, I decided I didn't want to bring more children into the world when so many others are suffering. I wouldn't mind adopting, but I don't want to add to the population. I should have gotten a vasectomy when I decided, but I didn't." When I look up, I see a full stream of tears running down her face.

Worried I said something wrong, I reached out to her. "Ney?"

She shakes her head and gulps for air. "How old were you when you watched that story?"

"Eleven, I think. Why?"

She sobs harder. Agony-filled eyes meet mine, and it hits me like an axe to the heart. Sharp, piercing daggers follow the blow. In a split second, my fork drops, and I kneel in front of her. My large hand wipes the tears from her face. "Sweetheart. Baby." My voice cracks a little. "It was you? Were you the little girl?"

She shakes her head, and I feel my heart drop. Dear God, the hell this woman endured at such a young age. It's no wonder that fucking woman scared her. That explains why she doesn't like being touched or trusting easily.

I lift her off her chair and into my lap, gently stroking her back to soothe her as she cries into my neck.

"I've never told anyone, Briggs. The only way Van would have known about her is if he had been digging into my life, and he would have had to dig deep. My name was omitted from the public reports. He's going to find everything and use it to break me. To break us. I need to let you go. This isn't what you signed up for. It's going to get messy, and I can't promise I won't lose it. I don't want to drag you down with me. You're too good," she says frantically.

"Journey, listen to me. No one, absolutely no one, will break you or us. If you lose control, I'll be right beside you, supporting you through it. I signed up to be your husband, and I intend to keep that promise. I don't remember the vows, but I think 'for better or worse' was in there somewhere. Please don't give up on us. Let me show you that you can count on me." I try to convince her.

Ney sucks in a strangled sob and sniffles as she tries to catch her ragged breath.

I can't lose her. My life won't be the same without her. When she handed me a shot of tequila and asked me to have an adventure with her, I was all in. I held her face in my hands, and my soul reached out to hers, begging it to keep me. She kept her brilliant gaze locked on me as she caught her breath and controlled the tears.

"I wished death on someone and admitted to thanking a man for murdering another in front of your parents. They probably already think I'm nuts." She sniffed.

I chuckle a little. "Sweetness, they don't think you're crazy. That man got what he deserved. It'll be easier if you keep me, Ney, because I'll follow you if you try to run. I'll be your biggest haunt."

She giggles and kisses me, then presses her brow to mine. "How are you real, Hercules?" she whispers. "Why do you care so much?"

"The same way you are. I care because you're worth it, Sunrise. I like it when you send me goofy pictures. Now it's your turn."

"I like it when you protect me."

I smile at her and run my fingers through her hair. "You're mine, Journey Leann. Now it's your turn," I tell her, then get to my feet with her in my arms.

"You're mine, Briggs Wilder. And it's Journey Leann Preston-Banks now."

A broad grin spreads across my face as I stand and lead us into the bedroom. She's adding my last name. My heart swells with joy at the thought. I lie her in the bed, then hover over her.

"I love that, Sweetheart. I'm going to let the dogs out real quick. Stay here and relax. Okay?"

"Okay," she says sleepily. Journey has had a tough night. I kiss her forehead because I know she likes it, then let the dogs out and clean up quickly.

In the bedroom, the girls jump to the foot of the bed and settle in for the night. I slide under the covers, pull Ney's silken body into me, and wrap myself around her.

I listen as her breathing evens out and she drifts off to sleep. Lying there, I start thinking of ways to make sure I never lose this woman before my own eyes drift shut and sleep consumes me.

Ten

Journey

Sunlight blares into my eyes as I peel my eyelids open. Good grief, why is it so bright? The sun is usually barely rising when I wake up.

When I reach over to the other side of the bed, I feel Briggs' empty space beside me. Fear seeps into my bones. Shit, what if he changed his mind? I scramble for my phone, check the time, and see it's almost 10 AM. Holy hell, I haven't slept past 6:30 since I was a kid or got too drunk the night before.

That explains why he's not next to me. As I scoot to the edge, I smile at the ache between my legs and at the reason it's there. Briggs is fucking huge. My face starts to heat, and butterflies take flight at the thought of having sex with him.

It was fantastic. I don't have anything to compare it to, but I know no one else could make me feel the way he does.

I stand up, stretch, and head to the bathroom to start my morning routine. I'm not sure what we'll be doing today, but it's going to be a hot one. After finishing my ritual, I gather my long hair into a messy bun on top of my head.

In the closet, I put on a pair of ripped shorts, a Five Finger Death Punch crop top, and my checkered Vans, then finally make my way out of the bedroom.

I don't see Briggs or the dogs anywhere as I move through the house. Maybe he took them for a walk? They already love him, and I'm pretty sure I do too, but I can't bring myself to say it. It's still too soon for the big L-word.

I also don't know what Van will pull out of his sleeve next. Briggs only knows about Sheila and Joseph. He doesn't know about my two half-brothers. One ran away when I was nine, and he was 15. He never took part in the torture I endured. A couple of months after he ran away, I sent the rest of my family, including our older brother, to prison.

He doesn't know how bad things got with Van. There's so much to unload that I'm unprepared for it.

I open the back door and step outside, surprised to see Briggs at the table with three women. Hot women. My body tingles with jealousy and possessiveness. Damn it, now I want to piss on him to mark my territory.

When his gorgeous eyes meet mine, he smiles broadly and walks over to me. He pulls me into his arms and kisses me tenderly. I wrap my arms around his waist, soaking in his presence, and giggle as he playfully bites my lip.

"Morning, my beautiful Sunrise," he says in a deep, sexy voice, rolling his pelvis into mine.

"Mm. Good morning, smoochie. Is everything okay?" I ask instead of saying, *'Who the fuck are these bitches?"*

He chuckles and whispers, tracing a finger along my lips. "Yeah, sweetheart. Everything is fine. They're just friends. I've known them for 21 years, and one of them is my brother's wife," he says with an amused grin.

My face drops. "Wha? I didn't say anything."

"Baby, it was written all over your face the moment you walked out the door. I like it when you get jealous and possessive." He smirks.

"I like it when you let me sleep until 10. When I have something that's mine, I tend to be protective of it," I admit sheepishly, because I do.

"See, I told you it was a good idea to keep me. Admit it. You wouldn't be able to live without me now, either?" He says, stretching his grin.

My mouth opens and closes. He truly wants to be with me. Nope, not giving it to him that easily.

"Hm, debatable at the moment, Mr. Cocky."

Briggs bursts into laughter and steps closer to me. "It's okay, sweetness. You don't have to say it. Just remember. I will haunt you. I'll make sure to give off super creepy vibes while I do it, too."

Now it's my turn to burst out laughing. "Well, hell, now I want to see just how far you're willing to go."

"Come on, I'll introduce you."

Briggs takes my hand and walks me to the table. One woman gleams, while the other two give me questioning looks. Fun way to start my Sunday.

Briggs points to the woman. "Journey, this is Birdie, Astor, and Annabelle."

"Sorry, we haven't had the chance to meet sooner. It's been a whirlwind," I say, giggling uncomfortably.

"Marrying a stranger would cause that," Astor says.

"And you two really plan to stay that way?" Annabelle asks.

I feel my neck heat up at the questions. Taking a step back, Briggs' face drops, and he wraps his arm around me.

"What the fuck?" he scolded them.

"Hey, I think it's great. I'm on your side. She seems like a nice woman, and you look happy," Birdie says, her hands raised in surrender.

Okay, I like her so far.

"It's just... It's wild, Briggs. You've been anti-commitment your entire life, and now you're married. It seems off. Serious isn't really your style," Annabelle snickers, and Briggs shifts uncomfortably.

Bitch say what?

The urge to punch this adorable cow is strong. I look at Briggs and see hurt flash across his face before he hides it. I don't like that. Not at all. No one makes my Hercules feel bad.

"Don't do that," I snap, glaring at her. Anna's eyes widen. "All it takes is the right person to fall for. We may not have known each other long, but Briggs seems to have his shit together. I'm sure he's gotten drunk with other women and never married them. That should tell you something."

Briggs gives me a sad smile. No. I'm the sad one in the relationship, not him. I may not be good at standing up for myself, but I'm good at standing up for the people I care about. And Briggs is mine.

Frowning, I look at Annabelle. "You just told your friend he's only good at fucking around. You don't think that might have hurt his feelings? That one of his best friends thinks so little of him? The way we ended up together may be unconventional, but it happened."

Shit, I'm pissed. I want to hit her right in her cute little nose. "Personally, I don't give a fuck if you think it's wild. He's my husband, and I'll defend him until my last breath. Snuggle Bug is an amazing person who deserves all the happiness in the world. And I'll make sure he gets it."

When I stop my rant, Briggs chuckles, turns me toward him, and runs his knuckles along my jaw.

"There is no other person in this world who is a better fit for me than you."

"Well, duh, that's pretty much what I just said, Robin Hood." Smirking at him, he looks at me with such affection, then pulls my face to his and kisses me again briefly. He's starting to love me. I can feel it.

"I like that you're always smiling with me, and I don't like that your friend made you feel bad. Now it's your turn," I tell him.

He gives me the beautiful toothy grin I love so much. "I like that you defended me, and I don't like it either."

I frown again, rub his biceps, and whisper, "Do you want me to hit her? I will if it'll make you feel better." I raise my fist and place it against my nose to show what I'm willing to do for him.

Briggs bursts out laughing and shakes his head. "No, Sweetness, I'll be okay."

"Ok, but if you change your mind, I'll do it."

"I believe you."

I nod, then turn in his hold. Briggs leaves his arm around my middle. Probably nervous, I will hit his 'friend'.

"I'd like to try this again. All I ask is that you keep your negative comments to yourself, especially about Briggs. He's mine, and that's the end of it," I say to the other two women.

"She's got spark and seems to genuinely like you. I agree it's not conventional, but that doesn't mean the marriage will fail," Astor says, smiling at us. "I'm a little jealous you got married before Noah and me."

"Noah's my brother. We've all known each other since we were kids," Birdie chimes in.

"That's great. You all stayed close."

"What about you? Do you have any childhood friends?" Annabelle asks.

When I look at her, I try to figure out her angle.

"Just my brother, but I have a friend coming in a couple of weeks with her kids. We met eight years ago. I spent most of my childhood focused on school, then on my career." With a shrug, I decide to see if I can win her over. "I have some items from my new collection upstairs if you'd like to take a look."

"I want to. Beau has the girls, and I have at least another hour or two before I have to pump again," Birdie says quickly.

"I'm in. I don't have kids yet, and Noah's with Freddie doing something." Astor says next.

"Annabelle, I'd like to get to know each other. You seem really important to Briggs, and he's important to me." I'm really trying to stay neutral toward her.

Annabelle finally lifts her lip in a half smile. "Okay, if you're willing to try, so can I."

Briggs lets out a sigh of relief behind me. Poor guy. It's a sticky situation, and I want him to be happy.

"All right, let's go play dress-up." Smiling at each of them, I turn to walk them inside, but Briggs stops me.

"Thank you. It means a lot that you're doing this," he says, tilting his head toward Anna.

"I'm not sure there's anything I wouldn't do for you, Hercules."

"I'll bring up something for you to eat."

"I'll be okay. You don't need to do that," I tell him, tracing his neck tattoo.

"I do." He kisses my nose, then lets me go.

My chest flutters, and my stomach dips. Pew, his kisses turn me on. Unable to control it, I flush, and he chuckles. Damn it. Will he be able to tell that he gets me hot and bothered all the time now?

Strolling away from him, I guide his friends into the house. As we walk up the stairs, they pause to look at the framed photos I hung.

"Are these Briggs drawings?" Annabelle asks.

I stop, look at them, and smile. "Yeah. They're too beautiful to keep in a box." I walk up to the Viking woman and trail my finger along her. "I don't know why, but this one is my favorite. I think it's the way he drew her eyes. They're full of pain, but she's a warrior, so she keeps a brave face." Looking at Annabelle, I see her features shift when she meets my gaze. I can't figure this chick out. I'm not sure I'll ever really get through to her.

As I open the door to the largest room, I see a glass desk and an office chair in the far corner, with framed photos of magazines I've appeared in and movie posters nearby. Beside it is a desk with a sewing machine and rolls of fabric behind it—long racks of lingerie, swimsuits, and loungewear line two walls—while accessories and fragrances sit on shelves along the remaining wall.

"I only have one of each size and style, but if there's something you want that isn't here, let me know, and I can get it. I'm pretty sure I have a stockpile at my office in Nashville." I tell them, then walk over to my desk. As I rest against it, I watch them look at everything. Then I see Annabelle eyeing a red clutch purse. I decide to be the bigger person here. I have to try for Briggs.

I inhale and walk over to stand beside her. "Do you like this one?" I ask.

"I do. It's adorable. When are you releasing it?" she giggles lightly. "I have a pin-up cherry dress that would go well with it."

Smiling, I lightly touch her shoulder and grab the clutch. "Here. They're already in production."

"Oh, no. I can't do that. I was an asshole earlier." She looks at me, embarrassed.

"We're all assholes sometimes. Doesn't mean we're bad people."

She blushes slightly, then accepts the clutch.

"You ladies can take anything you want."

"I'm not going to lie, I've been eyeballing a high-waisted bikini for the Fourth of July party. I still have the baby pooch," Birdie says, picking up the one she wanted.

"Have at it. Astor, I have a white corset with backless panties and a soft-pink lingerie set you might like. Maybe for the honeymoon." I wiggle my brows at her, and she busts out laughing.

"Yes. You're a rockstar. I saw them and was going to ask."

"They're all yours."

At my desk, I watch as they go through what's here and ask about some things that aren't. I make a mental note of the items they're asking about so I can see if I have any in the office.

When I hear a knock, I look up as Briggs walks in with a plate and a bottle of water. When he sees the magazine covers, he freezes, staring at them. I forgot he hadn't been in this room yet. He's respectful and didn't want to interrupt my work up here.

He stares at the photos of me in a full-length black sheer dress, sitting on a black horse and holding its reins. The photographer used fans to blow my hair and position my dress behind me. It's funny because the dress is one of Birdie's mom's designs, but she doesn't seem to notice.

Some might think my childhood would have kept me from modeling, but it didn't. I'm in a safe place, and I have full control when I model. I choose what I want others to see and whether I'll pose with anyone. It's professional.

"I haven't seen these," he says, bringing me the water and setting down a plate with a sandwich and fruit on the desk.

"They're gorgeous, aren't they?" Bridie says, standing next to him and staring.

To me, they're evidence of how far I've come and how hard I've worked to get here. I look away from them and take a bite of the sandwich.

"Stunning," Briggs whispers.

"Damn. I have to go. I leaked," Birdie says, shaking her head.

My brows pinch, and I look at her. Then I see the wet spots. Yup, glad I won't have to go through that.

"Journey, I am so glad I got to meet you," she says with a smile.

"Same. I look forward to getting to know you better," I tell her. Trying to be polite, I squeeze her hand instead of hugging her wet chest.

"I hope we can get together soon. Sorry, she's our ride," Astor says, hugging me. She's a short little thing.

"I'm sorry I came on so strong," Anna says next. Briggs' jaw slackens as he watches us.

"No worries. I get it," I tell Anna.

When they all leave, I finish the food while Briggs looks around the space.

"You know you can come up here anytime? Even if I'm working. I don't mind. I have to go to the office in Nashville sometime this week if you want to see that space, too."

"I don't want to bother you if you're working," he says, taking the plate from my hand, and we walk downstairs.

100

"It wouldn't bother me. Are we expecting any more visitors?" I ask as I slip off my socks and shoes.

He sets the plate in the sink and sighs. "I hope not."

Walking toward the sliding door, I open it and take off my shirt. Unsnapping my bra, I let it fall to the ground, meeting Briggs's bulging eyes.

Briggs groans and watches me as I walk backward, unbuttoning my shorts on my way to the pool. I let them fall, kick them to the side, and shimmy out of my panties at the edge of the pool.

Our eyes meet, and I smirk at him. "You coming, big sexy?"

I don't think I've ever seen anyone undress as quickly as he did. He doesn't stop when he reaches me. Instead, he grabs me and pulls me into the pool with him.

I tickle his sides underwater, and he squirms away from me and up to the surface. Coming up behind him, I laugh because I now know he's just as ticklish.

Briggs swims to me and pulls me into his embrace. I wrap my arms and legs around him, holding him as his raging hard-on presses between my legs. My body shifts, and I slide down him with ease. Okay, not with ease. It hurts, but I like it. My pulse picks up, and my breath catches as his thickness fills me. Fuck, he makes me feel so full.

"Baby, you should let your body heal." His voice comes out thick and husky. He says one thing, then grabs a handful of my ass, cups the nape of my neck, and moves his hips slowly.

God, he's impressive. There's no better feeling in the world. I know this will likely crash and burn in the end, but for now, I have to have him while I can.

I shake my head slightly as I kiss him slowly, moving with his gentle rhythm. "You feel so good, Briggs. I don't want to stop having you."

"Never, sweetheart. I love the way you feel. It's fucking amazing." He groans as I snap my hips. "And the way you move your gorgeous body." I feel his control slipping as he moans loudly.

He thrusts harder, his grip on my ass tightening as the water surrounds us. I dig my fingers into his hair and claw at his back with my other hand.

He groans and pumps faster. "I need you to cum with me, Ney." He latches onto my breast, releases my ass, brings his hand between us, and massages my swollen bud while I move up and down his length.

I feel my pussy clench and my stomach tighten. "Briggs, love," I moan as an explosion of glitter and sparkles flashes behind my eyes, and I cry out.

"That's it, baby," he groans, burying himself to the base and stilling, taking my mouth in another desperate kiss.

We breathe heavily as we ride out the high.

"I think we should stay home and do this all day," I rasp.

"Agreed, but we have to let your body rest in between."

I chuckle, and my insides warm at how he makes sure I'm taken care of. "Okay." Ok."

Eleven

Briggs

When I park in front of the shop, I see at least eight people waiting outside. We don't open for another 30 minutes, and we already have a fucking line. Thankfully, Jamie hired two people to help at the front. We've been so busy that we've had to start scheduling appointments.

Once I open the car door and step out, the dogs jump out behind me. I don't usually leash them when I come here. They listen well, but I grab the leashes from the front seat just in case. I look at the people standing there, watching the dogs as we approach. They're huge and could look scary to some people. As I suspected, they sit next to me while I unlock the front door and let them in.

"We close on the space next door on Wednesday," Jamie tells me as I walk into the shop. Then he looks at the two dogs beside me. "Are we running a dog daycare now?"

"That was quick, and Journey had to go to Nashville this morning. They won't get in the way. I'll put them in the office if they do." Who am I kidding? It's just an excuse. I love these two dogs, and I'm pretty sure they love me, especially Charm. She follows me everywhere.

He chuckles and shakes his head. "Cash talks." Jamie turns, grabs the pad from his desk, and hands it to me as I approach his booth. "What do you think of this for the new booth setups?"

I take the sketches from him and review them. The new design includes eight booths, two private rooms, and two offices. It's exciting to see we're busy enough to need more space.

"It looks good. How long do we expect it to take?"

"Baxter gave me Walker's number. He's coming in today to look at opening the wall between the two spaces. He'll give us a time frame and an estimate." Guess it's nice that your brother's best friend is a contractor.

"Sounds good. Got a fucking line out there already. It's going to be another busy day," I tell Jamie.

"Yup, it's crazy. It won't be so bad once we get the expansion and more artists."

"Here's to hoping."

As I whistle to the dogs, they happily follow me to my booth. Journey has taught me the commands to keep things consistent with them. These two are her beloved babies.

I set my belongings down and head to the front to get ready for my appointment, scheduled for about 15 minutes from now.

When the door opens, I look up and see our two new employees walking in. Slim is younger and just getting into tattoos. He schedules appointments, takes deposits, and records the estimate. Terry is older and covered in tattoos, like the rest of us. He is an experienced tattoo artist who can provide accurate estimates for the designs people request. He had to quit tattooing

104

after an accident fucked his hand up. He also serves as security for the place. He and his brother are friends with my dad, too.

"You brought the girls in today? They can hang out with us up front. I'll keep an eye on them for you," Terry says as the dogs trot out of the booth for pets.

"Thanks. Journey should be here sometime today. If she doesn't stay to hang out, she'll take them home with her."

"Okay. I'll keep my eyes open if she does. I may have a shaky hand, but I can still fuck someone up if I need to," he adds with a grin, and I don't doubt it.

Chuckling, I finish what I'm working on. "I believe you, and we appreciate it."

"Of course."

As I'm walking to my booth, Tink and Alice walk in, arguing about something stupid, and the stream of people moves toward the front. I notice the woman I'm working with today and call her back. I have her scheduled for 6 6-hour sessions because of the intricate detail of the Medusa tattoo she wanted.

As I get her set up, I hear the machines around me come to life. Once she's situated, I dip the ink.

"If you need a break at any point, let me know."

"Will do."

Leaning forward, I start working on the outlines. I appreciate that this chick isn't very talkative. If the customer doesn't talk, I can concentrate better on my work. However, I feel I should engage if they are nervous talkers.

Lately, I've had to ignore some because all they want to talk about is Journey, and I will not discuss our personal life with strangers who are digging for information.

Over the past week, Journey has taken it upon herself to spend more time with Birdie, Astor, and Anna. I love that Ney was quick to jump down Anna's throat after her little accusation last week, but she also expressed a desire to get along for my sake.

I've been preparing since the run-in with Journey's biological mother. She thinks she'll bring me down and that her childhood will change my opinion of her. It won't, and I want to be ready in case she decides to run. I wasn't kidding when I told her I would find her.

I want to look up what happened to her, but I've been resisting the urge. It's her story to tell me, and I refuse to be like the motherfucker digging into every inch of her life. I spoke to my parents about that night, and as I suspected, neither of them had a different opinion of her. Mom said Audrey told her a little about what Ney went through.

Killing Van is still on my to-do list. The way he said those chilling words to her told me what I needed to know. He hurt her. I can't even say how much of a relief it was to know she never slept with that man.

It's satisfying to know I'm the only man she's trusted to give herself to. And fuck me if she isn't giving herself to me every chance we get now. Sex with Journey is like a drug, and I'm addicted. Okay, I need to avoid that topic. Just thinking about her excites Vlad the Impaler.

By the time I sit up to stretch, the woman I'm working with has reached her pain limit, but she was a trooper and barely said ten words to me the entire time.

Once the woman is out of the chair, I start cleaning my station. Walker walks in just as I finish. I check the time and see it's five. Journey still isn't here. I feel a sense of panic and dig my phone out to text her.

Me:

> Is everything ok, Sunrise

Sunrise:

> Sorry, the meeting ran late.
> I'll be there soon, Stud.

Me:

> Ok, baby. Be careful.

A wave of relief washes over me, knowing she's on her way. I hate that she always feels she has to apologize. Striding over to the attached building, I step inside and look around the open space. It's bigger than I thought. Eight booths will fit nicely. Glancing over, I see Walker talking to Jamie. He's a tall, slim guy with long black hair and dark brown eyes.

"Hey, Briggs. It's good to see you," Walker says, stepping up to me and shaking my hand.

"You too. How's it looking in here?"

"It won't take too long to do what you guys want. Most of the work will be knocking down the wall. I told Jamie that if you can close for a week, we can get the wall down, then use a temporary closure to separate the space and finish off this half."

"I like that idea," Jamie says, stroking his beard.

"You need the wall down to add these booths?" I ask, pointing to the sketch.

Walker tilts his head, looks at the drawing, then at the wall. "Now that you have me looking at it again, we can take the wall out and do those at the same time," he says, pointing to two other booths.

"I'd say leave it until last, then. I'm worried about the noise and jumpy clients. We're not working with washable marks over there." I joke, kind of. The last thing we need is a customer jerking their body while we're using permanent tools because they were startled.

Walker chuckles and scratches his face.

"Well, I think we have a plan. When can you start?" Jamie asks him.

"Next Monday. I have a couple of other projects to finish this week."

"Sounds good. Will you be at the Fourth party next weekend?" I ask him. He and his daughter have never missed it.

"Yeah, Lea looks forward to it and's excited to play with Harley in the pool. That means I get to swim so I can keep an eye on her. That kid's a fucking daredevil." We all chuckle as we walk out of the building. When I see the Bronco pulling in, I say bye and make my way to my goddess.

Journey steps out in four-inch black heels and a tight red pantsuit, with a black corset underneath. She looks like she could rule the underworld, and she's mine. I bite my lip and smile as her bright amber eyes meet mine. She tilts her head up, but she looks like she's had a long day. I make my way to her, wrap my arms around her, and rub her back with both hands, instantly soothing her. She wraps her arms around my neck and leans into me.

"Long day, sweetheart?"

"Yes. Now kiss me." She demands with a toothy grin.

Chuckling, I bury my fingers in her hair and tilt her head up. I press my lips to hers in a slow, sensual kiss. Journey moans and arches into me, bringing the cervical destroyer to life—Ney protests with a growl as our lips part.

I hold her close and nip her ear. "If I don't stop, I will fuck you right here."

"Ugh, fine." She huffs.

"I still have a couple of hours of work. Then, when we get home, you can have as much of me as you want."

"Mm, I like that. You're forgiven, McLovin."

Holding her hand, I walk with her into the shop. She pauses, glancing at Jamie and Walker with a curious tilt of her head, taking a moment to study them. "Who's that with Jamie?"

"That's the contractor Walker. He's friends with Baxter. Why?"

"He looked familiar, that's all." She looks away, tightens her grip on my hand, and quickens her pace toward the front door. I glance at Walker and see him staring at Journey. Before I can think twice, he looks away and gets into his truck.

Fucking weird.

Inside, Journey plays with the dogs and looks even more badass with them by her side. I pat her ass, kiss her temple as I walk past, and give her a devilish grin. I speak her love language. Journey loves my touch, and I am more than happy to oblige. Hell, it's taking everything I have to finish this last tattoo instead of taking her home and sinking inside her.

She smirks at me, then sits next to Terry, and they start talking. At my station again, I set up for the guy waiting in my chair and get to work.

"Journey, want to go to Lucky Eights tonight?" Tink asks.

"Yup. Just the girls?" Ney asks. Before I can say anything, Jamie dives right in.

"No. Absolutely not. Briggs and I will take you two."

"Excuse you, big brother." Journey turns in her chair and stares at an unfazed Jamie.

"Don't give me that shit, Tiny. You know it's a bad idea to be out on your own right now. I'm not letting my little sister and girlfriend go out unprotected. Briggs, back me up here." Jamie argues with her, but drags me into it.

Journey looks at me, narrowing her eyes, daring me to side against her. She isn't going to like my answer. "Sorry, sweetheart. I'm with Jamie."

"Traitor." She grumbles and turns around, making me laugh. "Alice, do you want to come? And you two?" Journey asks everyone.

"Can't. I have plans," Alice says, and Slim follows her lead. "Same." Damn it, I hope they aren't hooking up. Work breakups suck to deal with.

"What about you, Terry?" she asks, then starts doing something on her iPad.

"Sure. I was meeting my brother there later anyway," Terry tells her, then looks at what she's doing.

I listen as she tells him what she's looking at. It's incredible to watch her interact with people. Don't get me wrong, there are some she wants nothing to do with, but others she instantly connects with. Terry is one of those people for some reason. Hm, maybe I should ask what made her so comfortable with him.

After wiping the tattoo I was working on, I applied a second skin and escorted the guy to the front. He stares sheepishly at Journey for a moment before opening his mouth.

"Would it be rude if I asked for an autograph?" he asks her.

"Yes," I tell him gruffly—this little shit. Ney turns to me and gives me a chilling look. Oh, damn.

"Not at all. Tink, can you toss me a marker?" she asks Tink instead of me. Yup, I just pissed her off. Tink grabs a marker and tosses it to her. "What do you want signed?" she asks the guy, and he hands her his hat. Journey signs it and adds a heart. "Want a picture too?" she asks him, and I fucking know it's to spite me. Clenching my jaw, I watch her shift in the seat.

"Hell yeah." She stands 6'4" in her heels and towers over the guy. "Damn, you're a lot taller than I realized." He looks up at her with his jaw agape. She chuckles and steps next to him. She keeps a two-foot distance, takes a photo of them on his phone, then hands it back.

Journey turns and glares at me as the guy leaves. "He was polite about it. People will ask for pictures or autographs, and you'll have to be okay with that. I understand there's a time to say no. You need to learn when that is, too. I'll see you at home." She walks over, grabs her bag, and calls the dogs. Terry, being the guard dog he is, walks her to her car.

"You just fucked up." Tink and Jamie laugh behind me.

"Yeah, I caught that." Groaning, I realize I let jealousy get the best of me. She had already had a stressful day, and I just made it worse.

"Are you two still coming?" Tink asks.

"Yeah. She might kill me if I try to get her to stay home."

"Oh, she will, or she'll leave your ass at home and come out with us alone. Journey has a mean streak, and she looked like she had a shit day." Jamie chuckles again.

"We'll see you guys there."

I grab my things and head to my car, feeling tense. I really want to find a way to make things right with her. I know I shouldn't have overstepped, and she's right about accepting who she is. It's tough, especially since many of these guys have seen her half-naked.

In the car, I start driving home. Others may have seen only half her body, but I'm the only one she's let have her, and I need to remember that.

As I step into the house, I notice her belongings casually tossed onto the island. She's had a busy day. Usually, she's so good about putting her things away. Standing in the doorway of our bedroom, I watch her walk out of the bathroom. She looks like a more confident version of Lara Croft, dressed in high-waisted cargo pants, a long black belt, a sleek black high-neck crop top, and sturdy black boots. Her hair is in a relaxed, chunky braid that drapes over her front. Honestly, I might have stopped breathing for a moment. When her golden, flaky eyes lift to meet mine, they soften with a gentle expression.

"Hey, baby." I approach her and gently cup her cheek in my hand. "I'm sorry I overstepped tonight."

She responds by rising on her toes and brushing her lips against mine. "It's okay. Get dressed. I need a drink and something to eat."

"You didn't eat today, did you?" I ask, stepping into the closet to grab clothes.

"I got busy and forgot." She sighs, confirming she had a long day.

I want to argue with her about making sure she eats. It's been a thing for me since I found out she was starved as a child. But I know not to push my limits any further. Let's hope tonight goes smoothly.

Twelve

Journey

I love riding with Briggs on the motorcycle. It's one of the most freeing things. He stopped so we could eat before we reached Luckey Eights. He always makes sure I eat. When I get off the bike, I wait for him. Once he dismounts, my arms slip around his waist, and he brings his hand around to thumb my neck. He knows I need his touch.

I shouldn't have snapped at him earlier. Briggs is possessive, and that's all he was doing. My day was total shit. The wrong photo was sent for the swimsuit collection, and I had some pissed-off models calling. I smoothed it over with them, assured them the images had not been approved, and said I would fix it.

We had to resend everything with the approved photo, and I have IT working on figuring out how the other one was sent from my fucking email.

On my drive home, I was almost run off the road by a road rager. I ran over a squirrel in the process and cried. Then tonight, the man talking to Jamie looked so familiar, and it irritated me that I couldn't place him. All of today's events were mediocre, but it still made for a shit day.

At the door, I pause and turn to him. Briggs's Caribbean eyes meet mine. He pinches his brows when I don't say anything right away. Holy hell, he's gorgeous. I love it when he leaves his wavy hair down. I trail my gaze over his thick, muscular arms and rippled stomach. Damn it, I need to reroute my brain from the constant lust it seems to be in.

"I'm sorry, too. I shouldn't have snapped at you. I try to keep my emotions in check, but I failed tonight because I had a bad day. That wasn't fair to you. I'll try not to let it happen again." I apologize.

"Sunrise, you had every right to put me in my place. I acted out of jealousy, not logic. I always want you to express how you're feeling." He states, squeezing my hip.

How can someone so good and pure exist?

"You're too good for me, Hercules."

Briggs grips my chin, pulls my mouth to his, and gives me a deep kiss before pressing his lips to my forehead.

"I wish you could see what I see inside you. It's the other way around, Ney. How about we agree we're good for each other?"

With a broad smile, I bow my head. "I can agree to that. Can you rub my back for just a minute before we go in?" I ask, needing his touch before we walk into the sea of people.

"Absolutely," he says as I rest my head on his collarbone. I take in all of Briggs. He's the only person I've ever let this close to me, and it's easy with him.

"Thank you." I breathe.

"You don't have to thank me for taking care of you. I want to. Do you feel better?"

He says I don't have to thank him, but I do. Very few people have been there for me in my life. He started taking care of me when I was still a stranger, and he didn't hesitate.

I shake my head and squeeze his waist before releasing him. "Very much."

He leaves his hand on the small of my back, holding me protectively against him. As we step inside, half the crowd pauses to look at us. Briggs kisses my head and leads me to our group. I'm surprised to see his brother, Baylor, sitting with everyone. I've only met him once.

"Bro. New sis. About time you two showed up," Baylor says.

"Everyone else just got here, shithead," Briggs tells his brother.

"Hello, Baylor. Did you throw those posters away like you were supposed to?" I raise a brow and smirk at him. A broad grin spreads across his face because he knows I only asked to mess with Briggs.

"I did. Well, all except one. I hid it under my mattress." He fake-whispers under his breath. Briggs is not amused, so I hold back my laughter.

"The fuck, Bay?" Briggs grumbles. "I'm going to get a drink. Can I trust you to watch her? Without touching her?" he asks his brother, and I lose it. I burst into laughter and stand next to his brother.

"You bet. You know I won't do anything, asswipe."

Briggs sighs and runs a hand through his hair. "I know. Don't let anyone near her unless we know them." He waits a minute, then concedes and goes to the counter.

"A bit overprotective, isn't he?" Baylor asks me.

"Yeah. I had to ask if he was going to piss on me so everyone would know I'm his."

Baylor chuckles. "I think it's bred into our blood. Beau's the same way with Birdie."

"I don't mind. It's nice to have someone who wants to protect you instead of hurting you." My eyes widen as I look at him. I shouldn't have blurted that out. "That came out wrong. Jamie and my parents have always protected me. I mean." I huff out a breath and steady myself. I need to learn to think before speaking.

Bays' features soften when his eyes meet mine. "I won't say anything."

I let out an exasperated sigh. "Briggs knows some and suspects others." I purse my lips and look at my feet. I'm making this worse.

"Hey, really, you don't have to explain. That's between you two. I will say you're part of our family now, and if anyone messes with one of us, they mess with all of us." Baylor smiles and bumps my shoulder with his.

"Thank you. I've only met everyone briefly, but your family seems kind."

"Eh, we try. So, do you have any hot model friends you can invite for a visit?" he asks, wiggling his brows at me, which makes me laugh. Thank fuck he changed the subject.

"I might have a couple. I'll see what I can do."

"Yes."

"Yes, what?" Briggs asks as he walks up to us with two beers. He hands me one and kisses my forehead.

"Ny has model friends," he says, giving us an animated look.

"Don't encourage him," Briggs says, leading us over to the rest of our friends. As we walk up to the group, Tink bursts out laughing.

"What's so funny over here?" I ask, sipping my beer.

"I was just telling them how I kissed you before I knew you were Jamie's sister." Tink's eyes light up every time she tells this story. I'm pretty sure her girl crush is still solid.

Briggs chokes on his drink and starts coughing. I pat his back and laugh with her. Jamie almost died that day.

"Yeah, she did that. You should have seen Jamie's face."

"You what?" Briggs' voice is hoarse from coughing.

"In my defense, he knew I had a girl crush on her, and all he told me was that he had someone he wanted me to meet. When she walked into the living room, I went full steam ahead. I thought she was my gift."

Tink loves making Jamie uncomfortable, and she is completely unashamed of her actions.

"She jumped off the couch so fast. Ran, jumped on me, and boom, tongue and all." I crack up at the memory. Glancing at Jamie's disgusted face, I laugh harder and point. "He had that same look then, too."

"Bro, she made out with your wife." Baylor barks out a laugh, then looks to Jamie. "And your sister. That's fucking funny."

"It's not." Briggs and Jamie grumble in unison. Terry chuckles and shakes his head.

"This is my brother Hendrix. I figured I'd better introduce him so you wouldn't think he was some old weirdo," Terry says to me, pointing to a tall man with a lean frame. He's tanned, with black hair and amber-colored eyes. My eyes bounce between the two. I can tell they're brothers of Native American descent. Maybe that's why I'm comfortable with Terry. We share that, in some ways.

"It's nice to meet you, Hendrix. Don't tell the others, but Terry is my favorite person at the shop," I whisper, shaking his hand.

He chuckles and zips his lips. "You can call me Henry."

Smiling at him, I nod. He and Terry have a calming aura.

"Henry is a fire captain. Baylor works with him," Briggs tells me.

"Oh, that's awesome. Do you like your job?" I ask, leaning against the pool table. I'm aware there are more people here, but I haven't talked to this guy yet. I trust Terry. Let's see if I can trust his brother, too.

"I do, but it's stressful at times. Watching over a firehouse is like watching over a roomful of toddlers," Henry says, and Bay gasps dramatically.

"We are not that bad. We're like ten-year-olds," Baylor jokes with Henry.

"Please. I'm lucky you dickheads know how to wipe your own asses." Henry and I both laugh at his quip.

"Is it anything like the TV shows? I know the chances of a bee tornado or raining frogs aren't real, but is it like having a second family?" I ask, taking another sip of my beer.

"Yeah. You have to trust the people you're working with. Do you like being a designer?"

I smile and nod. "I do. When I was young, I thought I wanted to be a police officer, then a lawyer, and so on. I ended up in modeling, then acting, and finally designing. I like to stay busy."

"Why a cop?" Tink asks.

"I was nine. I didn't know what cops actually did. I just thought they looked like badasses in all their shit." I chuckle at her. "After I learned they could get shot, I scratched that thought."

Tink gives me a questioning look, then giggles. "Sissy."

"For sure. The most dangerous thing about modeling is twisting an ankle on the runway." I shrug and finish my beer as they all laugh.

"Don't let Ny fool you guys. She's got brass balls when she needs them. We were what?" Jamie thinks for a minute. "11 and

13 when Ny saw some kid trying to bully me. The little shit came flying at us out of nowhere, tackled the fucker like a football player, and started whaling on him."

Briggs holds my waist as pride fills me. Jamie and I have always watched out for each other. I huff. "Mess with my brother, and you get these guns," I say, flexing my biceps, which makes everyone burst out laughing.

"How long have you two been siblings?" Henry asks.

"Tiny was nine when she came to the home I was in, so seventeen years." Jamie pinches his brows, tilts his head from side to side, then nods, confirming he was right.

"They tried to separate us once. I went on a hunger strike, and Jamie kept running away."

Jamie chuckles with me at the memory. After the foster home was shut down, they tried to place us separately. They quickly realized it wasn't a good idea and put us back together.

"Are we playing pool or what?" I ask them. I'm about to kick all their asses and change the topic.

"Finally," Baylor says, then starts racking the balls.

"Why did they try to separate the two of you?" Briggs whispers to me.

"The foster home we were in got shut down, and they had to move all the kids." I leave it at that.

I watch his shoulders drop, and his sad eyes meet mine. The face of fucking pity. He knows, just like he has an idea of what Van's done. I hate that look in his eyes. That's why I don't talk about my past. The foster home was filthy, food was restricted, and kids were always getting hurt or bullying the smaller ones. The foster parents left us alone for days at a time. It was all around a shit home.

"Ny, you and me," Baylor says, handing me a stick.

"Sure thing, chicken wing." I plaster on my fake smile and set my empty drink on the table. Briggs steps aside without touching or kissing me. Now he's starting to see. Right now, my heart feels like it's already cracking.

I wait for Bay to break without pocketing any balls. Moving forward, I assess the table. I lean forward, set my stick in position, pull back, and then strike at my targets.

"Damn."

With a confident grin, I stroll around the table, feeling completely at ease with the game. I make two more moves, savoring the moment before I scratch.

"You could have warned me, Jamie."

"Where's the fun in that? Tiny's a shark."

"I see that now." Bay whines.

I watch and wait as he misses his shot. I pat his shoulder, get into position, and pocket each ball. I stare at the table before calling my last one. It looks impossible, but I know I can make it. My body stretches over the table. I draw the stick back and hit my mark. We all watch as the cue ball jumps, bounces, hits the eight ball where I want it, and then rolls into its bed.

"I win, baby carrot."

Baylor stands there, his jaw agape and his eyes wide with shock. "Seriously, how?"

"We had a pool table at home, and I got bored easily. I liked the strategy of it."

When I glance around, I don't see Briggs with the rest of the group, but I do see him at the bar, talking to a woman. She is beautiful, with short blonde hair, a heart-shaped face, and a cute button nose. My heart sinks, and my breath leaves my lungs. Surely he wouldn't flirt with her while I'm here. Right? Then they start laughing, and her hand goes to his arm.

Pain, fear, and anxiety have my heart sinking to my toes. What should I do? Should I interrupt or walk away? I suck in a breath, spin on my heels, and slam into Baylor.

"I'm sure it's not what you're thinking, Journey. Briggs would never hurt you," he says mildly.

"Sure," I mutter, giving him a weak smile. Sighing, I set the stick down and walk to the restroom. After I finish, I stare at myself in the mirror as I wash my hands.

I have no right to think that man loves me after only a few weeks, and I have no right to ask him to carry the burden of my past. Some people can't handle it, and I know that. I was fully aware that Briggs was too good for me by the second day we were together, but I have a habit of clinging to the people who make me feel safe and loved. I've already committed to riding this out until it ends, so I pull my shit together and go face my fears.

As I leave the restroom, a broad figure blocks my path, preventing me from passing. It's not Briggs. No, I know the scent of this cologne. My heart thunders in my chest so hard I can feel it in my ears. Stay strong. Stand your ground. I've done it before. I can do it again.

I look up and meet Van's gaze. He raises his hand, grips my throat, and pushes me into the shadowed corner. "You think you're clever, don't you, mouse? Marrying that man was a mistake you shouldn't have made," he says, his voice sharp with anger.

Stay strong. Stand your ground.

"Too late. He's mine now. You were never going to break me. I'm smarter than you, Van. You played a weak game. You're an abusive loser who couldn't hack it as a fighter and hasn't had a movie deal in years. You're nothing," I hiss through gritted teeth.

121

His grip tightens, cutting off my air. When he steps closer, I squeeze my eyes shut and turn my head.

"Oh, little mouse. I will get my claws into you again. You will be mine, Journey. And when you are, I will take everything from you."

The hell he will. I still have Briggs for now. I open my eyes, drawing on the strength Briggs has given me, and look Van dead in the eyes. "Fuck you," I rebuke him in a choked scream, spitting to make sure my saliva hits him in the face.

Van draws his hand back, but before either of us can do anything else, he's ripped away from me and flung at least fifteen feet. Relief floods me when I see Briggs's large frame crowd me. He cups my neck and locks eyes with mine. "Are you okay, baby?" Unable to find my words, I clutch my throat and nod. He kisses my temple, then turns and stalks toward Van, wrapping his left hand around the man's throat. Damn, Briggs just went from Hercules to Hades.

Both are equally sexy.

"You think you're a big man, cornering and holding a woman down by her throat so you can threaten and hit her. Not just any woman, but *MY* woman. *MY* wife." Briggs thunders, baring his teeth at Van. "Nah, that's not how we do things here. Around here, we protect our ladies."

"Screw you. I'll kick your ass and then get her while you try to recover." Van barely gets the words out before swinging and hitting Briggs' jaw. I watch his leg come up and connect with Briggs' ribs. I gasp, but Briggs seems unfazed. He doesn't lose his hold on Van's throat and lets out a twisted laugh. Van's eyes widen as his moves do nothing to the brick house in front of him.

As I look around, I see the other men stopping what they are doing; they shift or cross their arms and glare at Van. Without warning, Briggs pulls back and punches Van in the nose, causing blood to pour out.

Jamie comes up, helps steady me, wraps his arm around my shoulders, and rubs my bicep.

"You just fucked up, compadre," Baylor whistles, then crosses his arms over his chest and scowls at Van.

"You're not going anywhere near her again. I warned you once." Briggs' voice cracks like a whip, then he punches Van twice more and releases him. "Get the hell out of here."

Van stumbles, holds his nose, and glares at me.

"I'll get you, mouse," Van tells me, because he's an idiot who has to have the last word. I flick my wide-eyed gaze to Briggs, whose eyes darken to a color I've never seen, and he snaps.

"Motherfucker." Briggs roars. He lunges toward Van, swinging a left and two right hooks. Van collapses on the last swing. Briggs squats beside him, watching him groan and hold his face. "Not so tough now, are you, you piece of shit? I will end you if you come near her again. This is your last warning." Before Briggs stands, he slaps Van hard across the face, for good measure, making his head swing to the side and bloody saliva fly from his mouth and nose. A bitch slap is pretty degrading for a man like Van.

I watch as Henry and Terry laugh, get Van to his feet, and toss his ass out the front doors. Glancing around, I see everyone return to what they were doing as if nothing had happened. Damn, I love this small town.

Jamie lets me go when Briggs stalks up to me and pulls me into his arms. He rubs my back and rests his cheek on my head. His body is tense, the rage still rioting inside him.

I bring my arms around him lightly so I don't hurt his ribs, then gently touch the red mark on his jaw. "I'm sorry. You're hurt," I whisper to him.

"There's nothing for you to be sorry for, Sunrise. And I'm okay. I have three brothers. We kicked each other's asses all the time. That was nothing." Briggs studies the red mark on my neck and sighs. I watch as the color of his eyes seems to shift again. He brings his hand up and thumbs the mark. "I'm sorry he got to you before I got to him. I won't leave you again, baby."

"It was my fault. I wouldn't have left the group if I'd known Van was here. I saw that woman touch you, and I just... I don't know," I say weakly. What I should say is that I got hella jealous.

Briggs gazes into my eyes. I love his Caribbean irises. "Oh, sweetheart. That was Alice's mom. I apologize if it looked like something it wasn't. You're the only woman I want. My heart. My Sunrise. My wife." He kisses my face with each admission. My lungs ease as he explains what I saw and calls me those sweet words. My chest thunders, and I feel that flutter in the pit of my stomach.

He offers me a warm smile as I hold his face in my hands. "You're my heart, too. Thank you for being so good to me."

"Sunrise, don't ever thank me for that. Let me take you home and hold you," he whispers.

"Ok," I whisper.

After we say goodbye and make it home, Briggs cocoons me to him and gently rubs my neck. His body is still stiff, and he's still pissed that Van managed to get to me. Scooting closer, I snuggle into his neck.

Thirteen

Briggs

Warm, silken lips wrap around my stiff shaft, making my hips jerk and waking me from my slumber. My eyes flutter open, and I look down at my sweet goddess of a wife with my cock in her mouth.

Waking up like this has got to be the best fucking way to start a new day. I've told Ney she could wake me up anytime she wanted, and son of a bitch, she's finally doing it.

"Fuck, sweetheart. That feels so good, baby," I rasp in a sleepy voice, digging my fingers into her lustrous hair.

She wraps her slender hand around the base and twirls her smooth tongue around my crown, making it twitch and stealing my breath.

"Mm." She hums around me, adding to the sensation. Her blazing globes stare up at me as her lips cover my tip, and she glides her warm, wet mouth down my throbbing cock.

My girl isn't just sucking my dick. She's claiming me as hers, and I love it.

I tangle my fingers deeper into her hair and hold on a bit tighter than intended, but she moans and speeds up, swallowing every inch of me. Today is the first time she's given me a blowjob, and it's incredible.

"Yeah, baby, just like that." I groan because, damn it, it's the best thing I've ever felt. My hips jerk, and my stomach spasms.

"You're doing so well, sweetheart." I groan and praise her as my toes curl with each stroke of her mouth moving up and down me.

I almost cry out like a little bitch when she lightly grazes her teeth along my hardened cock and squeezes my balls. I'm pretty sure I fucking whimpered from the sensation.

Ney is a cock-sucking queen, taking me like a motherfucking magician doing a disappearing act. Holy hell, that has got to be the hottest thing I've ever seen.

"I'm going to cum, sweetheart." Her hands grip the insides of my thighs, squeezing, digging her claws in to keep me in place. "Ney, fuck." I tilt my head back and squeeze my eyes shut. Thrusting my hips once more, I feel my stomach and balls tighten as my cock spasms, and I release down her throat. Sparks and flames erupt behind my eyes. "Damn, Journey, you're perfect, baby. That was amazing." She smiles around me, sucking me clean, then releases me with a pop before licking her lips.

"Mm. I wanted to give you a good wake-up. Get dressed, love. I'm taking you somewhere." She purrs, crawling up my body, then gives me a deep, soul-shattering kiss. I dig my fingers into her ass and hold her close.

When she breaks our kiss and looks down at me with her glowing eyes, I feel it. She is everything. I love her. I love her more than I've ever loved anything in my life.

"Journey, I." She places her thumb over my lips, whispering it over them, stopping me from saying what I need to say.

"Get dressed, dreamboat," she whispers. Giving me an open kiss, she rolls off me and heads to the closet.

I can tell whatever we're about to do is important to her. I jump off the bed and stride into the closet, still naked, then grab her from behind, making her giggle.

"You should let me take care of you," I tell her, nibbling her ear. Twisting in my arms, she runs her fingers through my hair, making me moan. The scrape of her nails across my scalp feels amazing.

"You do, love, in the best way. This morning was for you. I've never done it before, but I've watched videos and wanted to try it."

My mouth opens and closes for a minute. There's no way that was her first time. Hell, maybe it was. Ney is the best at everything I've ever had.

"Never? That was phenomenal, sweetheart."

"Yeah. All the things we've done have been my first, except kissing." Shrugging, she looks down at her feet. She's so freaking adorable and innocent. "I've never trusted someone enough. Van was the first guy I'd dated, and he was more interested in mind-fucking me."

My face instantly heats at the mention of his name, and images of what he did to her last night flash before my eyes. I want to kill the fucking prick. I almost did. He was lucky we had a roomful of people watching me beat his ass. I wasn't kidding when I said I'd end him next time.

"You're mine now, my heart. I will always protect you and make sure you're taken care of and happy." I peck her nose, then release her so we can get dressed.

"I like that." She giggles lightly.

"What?" I ask, stepping aside and picking out a pair of jeans and a shirt.

"When you say my heart, that you take care of me, and how happy you make me. I like all of it. You're my heart, too, gorgeous. I hope you know that."

I walk over to her, press my lips to the top of her head, and inhale the lilac scent. "I do, sweetheart. I can feel it here." I reach around and place my palm on her heart. "We were destined to be together, Journey. Two halves of the same heart, now whole."

"You think?" She said in a weak voice, leaning against me.

"I know. Where are you taking us today?"

She sighs softly and chooses a comfortable pair of jeans and a fun graphic T-shirt. "I need to start letting go, and I want to share it with you." Her words carry so much emotion.

"Okay, baby." I give her a quick rub, then head to the restroom.

Once I've dressed, I brush my teeth and pull my hair back. In the mirror, I see a slight bruise on my jaw and feel the one on my ribs, but I've had worse. It was worth protecting her. I step out of the bathroom and head to the kitchen, where she has bagels and fruit ready for us.

After a quick breakfast, we set off on our drive. Twenty minutes later, we're pulling down an overgrown, bumpy drive when a shack of a house comes into view. The place is barely standing, and all the windows are broken out. My stomach sinks as I think about what this is and why she needs to let it go.

Journey parks and stares at the place before opening the door, and I follow behind her. We stop in front of the Bronco, and I gently wrap my arm around her to offer comfort and support.

"I called my therapist this morning and asked her how to let go of not feeling worthy enough. How do I start feeling like I deserve you? She told me I needed to let go of the past that still

128

controls my fear and that sharing it with you may help. Van undid a lot of the progress I've made over the years. I need to start over. This place is one of the things I need to let go of." She says, then stares off into space. I want to destroy everyone who's ever hurt her. I want blood from all of them.

"I'm right here, sweetheart. Let me take some of this from you," I murmur, kissing her shoulder.

Her shoulders relax slightly, and she points to the house. "This is where I lived from the time I was born until I was nine. The last time I was here, it was right before school. It was the first day of fifth grade, and I had just finished a two-week punishment."

She stops for a moment and leans into me. Holding her close, I try to pour my love into her.

"I could barely move my limbs. I hadn't eaten. Not real food, anyway, and I was in a lot of pain from the discipline." She sucks in a breath and wipes her eyes. "I walked to the bus stop, though. None of my teachers paid much attention to me, or maybe they didn't want to know the truth. Until Mrs. Everson. I could tell she knew as soon as she looked at me." Her sweet, raspy voice cracks.

"I asked to use the bathroom, but I couldn't get back up. It hurt so much, and at nine, I asked death to take me. But Mrs. Everson found me instead. When she opened the stall, she burst into tears at the sight of me. She helped me up and rushed me to the nurse's office. That was the day Sheila, Joseph, and one of my half-brothers, Gary, were arrested." She admitted with a shuddering breath.

The air leaves my own lungs. Brother. She has brothers who did this to her. My heart sinks, and anger boils inside me. I don't know what to say right now. What do you say to this? All I can do is be the man she needs me to be and love her.

"Ney, I'm so sorry." I look at her, then gently reach out to wipe away her tears.

"They always told me I wasn't good enough and that I deserved everything I got. That no one would ever love someone as pathetic and broken as me. I was a burden and a mistake. I heard those words for nine years. Joseph and Gary were obsessed with me and nicknamed me Lila because I smelled like lilacs. Sheila punished me twice as hard because of it. They never touched me. They just made comments." She reiterated. It's good she did, because my brain was about to take a dark-as-fuck turn, and I was going to have to start hunting people.

How could anyone do this to a child? I can't let her see how much this is tearing me up inside. She needs me to carry some of this so she can let it go, and I will, for her. I would do anything for her.

"My heart." My own voice cracks. I feel moisture gathering in my eyes. She turns and steps into me, hugging me. I rest my chin on her head and leave it there. I know she loves the sentiments. It's hard to find out why she needs so much affirmation and reassurance, and I will always give it to her.

"Gary was eight years older than me and would help Joseph. Then he'd help Sheila. He would laugh. God, he would laugh so hard while he watched me cry. Eventually, I just stopped. I stopped talking, crying, and screaming for Craig to help me."

"Oh, sweetheart. I wish I knew you then. I would have noticed. I would have helped save you."

"I know you would, baby. You're saving me now. Jamie and my parents are the only people I've shared some of this with. I never mention Gary or Craig," she admits. Ney is trusting me to keep this secret, and I will. I'll take it to my grave.

"Is that your other brother's name?" I want to find out where each of these fuckers is now.

She inhales deeply and kisses the base of my neck, ever so lightly. "Yeah, Craig is six years older than me. He never helped them. He was never mean to me. I used to think he was a coward, but I can't blame him. I was locked away most of the time, so I don't know whether they did it to him, too. He ran away a couple of months before school started, and I haven't heard from him since."

Journey turns and faces the dilapidated building. "There is so much pain in there. I needed you here so you could see and know why I still struggle. This house and those people were the first to break me."

I can feel the pain inside her. I'm outraged, but I can't show it. She picked up on me being upset last night, and I won't let her feel it today. I wrap my arms around her and offer the only thing I can. Support. I love her so much, and I hate the pain and fear she's felt. She gently takes my hands, unwraps them from her, and then walks with me up to the house.

The place is vacant and in disrepair as I step inside. The smell of mildew irritates my throat and makes my nose wrinkle. Dust cakes the few remaining surfaces. You can tell it's been used as a party house for teenagers and possibly as a temporary home for people with nowhere else to go. She walks me to a tiny space that would never be considered a bedroom.

"This was my room," she says. When I glance down, I see the stains on the floor and refuse to acknowledge what they are. "Sheila refused to tell anyone who my biological father was, so I ended up in the same home as Jamie." With a heavy sigh, she moves through the place until we're outside.

"People think it's weird how close we are, but Jamie was the first person to care for and protect me. After that, I clung to him. Then, when we were adopted, I clung to my parents. I'm sorry,

Hercules, I've done it to you, but in a whole different way." She whimpered as she tried to hold back her sob.

"Cling all you want, sweetheart. I want you to. I want to be your strength, your protector, and your love. I want to be everything you need. When you start to worry, please let me know, and I'll reassure you. When you're scared or anxious, I'll comfort you. Journey, staying married to you was never about anything other than me wanting to protect you and win you over." She giggles and steps into me, her face tear-stained. "Baby, I want to stay married to you because I love you. I love you so fucking much. I didn't know it yet, but I fell in love with you the moment you sat next to me at that bar. Honey bottom, I will carry all your burdens with you." I vow, meaning every goddamn word.

More tears stream from her whiskey eyes. "You love me? Even after everything I told you? Why?"

I gently rub her back and nuzzle my cheek against hers. "Because you're worth it, sweetheart. There's nothing you could say that would change that. You're mine, and I'm yours."

"I love you too. I was too scared to tell you. I didn't think you could love me. I thought you'd think I was too damaged. I still struggle with the idea that anyone could love me." She surrenders, clinging to me like Velcro.

"How could I not love you? You're incredible. I don't think you're anything but perfect, Sunrise. I think you needed the right person to make you whole, and that's me." I tell her, tucking her stray hairs behind her ears.

"I have a few more things, but I think you already suspect them." She sniffed.

I do. I know her shitbag of an ex laid hands on her and subjected her to mental torture. Between what her father said, what he told her at the restaurant, and last night, I know what that prick did.

"No one will hurt you while I'm around. I'll protect you with my entire being," I promised.

"I know you will. Thank you for being here with me and loving me anyway."

"Being here for you and loving you is the easiest thing I've ever done. Let me take you home and cuddle you."

She giggles in my arms. "You want to be my big, strong cuddle bug."

Chuckling, I take her hand and lead her away from the shit shack. "I do. I thought you liked my cuddles? We can watch all your favorite movies and eat all the junk food you want. Later, we can soak in a bath together. I'll give you a massage, paint your toenails, and give you all the forehead kisses you want."

"I do love your cuddles. You're really trying to wow me today. You just named all my favorite things." She laughs as I open the passenger door.

"I will never stop trying."

I shut her door, walk to the driver's side, and start the ignition. I wish I had expressed my love more romantically, but she needed to hear it now, especially after everything she had shared with me.

"Ney, what's your brother's last name?"

"Gary's is Thompson, and Craig's is Franklin. Why?"

"I was just curious. Since they had different last names, did they know who their fathers were?"

"Oh, I guess maybe they did. Sheila's last name is Brown, but that was also Joseph's. My previous name was Middleton before I was adopted, so maybe that was her name before she married Joseph? I didn't look into it once I got older. I have my true brother and parents. That's all that matters."

"Can I ask one more thing? You don't have to answer. I'm only asking."

"Okay, I'll tell you anything, but only you."

I reach out, take her hand, and tenderly kiss it. "I know, sweetheart. All your secrets are safe with me. What if your biological father didn't know about you? Would you want to meet him? Would you want to give Craig a chance to explain his side?" I ask, knowing these questions may be difficult since I will be researching the brothers. I want to know whether she wants to see Craig. I might eliminate Gary and dispose of him on a pig farm if I find him. Maybe I'll include Van in that task.

Ney sucks in a breath and thinks about it. "I guess if my biological father didn't know, I wouldn't mind knowing him, but I would worry about hurting my parents' feelings. I don't like to hurt people. And as for Craig." She thinks again. "I would like to hear his side. If he was hurt too, I can't blame him, and I'd like to know him... maybe. What if he was locked up, too? But then I would worry about hurting Jamie."

"I love that you always think of others. You have a gentle heart, Ney."

"I try to."

Ney leans over, hugging my arm. She nuzzles her nose into my bicep, just like she did the very first time we made our way home together. Who would have thought that accidentally getting married could turn out to be the most wonderful thing I've ever done in my life?

Fourteen

Journey

When I hear the tires crunching up the drive, I jump off the stool I've been perched on, impatiently waiting for Winter and the boys.

"They're here," I tell Briggs, then run to the front door, with him chuckling behind me.

It's been a few days since I started unlocking my secrets and sharing them with him. He's been right beside me the entire time, loving and supporting me through it all. He's been clinging to me just as much as I have to him. He truly is the love of my life, and I'm working to help my brain comprehend that.

I fling the front door open and bounce on my heels when I see Dylan and Daniel step out of the car. They let their hair grow into curly brown shags. Their hazel eyes meet mine, and they both smile at me.

"Aunt Ny." They both say it in unison and run up to me.

I rush over and hug them both. "You boys have gotten so big. It's only been six months, but I swear you each grew five inches. I missed you."

"We missed you, too. Is that your husband?" Dylan asks, flinging his head to the side to clear his hair from his eyes. Glancing back, I see Briggs right behind us.

"It is. His name is Briggs." I release the kids and step back. "Briggs, this is Dylan and Daniel."

"Look at all his tattoos. That's awesome," Daniel says, stepping closer.

I scoot past them and hug my best friend. Winter is 5'6 with medium-length, wavy white-blonde hair and crystal blue eyes. She's stunning, but she's lost weight since I last saw her.

"Ny, I gotta say he's hotter in person. It's no wonder you call him Hercules," she says, bumping me with her shoulder.

"He has two single brothers. We can call them Apollo and Ares." I whisper through cracked lips, wiggling my brows at her.

"Do they look like him?" she asks, arching a brow at me. I giggle and loop my arm through hers.

"Close. You'll meet them at the party tomorrow." As we stride over, we hear both boys asking Briggs about his tattoos. I release her and step up to Briggs, and he places a hand at the base of my ass.

"Cuddle whisperer, this is my best friend, Winter," I chirp. Briggs chuckles and shakes her hand.

"It's nice to meet you, Briggs," she says, narrowing her eyes and sizing him up.

"You two. Ny's told me a lot about you all," he tells her.

"Are the dogs inside, Aunt Ny?"

"Yeah, go on in and make yourselves at home. I'll help your mom get your stuff. There's a shit ton of snacks in there, too," I tell them, then start walking to the back of the SUV, with Briggs and Winter following behind me.

We gather what we need and walk to the other side of the house to enter the guest suite. "It's a three-bedroom, so there should be plenty of space, and you're. You're welcome to stay as long as you want."

"Briggs, I'm sorry to ask this, but could I talk to Ny alone for a few minutes?" Winter asks, fidgeting with her hands.

"Absolutely. Would it be okay if I took the kids to the shop, then to lunch? It'll give you two some time to catch up," Briggs asks her, then kisses my forehead. I can't help the smile on my face or the flutter in my heart. He's always doing that, and I love it.

"Actually, I'm sure they would love that. Thank you," she tells him, tossing a bag onto the couch.

"You're welcome. I'll let you know where we're eating, and I'll bring you both something." Briggs briefly presses his lips to mine. "I love you, sweetheart. If you need anything while I'm gone, let me know."

"I will. I love you, Hercules." Giving me one more kiss, he leaves us.

He's struggling to let me out of his sight, and I understand. He's doing it for us because my friend needs me. When we're alone, I make us both coffee, and we sit at the kitchen table. I glance at Winter, sipping my coffee while she plays with her cup. I won't push her to tell me what I suspect.

"Troy broke into the house while the boys and I were out, stealing everything valuable. Then he showed up at my job high, and I got fired."

I reach across the table, take her hand, and sit quietly.

"He was arrested before we left and won't be out for years. When I asked if the kids wanted to move here, they didn't hesitate. Everything we wanted to keep is in my car." She says in a shaky voice, trying to keep her composure.

"You came to the right place. If you need a job, I have an opening for an assistant, and I also need someone to manage my social media." I'm not lying. I hate social media and the time it takes to keep up with it.

"Thank you, Journey. I'm so sorry. I didn't know where else to turn, and the boys love you."

"Oh, sweetie. You're like a sister to me. You and those boys are my family. Stay as long as you want. I'm serious about hiring you." I lift a brow. I'm not letting her out of this. I'd happily pay her whatever she wants, so I don't have to do it myself.

"I've tried to help him, but he never really cared about us. The boys need this fresh start. When you offered, I just... I knew this was what we needed. Are you sure you and Briggs don't mind?" She sighs.

"Not at all."

"You're the best person I know, Ny. I know my sister is out there somewhere, living the life our parents tried to stop her from having, and I could never count on them to help me, but you? You don't even think twice." She says, wiping away her tears.

"Because I love you and those kids. Is there anything you need?"

She shakes her head. "No, but I'll take you up on the job offer. I used what I had in savings to finish out the lease on the apartment and get us here."

"Done. I'll text you all my logins and get you set up on payroll by Monday morning. How about you and I change into our swimsuits and day drink by the pool while they're at the shop?"

Winter lets out a relieved sigh. "I need a suit."

I stand quickly and extend my hand. "There are plenty of suits in the design room." She takes my hand, and I guide her to the other half of the house.

I leave her alone in the room, go to mine, and change before texting Briggs and asking him to take the boys shopping for whatever they want. He doesn't ask questions. Instead, he says he'll take care of it.

While he's hanging out with the kids, Winter and I relax by the pool with the dogs at our heels. By the time Briggs and the kids come home, we're two sheets to the wind and having a hell of a good time. The rest of the night is a blur of drunken laughter. At least no one got married this time.

"Do you think this is okay?" I ask Briggs, stepping out in my jean shorts with a flag painted on them, a red crop top, and my white bikini underneath.

I can't help but soak in his yummy, tattooed goodness as my eyes rake down his muscular body. He's wearing flag-themed swimming trunks and a red sleeveless shirt to match my outfit. We're that cheesy couple today.'

I watch as Briggs licks his lips and his gaze trails up my body. "Hell yes," he groans, pulling me into his arms. "You are absolute perfection. I might have to kill someone for looking at you today, but it'll be worth it." He looks down at me and flashes a toothy grin that makes me giggle.

I run my fingers along his neck tattoo like a feather. Goosebumps rise on his skin, and his body quivers.

"I like it when you do that," he whispers.

"I like it when you threaten to kill people on my behalf," I say with a smile. I know he would never actually kill anyone, but it's the thought that counts.

"I mean every word. Are you ready?"

"Yup."

Briggs takes my hand and leads me into the living room, where Winter and the boys are waiting. We drank way too much last night, but we had a hell of a good time. The boys were happy to have a gaming system again.

Briggs says they argued with him about picking anything, so he just started tossing shit into the cart. He really is a fantastic man.

Once we're all loaded up in the Bronco, we head to Briggs' parents' house. I'm trying to play it cool, but I'm nervous as hell being around his family like this. Our first introduction was quick and awkward, and then dinner with his parents got fucked up when Sheila and Van showed up. Things have been quiet, but I never know what the prick is planning next.

As we enter the spacious house, a cute little girl bounces over to greet us. I assume this is Harley.

"Uncle Bigs," she screeches.

Briggs lets go of my hand and scoops her up.

"Hey, munchkin. Did you miss me?"

"Yeah, um, Blue cries a lot," she says matter-of-factly, and Briggs laughs. "Um, are they your, uh, friends?"

"Well, Ny is my wife and your aunt now, and those three are my friends," he tells her, then starts naming everyone.

"Like Aunt Astor?" she asks, staring at me with a bright smile.

"Yup." Briggs sets her on her feet when she starts to wiggle. Harley walks over to me and looks up.

"It's nice to meet you." I look down and tell her, which makes her smile broaden.

"Yeah, I'm nice," she says, making everyone laugh. "Um, hi. My friend is Lea. I'll show you," she says, taking my hand. We all chuckle as she leads us outside, where everyone else is in the yard. I've met most of the people here, except the guy with Astor, whom I assume is Noah. Stopping a few feet from another little girl,

"Lea. I have a new aunt." Harley calls out to her. I watch as a little girl, her raven-black hair and amber eyes bouncing toward us. When she stops, Harley swings my hand in hers.

"Hi, you're pretty," Lea says, shyly shoving three fingers into her mouth.

I giggle and squat down to their level. "Thank you. You are both very beautiful, too. It's nice to meet you, Lea."

"You look like my daddy," she tells me.

That's a weird thing to say. Maybe he has a tan and dark hair. Kids see things differently. Stepping up to me, she starts touching my face and hair. I have no idea what to say to this child, so I just let her poke and prod my face.

"Lea, honey, leave the nice lady alone," I hear a deep voice say.

"Daddy, she's like you," Lea says, then drops her hands. When she finishes staring, she runs off with Harley into the house.

"You guys can go swim," Briggs tells Dylan and Daniel, who waste no time moving past us.

"I'm going to lie on one of those chairs. Do not let me burn," Winter tells me, then follows them.

Standing at my full height, I meet Walker's gaze. He's the man I couldn't figure out the last time I saw him. We stand there, staring. I take in his bone structure, deep tan, and black hair. Why is he so familiar?

I search through all my memories as my eyes wander, my lips part in a gasp, and I lose my breath.

The weight of the memory almost brings me to my knees. I step forward, and my eyes lock with Walker's. He's older now, but I remember.

Shame flashes across his face before he closes his eyes and hangs his head. I never felt fear or pain from this man, so my anxiety doesn't rise, and my heart stays steady.

I notice Baxter and Baylor walking up behind Walker out of the corner of my eye, but I keep my attention on the man in front of me.

"You." My whisper is barely a shadow of the word.

"I was hoping you would have forgotten." He hangs his head and slumps his shoulders.

"Why?" That's all I have to ask.

Walker shakes his head and looks up at me. He knows what I'm asking. "I tried. I tried so many times."

He tried to save me, but he couldn't. They hurt him, too. I can see it in him.

"What the fuck is going on?" Briggs asks, stepping up to me. I ignore him and keep staring. Baxter and Baylor are on alert, watching.

"What happened when you left?" I keep my voice even and let him explain.

"I had everything planned to get us out, but they found out. When I went to get you, your body was limp. They shook you, but you didn't move." His voice cracks. "They told me it was too late and that you were already gone. I believed them because you wouldn't move."

"Walker, what are you talking about?" Briggs' voice comes out dark and furious. He steps forward to go after Walker, but I grab his arm.

"Yeah, Walker, what are you talking about?" Baxter asks now. We both ignore the pissed-off brothers.

"They were hurting you, too," I ask, keeping a firm grip on my husband's tense arm.

Walker nods. "I tried to get help from the sheriff, but he was friends with Joseph and didn't believe me. They almost killed me that night. Every time I tried to get to you, it got worse."

Nausea begins to roil in my stomach at his confessions. My heart starts to race. He's been here this entire time. He tried to be a good brother.

"Why did you stay away?" I ask, needing to know why he never tried to find me.

"When I saw the news that they were finally arrested and that you were still alive, I was filled with regret and shame for believing them, and I just left you. I thought you would go to a good home and be safe." He scrubs his hands over his face and shifts.

"Then, a few years later, I heard about the foster home. I was 18 when I went to your social worker and explained who I was, but your parents were already adopting you. She told me they were good people and that I needed to let you go so you could finally be free and have a good life." He shrugs and shifts again.

"She was right. You needed to forget that part of your past, and I would have been a constant reminder of the pain. When I saw you in your first movie, I knew I had made the right choice to let you forget me."

"You're Craig?" Briggs says, bringing his arm around me.

"Walker is my middle name," he says, not taking his eyes off me. "I tried Journey. I promise I tried. Letting you go was the hardest thing I've ever done, but I never stopped thinking about you." Tears well in his eyes, but he keeps them from falling.

"You're her brother? We've been friends for seventeen years, and you've never mentioned any of this," Baxter says to Walker in a harsh tone.

"It's not his fault. You have no idea what it was like. Would you have wanted to hear the horror stories? They would have given you nightmares. He did what he thought was best. We were young and fragile. All that matters is that he tried. That's all I ever needed to know." I snapped, and Baxter slammed his mouth shut.

I walk up to Walker, wrap my arms around his shoulders, and hug him. As his arms close around me, we both let out the sob we've been holding back.

"I'm so sorry I let you down," he whispers. I shake my head and squeeze him.

"You didn't," I whisper back, then release him.

Briggs comes up and pulls me into him. The warmth of his rigid body instantly calms me. He reaches out and wipes away my tears. "Are you okay, baby?" I shake my head and turn slightly in his arms.

"I'd like to know you now, Walker, and I'd like to get to know my niece. Jamie might try to kick your ass first, though." I chuckled, trying to ease the mood.

"He has every right to. I want to get to know you, too, and I'd like Lea to meet her aunt. You should know something. Your ex, Van, already found out who I am. He tried to pay me to mess with you. I told him to fuck off, but I have a feeling he knows about Sheila, Joseph, and Gary," Walker says.

"Yeah, he already brought Sheila to see me. Her parole was granted a few months ago. Joseph was murdered in prison. I have a feeling Gary's next."

"Fuck." He hisses, then looks for his daughter. His body relaxes when he sees her by the pool, talking to Winter. "Joseph got what he deserved," he says, clenching his jaw.

"I take it Gary is another brother?" Baylor asks.

"Yeah," I say with a heavy sigh. "I'll be right back."

Briggs stops me and gives me a look. I smile at him and give him a sweet kiss. "I have to pee. I'm okay," I whisper. He kisses me once more before letting me go.

As I walk up to the house, my mind is buzzing with everything that just happened, and I'm already wondering how my parents and Jamie will feel about it. Deep in thought and not paying attention, I walk right into someone as I enter the house.

A thick arm wraps around me, and a hand wraps my braid around it. When I try to pull away, there's a hard yank, and the person holding me speaks.

"You should watch where you're going, Lila," a gravelly voice says. My heart stops at the nickname. Fear and panic hit me like lightning. No. No. No. Not here. Not now. Refusing to look up, I try to back away, but the grip on my hair pulls my head back, forcing my eyes to meet the black, dead ones before me.

My jaw clenches when I see my older brother's weathered face.

"You shouldn't be here," I spit, trying to pull away again. My heart is on the verge of exploding from how hard it's beating.

"I had an invitation." When he leans his face into mine, I turn my cheek. "I always did love your long hair. So beautiful." Gary inhales deeply. He's sick. I'm his fucking sister. I'm going to barf. "It still smells like lilacs. It's going to be fun watching you squirm." He pulls my hair tighter, making my neck crane, then lets go and shoves me back, making me stumble. "I'll see you out there, Lila." He slams into my shoulder as he walks past me.

My body quivers as I run to the bathroom, slamming the door shut and locking it behind me before the tears spill out. I try to steady my breathing, gripping the counter so hard my knuckles turn white. Glancing in the mirror, I resist the urge to smash the image. Then I know what I need to do.

As I open the cabinets, I start searching for what I need. Gary is just as vile as he was back then, if not worse. How is he here?

Who the hell would want to be near that man? When I finally find what I'm looking for, I take a shaky breath.

I can do it. I need it to free myself. Glancing in the mirror one last time, I start cutting.

Fifteen

Briggs

What a crazy fucking way to start a party. Discovering that Walker is Journey's half-brother was not what I expected. I already asked Beau and Noah to look into the names I gave them. They can scratch that one off now.

I glance around, watching people milling about, eating, and talking. My eyes land on Anna, walking toward us with a guy I've never seen before. He's of average height and slight build, with dark brown hair and black eyes.

When they get closer, I start to feel on edge around him. Baxter and Baylor step closer, and Walker folds his arms across his chest and tightens his shoulders.

"Hey, guys, this is Dean. Where's Ny? I didn't see her," Anna asks me.

"Bathroom." I give a one-word answer. I don't know this prick she's with. Hell, Anna has never brought a man to one of our events, so why the fuck would she bring him today?

"Dean, huh?" Walker says beside me. "How did you two meet?"

"Oh, Dean came into the bakery a couple of weeks ago. It was so cute how shy he was to ask me out," she says, beaming at the man. When he looks at her, his eyes are completely devoid of emotion. I can see past the fake look on his face. Fucking psycho eyes.

"She's just too adorable to resist," he says, rubbing his nose against hers, making her giggle and me want to gag. Baxter grunts beside me and shifts on his feet.

"So, you live around here, then?" Walker asks. Hell, he's doing all the work for us with the third degree.

"A couple of towns over. I was here on a job and met Annabelle," Dean says, bringing his arm around Anna.

"And what do you do for work?" Walker asks, taking a step forward.

"I'm a pastor at The Church of God. I was in town for a funeral."

Walker snorts a laugh. Okay, so Walker isn't religious. This man doesn't strike me as spiritual, either. I'll figure him out. He's hiding something.

"Oh my god, Journey, what did you do?" I hear Winter's high-pitched screech.

My head whips up, and my eyes start searching. The organ I call my heart feels like it's about to pound out of my chest as I step forward, searching for her. Fear begins to sink in about what the hell could make her scream like that.

When I land on Journey, my heart races for a whole new reason. "Fuck me," I whisper. Taking her in, I see she no longer has her straight, waist-length hair. No. She cut it straight across, to the middle of her long, slender neck. She was hot before, but damn, she's even hotter with short hair.

She laughs with everyone, then her eyes lock onto mine, and she brushes past them all to reach me. She increases her pace and jogs toward me. Stepping away from everyone, I catch her as she throws herself into my arms and wraps around me. My hands don't hesitate, digging into the short locks.

I press my lips to hers and kiss her passionately—her sweet, succulent mouth tastes of berries and tequila. The little temptress took a shot without me. I pour all my love, desire, and need into our kiss, hoping she can feel it all.

As we part, I keep running my fingers through her hair. I can't take my eyes off her. Hell, I can't get enough of this woman. I find myself captivated by her warm amber eyes, my heart skipping a beat as butterflies flutter anxiously in my stomach.

"Do you like it?" she whispers.

"I fucking love it. You're always stunning, but this. Baby, it looks incredible. Do you like it? What made you want to cut it?"

She shakes her head, the biggest smile I've ever seen on her face. Her features are even more prominent now that they're not partially covered. So much beauty in one person shouldn't exist, but it does. Fuck, I have a raging boner at a family party.

"I love it. I'm letting go of the past. My hair was part of it. I feel free," she says, still smiling broadly as a tear slips out.

I wipe it away, then bring one arm around her back to support her. She weighs almost nothing, but I want to hold her while my other hand keeps playing with her hair. "Good, sweetheart. All that matters is that you love it and are happy."

"I like that you're always supportive," she says, tracing the tattoo on my neck.

"I like that you're healing," I whisper to her.

"It's because you give me strength, too." She whispers back and kisses my forehead, this time making me chuckle.

Gently easing her legs away from my waist, I help her stand, feeling a warm sense of closeness. "I need another minute before you move," I tell her, then close my arms around her.

She presses her body against me and giggles. "Mm, Russel, the one-eyed wonder weasel, likes the hair, too," she jokes, and I bark out a laugh.

"He does. He likes everything about you, sweetness." I give her a quick peck, then turn her in my arms and guide her back to the group, keeping her firmly in front of me.

"Ny, your hair looks good like that," Anna tells her when we get back.

Journey's body stiffens, then she tries to relax, but I notice. Frowning, I look at her. Then I see Walker moving closer to us.

"Thank you, Anna," she says politely.

"This is Dean. Ny is Briggs' wife." Anna introduces them. Journey doesn't say anything or move when he holds out his hand.

"It's nice to meet you, Ny," he says in a sickly-sweet tone. Journey pushes back into me, shifts, and looks at her half-brother. Something passes between them, and he nods, moving a little closer. What the fuck is happening right now? Turning to face Dean again, she looks at the still-outstretched hand.

"I don't like being touched. Germs," she says in a flat tone. No, my baby doesn't care about germs. She doesn't want this man touching her. I wrap my arms around her chest and stomach, holding her protectively.

Dean drops his hand and tightens his jaw. "That's no bother. You recently cut your hair?" he asks her.

"I did." She says sharply, sending me on alert. This isn't my Ney. Journey is never abrupt.

"You know, at my church, we believe a woman's beauty lies in her hair. Why would you cut it?" The disgust in his voice is hard to hide.

Journey snorts a laugh. "Because I hated it, and I guess it's a good thing we're not at your church," she quips. I do not like this son of a bitch. Rage flashes in his eyes.

Hell no. Now it's my turn to talk.

"My wife's beauty is none of your concern. If she wants to shave her head bald, she'll still be gorgeous. Anna, how much do you know about him?" I ask in a clipped tone, looking into my nervous friend's eyes.

"Well, um, we're still getting to know each other," she says anxiously. She's clearly uncomfortable with the situation.

"You don't have to explain anything to him, Annabelle," he counters. Baxter and Baylor step forward as he does.

"This is his parents' house," Anna says in a small voice, stepping to the side away from him.

I see Baxter take another step from the corner of my eye, then take Anna's hand and pull her to him.

"You shouldn't have cut your hair, Lila," he growls. White-hot fury flashes through me. His name is not Dean.

"You know, you may be able to change your name, but it's still the same demon inside that meat suit. I thought you would want a reminder, Gary." Journey seethes. She digs into her pockets, pulls out her braided hair, and a lighter.

"You had it wrong when you held me by this braid. It's going to be fun watching you squirm." She holds out the braid, sets it on fire, and drops it at his feet.

He touched her. Here, today, while I wasn't with her. Pissed doesn't even begin to describe what I'm feeling right now. The fury has turned into a bloodthirsty monster, screaming for me to kill this fuck.

"You bitch. You're going to regret that." He raged.

Adrenaline hits me like a hammer, sending me into a full-blown frenzy. I swiftly pass Ney off to Baylor and swing out, landing a right hook to his jaw, then a left. Gary stumbles back with each hit.

"You touched my wife. You sick fuck." I roar. I'm going to kill him. He's going to die today. I land a few more blows to his nose and mouth before Walker stops me. "Let me go," I yell, trying to shove him off. Skinny shit is strong. My eyes don't leave Gary's as the wicked, bloody smile spreads across his face. The freak likes it.

"It's not worth it," Walker says, but it is. It's worth it to protect her, and if killing him is the only way, I'll do it. I want to. He needs to hurt, to feel the pain Ney felt as a child.

"You twisted piece of shit. She's your sister. If you come near her again, you're dead. I'll kill you." I bellowed, not caring who heard the threat.

"Actually, she's not. Sheila saved me from my parents when I was three. You can't be with her all the time. Van has plans for you, Lila. If I decide to let him have you, that is. I'll have you first, and when I do." He closes his eyes, inhales, groans, licks his bloody lips, and then brings his gaze back to Ney, smirking at her. Journey whimpers, and I lose it all over again.

"I'm going to pluck your eyes from your skull and make you eat them," I shout, fighting the hold on me. I turn and throw a punch at Walker to get the prick off me, but he dodges. Then I notice Jamie holding me, too. When the hell did all these damn people get here?

"Briggs, stop. I want to kill him, too, but this is not the place to do it," Jamie whispers.

"Get the fuck off." I throw another punch at my friends.

Gary laughs and looks at Anna. "It was fun playing with you, kitten. You were too easy. So eager for affection. You should really get to know someone before you spread those sweet thighs. Did you really think a church pastor would choke someone while fucking them from behind on the first date?" He tsk's at her, then laughs at Anna's expense.

"I'll kill him for you," Baxter growls and lunges.

"Bax, stop," I hear Bay.

"Aw, that's cute. You found your real daddy. Hendrix thought you died, too. You remember Jen, don't you, Henry? This is going to be fun. Be ready for me, Lila," Gary chuckles wickedly and twitches toward Journey, making her yelp, flinch, and choke back a sob.

"Get out of here, now." My dad's voice booms through the air. He grabs the back of Gary's neck, spins him, and shoves him forward. I fight harder against Walker and Jamie while Baxter fights Baylor and now Beau, as Dad and Sul watch him leave. I see Terry holding Anna, and Hendrix holding onto Ney. "Get the fuck off me," I snap at them. I don't care that Henry is holding Ney. I know she's safe with him. I care that Gary scared her. He's threatening to torture my wife and then give her to another man. He used my friend to get to her.

Wait, fuck, he called Henry her dad.

"Briggs, Baxter, both of you, calm down. He's gone," my dad says calmly.

I breathe raggedly, my chest heaving as anger boils over. Jamie and Walker still have me in a hold, so I don't chase the dickbag. "He touched her. He threatened my wife."

"I know I heard him. He got what he deserved, but Walker was right; he wasn't worth it. You have to be there to protect her, and you can't do that if you're in jail. Baxter, you need to calm down, too. Take Anna to the house. If she wants to go home, stay with her." Dad says in a controlled, logical voice.

Damn it. I hate his logic. My gaze searches until I find Ney still in Henry's grasp. From the corner of my eye, I see a pissed-off Baxter holding a weeping Anna and walking toward the house. Henry lets go of Journey and steps aside as Jamie and Walker release me.

"I'm sorry. I told you Van would do this, and it would be bad. Gary won't be happy with my broken bones and blood anymore. He'll come for yours, too. I'm so sorry," she cries, tears in her eyes. "I need to let you go, Briggs." Her eyes dart. I can tell she's about to bolt.

"Don't, please, my heart," I plead, stepping toward her. It's like watching a caged animal try to escape. I'll catch her, but I hate that she thinks this is her only option.

"I can't let him hurt you, too. You have to let me go so I can protect you." She shifts on her feet and looks at the car. Fuck, she's going to do it. In the blink of an eye, Ney turns and takes off running. Damn it. She's terrified and thinks this is her only option.

As soon as she moves, I run after her and scoop her up mid-run. "No, I won't let you go. You can't run from me, Ney. I'm your haunt. Remember? I will always be where you are. I will always find you. Baby, there is only darkness in my life if the sun isn't with me to rise." I insisted.

She turns to face me, shifting her body so her arms and legs encircle me like a koala. I hold her trembling body gently, as close as possible without hurting her, while she sobs into my neck. My heart can't take it.

"I need you," I murmur into her hair.

"It's my fault. I'm sorry. I'm so sorry. I taunted him." She lets out the most painful sound I've ever heard. It's breaking me to see her like this.

"It's not your fault. He's a psychopath. That's not your fault. You didn't do anything wrong, Sunrise. Stay with me. I'm begging you, don't run from me," I beg her. I need her as much as I need air. "Look at me, sweetness."

I raise one hand and gently stroke her soaked face as she lifts her head. "You didn't do this. They did. You have nothing to be sorry for. Nothing. We protect each other by staying together. I love you, my heart. No one will hurt you as long as I'm around." I proclaim. "You're mine, Journey Leann. Now it's your turn."

God, please don't let this break her. She's been hurt too many times. My heart thunders and slams against its cage as I wait for her response. I reach up and gently brush my thumb over her bottom lip, trying to steady the frozen emotions inside me. "Sweetheart," I whisper to her.

"You're mine, Briggs Wilder. I love you, my strength." She hiccups through a sob.

I pull her face closer; every kiss I pepper her with is laced with relief. "That's right, baby. I'm yours."

When she buries her face in my neck again, a sigh escapes me, and I look to the sky. I gently run my hand through her hair and wrap my arm around her back, drawing her closer.

Please, let her stay.

I need to talk to Sul about bodyguards for Ney when I'm not around. I have no fucking idea what the next move will be. All I know is that I need to protect Journey. I'll spend every last dime I have to keep her safe.

It's not Journey's fault this shit is happening. All she's ever tried to do is survive. Van is slowly getting to her. Fucking bastard.

"Baylor, can you make sure Winter and the boys get home? Don't leave them alone there. Stay close." I call out to him.

"Yeah, I can do that," he says without question. "Where are you going?"

"To take care of my wife. If you can't stay on the couch with them, pick a room in the main house. Take the dogs with you." I shout, then start walking with Journey still wrapped around me.

I don't bother listening to anyone around me. I keep my pace and head straight to the car. I open the passenger door and set Ney in the seat. She curls her knees up and holds them. When I close the door, I pull out my phone, swipe a few times, then send Audrey a text.

As I get into the driver's seat, I start the engine and drive. Ney leans over and hugs my arm. She needs my touch. I stretch my arm and hold her outer thigh. I know where I'm going. She needs this. We need this. I've never planned a murder, but I might have to. I will find a way to make all three of those people pay for ever hurting her. Hell, I know every pig farm within a hundred-mile radius. All I have to do is pull those fuckers' teeth first, and the swine will do the rest.

In the parking garage, I find a spot and park. Twisting in my seat, I spot Dylan's hat and grab it. I get out and open the passenger door.

"What are we doing?" she asks, sniffling.

"Would you be up for an adventure?" I ask.

Her lips twitch, and her red-rimmed eyes meet mine. "What did you have in mind?"

"You'll have to trust me. I'll make sure you have the time of your life," I tell her, echoing her words from a month ago.

A small smile dances on her lips. "Okay."

Placing the hat on her head, I take her hand and help her out. I don't have a plan. That's why I texted Audrey. I booked the first available flight out of here and asked her to arrange a hotel and whatever else she could think of for the next three days.

This time, walking through the airport isn't as rushed. Once we've boarded, Journey clings to me, and I love it. Earlier, the fear of losing her had me on the edge of a cliff, and I could almost feel myself jumping off it.

When the seatbelt sign is off, I unbuckle her, bring her into my lap, and cradle her to me. I need to feel her as much as she needs to touch me.

Her sweet lilac scent fills my nostrils. They even used her scent against her. Ney plays with my hair while I rub her back soothingly and run my fingers through her hair.

Sixteen

Journey

After the plane lands, Briggs guides me to a large SUV. A man waits by the back door and opens it as we approach.

"Mr. and Mrs. Banks," he confirms as we approach.

The scent of the salty ocean is thick in the air, which is great because I love Miami. I don't love how this day turned out.

"Thank you," Briggs tells him in his husky voice, then guides me into the vehicle. I guess it's his turn to swoon me. No, he isn't swooning; he's caring for me. That's exactly what I need.

Briggs slips in next to me and pulls me back into his arms. "Do you like the beach?" he murmurs into my hair.

"I love the beach, Hercules. But no fish," I say.

Briggs chuckles. "Good. We'll be here for the next three days, and I promise, no fish."

Briggs hasn't stopped touching me since the whole ordeal. I know he's trying to reassure himself that I won't run to protect him and his family from mine. If I did at this point, it might put

Anna, Winter, and the kids in danger. Or maybe it would lure Gary away from them?

All I want to focus on now is that we get to live in the afterlife for three days, worry-free. The Vegas trip will always be my favorite, but it lasted less than 24 hours. I should feel guilty for how we left, but I'm too exhausted to care.

I'll text Winter when we arrive. For now, I want my husband. He was quick to jump in and protect me today. Watching two men barely hold him back had my heart pounding. I'm glad they did. He would have killed Gary and ended up in prison.

I hate that this is the family I was born into. It makes me glad I can't have children of my own. I guess I can't say that. Gary isn't even related to me. Walker and I look similar, and you can tell we're related, but Gary's features bear no resemblance to ours. I suppose it's like comparing John Cena to Dwayne Johnson, or me to Jamie. Sheila always called him our brother, so that's what he was.

All of this is a mess. I'm dreading what Van has planned. What if Gary gets me when Briggs isn't around? What if he gets to Briggs first so he can get to me? The thoughts are too much. He's going to do far more than torture me. I should have known he would get worse. The defeat I feel is overwhelming.

I won't be able to show my face around the Briggs family anymore. They likely already had their doubts about me, and this only made them worse.

Another thought hits me as I stare out the window at the traffic around us. Was Gary lying about Hendrix? Was my father that close all this time? How different would my life be if I had ended up with him when I was nine? I can't imagine not having Jamie or my parents. I shouldn't have moved here. If I had stayed with my parents, none of this would be happening now. Family secrets wouldn't have surfaced, and Briggs' life wouldn't have been turned upside down.

Inhaling, I try to find comfort and smile to myself as the familiar resort right on the beach comes into view. I've visited this place with my family over the years. Briggs must have asked my mom to book something while we flew here. I have no doubt she got the presidential suite.

When we stop, the man in the passenger seat opens the door for us, and both follow us inside. Guess they're the bodyguards while we're here. That was likely my dad's doing.

Walking up to the concierge, I recognize the familiar face.

"Ny, it's good to see you. You must be Briggs. Everything Audrey requested is in the presidential suite," Bennett says in his usual cheery voice and with a huge smile.

"Thank you, Bennett," Briggs tells him, making the shy man blush. It likely surprised him that Briggs knew his name, or he thinks Briggs is hot. I'm going with the latter because Briggs is fucking gorgeous.

"You are welcome. If I missed anything, please let me know."

Briggs nods and takes my hand, leading us to the elevator as the two men follow. Stepping inside, he holds me protectively against him.

The room is huge, with multiple couches and chairs. The suite features two bedrooms, a full-sized kitchen, and a balcony with a hot tub. The entire back wall is windows.

As I move through the suite, I step out onto the balcony and walk to the railing. The ocean is beautiful from this height. The hot, salty wind blowing over me starts to ease my tension. I inhale and close my eyes. I love the feel of being near the beach.

Briggs's large arms wrap around me, and he leans down to kiss my shoulder.

"It's not Vegas, but it's still nice," he says.

Giggling, I hold his arms. "Vegas will always be the best, Hercules. But the beach is pretty great. Do you like it?"

"This is my first time on a beach, sweetheart."

Turning into his arms, I gaze at his gorgeous face with admiration. "What do you think so far?"

"It's hot but beautiful," he chuckles.

I smile at him. "Yeah, I could never live in this climate, but it's nice to visit."

"What's your favorite thing about being here?" he asks, lifting me. I wrap myself around him and hold on as he walks back inside to the bedroom.

"The shops. You can find some cool, weird stuff and the scent of the ocean."

"Okay, tomorrow that's what we'll do. We'll go into every store on the strip, and I'll buy you whatever you want." Briggs sets me on the bed and kneels in front of me. "Maybe I'll get one of those rad shell necklaces. Think I'll look like a surfer dude?" His eyes twinkle with humor.

Chuckling, I tuck his hair behind his ear. "I'm not sure they still sell those, but if they do, I think you'd look totally rad with one around your neck. And now you definitely need one. I'll get an anklet to match your look."

"We can get bright clothes and roller blades like in the Doll movie you made me watch," he says, lifting my shirt over my head and then removing his.

Oh, yes, I could use some naughty time right now. But I have a feeling Briggs is more focused on comforting me with his heart than with his cock.

I burst out laughing, my hands rubbing his solid shoulders. My eyes bounce between his Caribbean orbs. "Do you know how to roller blade?"

"Nah, but it looks easy enough." He shrugs, reaches behind me, unties my top, and lets it fall.

"We can dress you up in a sexy, cheap outfit. I'll put on a suit and take you shopping at all the fancy stores like the guy does in your favorite movie." He says, then kisses each breast before unbuckling my shorts.

My breath hitches at the contact. Okay, maybe Russell is helping him comfort me, too. I lean back, lifting my ass so he can drag my shorts and bottoms down. My heart races with anticipation of his touch.

"Mm, I charge a little more than she does," I tell him, digging my fingers into his hair as he spreads my legs.

"What's your starting rate? We'll see if we can negotiate." He asks, then slips his thick, rough, yet somehow soft fingers through my slit and rubs my swollen bud. My lips part, and my head tips back slightly.

"Hm, a grand per night," I moan when he slips a finger inside me. Briggs is the master of seduction. He grabs my ass, slides me to the edge of the bed, and takes my breast into his mouth.

Briggs twirls his tongue around my stiff peak, teasing my pebbled nipple. He releases it, meets my gaze, and gives me one of his heart-stopping smirks.

"That's too low, sweetheart. Three grand a night." He takes my other breast into his mouth, giving it the same attention, then slips another finger inside me and massages my canal while his thumb slowly circles my clit.

"Two." I counteroffer breathlessly, moaning again when he hits my G-spot. My hips jerk and start grinding against his hand.

"No, sweetness, you're supposed to go up. Try again," he says, then sucks my nipple hard, nipping it with his teeth and making me cry out with pure pleasure.

Holy fucking hell, my husband is a sex god.

Rolling my hips, I move closer to him. Briggs releases his hold on my ass and reaches down to remove his trunks. Yes, finally.

"Thirty-five hundred," I groan, tugging his hair. Fuck, I'm close. I can feel my pussy clenching already. Once his pants are off, he guides me to lie back.

"Do you want my cock, baby?" he asks, then lifts my legs over his shoulders and swipes his tongue over my clit. Dear God in heaven, how is he my husband?

"Yes, yes, I want your cock, baby."

My back arches, and my breathing quickens as his tongue lashes and assaults me. My eyes roll back as I try to hold back the orgasm.

Briggs pumps his fingers faster. "Anything that tastes as good as you should cost more. Your pussy is a delicacy. Try the number again. Once you reach an appropriate amount, you can have it." It might be too late for that. I'm already seeing stars, but then my devilish husband pulls his fingers from me and stops. I groan in frustration. Fucker knew I was about to cum.

I growl softly, lean up on my elbows, and glare at the smirking man worshipping me. "Ten grand."

His grin widens as he rises to his feet. I bite my lip, and my eyes glaze over at the sight of his full erection. He slips one arm around my waist, lifts us, and moves to the center of the bed. Hovering above me, he supports himself on his forearm, lines up, and gently pushes the tip of his erect shaft inside.

"That's more like it, Sunrise. But it still seems like a low price."

Briggs brings his lips to mine and kisses me with such emotion, pushing in to the base in one swift motion. We moan into each other's mouths.

He doesn't break our kiss as he rolls his hips, moving agonizingly slowly.

Briggs trails his fingers down my body, sending goosebumps spreading and butterflies taking flight. His hand stops on my hip, and he holds me there as he thrusts at an unhurried pace.

This isn't sex or fucking. Briggs is making love to me to express what he feels inside. I lock my legs around his waist, dig my fingers into his hair with one hand, and drag my claws down his back with the other.

He breaks our kiss, looks down at me, and picks up the pace. "You're the love of my life, Journey. I need you. Always. It will only ever be you." He groans and bites his lip. His body jerks as he pumps faster, and sweat beads on his forehead. He's close, and so am I.

I hold his back with both arms now, gasping and moaning as he hits my G-spot. My body tenses, sparks of pleasure igniting.

"Oh God," I say breathlessly as the orgasm hits and my eyes roll back into my head. "You're the love of my life, too, Briggs. I need you like I need air. You're my everything." I profess.

As soon as the words leave my mouth, the pending explosion detonates. "Briggs, love," I cry out, digging my claws into him. My pussy grips him tightly, pulsing around him as stars and sparks flash behind my eyes.

"Fuck, baby," he groans, thrusting once more before his body stills and he releases inside me.

Briggs rolls his hips as we ride out the sex-filled endorphins of our climax. I was right. He's a fucking sex god.

He slides his arm under me and rolls us onto our sides, keeping us connected. I reach up and push the wet hair from his face.

When my eyes meet his, I see love, protectiveness, want, and need, but also his fear. He's scared I'll leave him.

"I'm not going anywhere, sweet toosh." A small smile creeps across his face, and he cocoons me, pressing his lips to my sweaty forehead. "Please, don't. It will break me, sweetheart. I don't think I can survive without you. You're my heart."

"I should, but I won't. You're my strength, but I'm blowing up your life," I whisper.

"You're not. You've made my life better. If you leave, I'll tear the world apart to find you." He loosens his hold on me, grips my chin, and tilts my head to look at him. "None of this is your fault, Ney. Even if it were, I'd still be right beside you. If you want to kill them, I'll be there with you. Then I'll help dispose of the bodies." I giggle at his admission. Briggs kisses my nose, then slips out of me and off the bed.

I stay on my side and watch his sexy, tight ass walk to the bathroom. "It must be true love if you're willing to murder with me," I say, hearing the water running and his chuckle.

"It is, baby. I want to get rid of all of them. Van might be a little tricky since he's famous, but I'm sure we could come up with something."

Briggs steps out of the bathroom, a cloth in his hand. He sits on the bed, lifts one of my legs, and cleans me. He tosses the cloth back into the bathroom, lifts me, and settles me into his lap so I'm straddling him. He runs his fingers through my hair, massaging my scalp. Scalp massages are the best.

"I'm sure we could. Maybe we could stage a yacht accident. I know a few people who would get in on that." I tell him, wiggling my eyebrows, making him bark out a laugh.

"We'll keep thinking. Do you want to get drinks and sit by the pool? Or should we order room service and stay in tonight? What will make you happy?"

"It would make me delighted to be with you tonight," I tell him as I trace his tattoos.

Miami is great, but it was a shit day, and I only want him right now. Tonight, I need to clear my mind of the day's events.

165

"Okay, baby. Why don't you go start a shower for us, and I'll order something to eat."

"Thank you, Hercules. For everything," I whisper to him.

"Everything I do is because I love you. Never thank me for that," he says, kissing my chin.

Briggs stands and sets me on my feet before he takes my mouth with his. His soft lips feel like silk on mine, his warm tongue like velvet.

He draws back, stopping the heated moment. Taking a step back, I soak in his naked yumminess before walking to the bathroom.

As I start the shower, I hear him on the phone. When I step under the water, I try to silence the broken piece of me whispering that I'll never fully deserve a man like him. I'm learning to ignore it, but today has made it hard.

It's not long before Briggs slips into the shower with me and starts washing my hair. I'm beginning to think he's obsessed with it. I should have cut it sooner. I felt the weight of the world lift off my shoulders when I did.

After we're clean, Briggs dries us both off, wraps a white plush robe around me, then grabs a black one and puts it on. He guides me outside and pulls me into him on the outdoor daybed.

"Can I ask why you dislike fish so much?" he asks, then resumes playing with my hair. I stiffen at the question.

"It's not good. Are you sure you want to hear it?" I ask, offering him a chance to opt out of my horror stories. He takes a deep breath and pauses to consider.

"Yes, but only if you want to tell me."

With my head resting on his chest, I gaze at the rippling water. "Sheila called it whale stew. She thought I was gaining too much weight, and if I was going to be the size of a whale, I should eat like one. I was underweight, but to her I was never small enough." I can't sugarcoat this.

"The stew was just salt water and fish. If I didn't eat it by the second day, Sheila would puree it, and Gary would hold me down while she fed it to me. My raspy voice isn't natural; it's from damage to my esophagus." Briggs' arms tighten, and I feel his heart pounding beneath me.

I warned him.

"I can handle being around fish sticks, but that's it. It causes me severe anxiety that ends in a panic attack when I'm around them." I am fully aware how stupid it is that fish on the dinner table does that to me. I've tried to work past it, but I still struggle with it.

"Fuck, sunrise. I'm sorry. Most of your stories are like that, aren't they?" He runs his fingers through my hair and holds me with his other arm.

"Until I was nine, yes. Nine to twelve and a half was a little different, but still not great. Then, from twelve and a half to now has been mostly good."

"I swear to give you only good memories and stories."

"I believe you. How about I tell you a good story now?"

"I'd like that."

I snuggle into him and smile. "I fainted for the first time at Disney World after Cinderella hugged me. She was my favorite princess, and I envied her." I gush over the memory.

Briggs chuckles. "That's adorable."

"Uh, not when you're thirteen. I was mortified when I saw everyone staring at me. But what made it okay was seeing my parents. I saw how concerned they were about me. That night, I asked if I could call them mom and dad."

"I love that story."

I love that story, too. My life may have been total garbage at one point, but once I had my parents, I felt loved from then on. As my eyelids grow heavy, I close my eyes, relax into my husband's embrace, and drift off.

Seventeen

Briggs

A faint noise has my eyes flying open. I reach over and feel the space beside me. I fling myself up, tear the covers back, and look around the empty room.

The sun is just starting to rise, and Journey isn't next to me. I jump out of bed, grab the joggers from the floor, and slip them on.

My legs move with purpose as I rush through the suite, my heart taking flight with trepidation. Ny wouldn't run. Not right now. Not while we're away and she feels safe.

As I enter the empty second room, my chest tightens. I let out a controlled breath, trying to calm my pounding heart. At the balcony, I step outside and let my eyes scan the area, searching for her.

My heart finally settles when I spot her in the silk nightgown she wore to sleep in, her hair blowing in the wind, sitting on a bench with her knees to her chest and her arms wrapped around them. Her eyes are closed, and her head is tilted skyward.

Ney's eyes open, and she turns to look at me as I approach. Golden flecks sparkle in her amber irises. My beautiful goddess's brilliant gaze meets mine, and the corner of her lip twitches up.

"I hope I didn't wake you." Her raspy, feminine voice is like a melody to my ears.

"You didn't, Sunrise. What are you doing out here?" I ask, straddling behind her. Leaning in, I kiss her shoulder, and a shiver rakes her body.

"I couldn't sleep. I can't stop thinking about what Gary said yesterday," she says, then leans back against my chest.

Of course, she can't stop thinking about what the fucker said. He said a lot that's running through her mind. It pisses me off that that man was ever part of her life.

"What part, baby?" My finger lazily traces circles on her smooth stomach while I wait for her response.

"About Hendrix." Fuck, I forgot about that part, but now that I'm thinking about it, she does resemble him and Terry. Okay, I can handle this conversation. At least she isn't thinking about the threats he made. And maybe having Walker, Lea, and Henry will keep her from running.

"You're wondering if he was telling the truth?"

"Yeah. I can't help but want to know, and I feel guilty because of my parents. It's just. I instantly connected with Terry, and when I met Henry, I felt an even stronger connection. I don't do that often. I don't know. Maybe there was more of me hoping to find my biological father than I thought, or I'm letting Gary get into my head again. Why would he tell me now? What was the point of telling me who Henry is?" she says, frustrated, and sighs.

I hate that this is her life. That she still has so much doubt and insecurity. She can dominate the modeling scene, act in movies, and excel in the design world, but when it comes to her heart and mind, she struggles immensely. She doesn't believe she deserves the good in her life. I inhale, hold her, and watch the sun rise. The pinks, purples, oranges, and yellows on the horizon are stunning.

"I don't know why, baby. Maybe he thought you knew because you were hugging Henry. Don't think about Audrey and Sul. They will always be your parents. Wanting to know him is no different from wanting to get to know Walker. He'll never replace Jamie. Without that, would you want to know whether Henry is your father?"

She thinks about it as we watch the sky. The warm breeze and salty air, mingling with her lilac scent, are far more relaxing than I expected.

"Yes, but I'm still struggling with how my parents would feel," she says, rubbing the outside of my thigh.

"Sunrise, we left after he said that, and both your parents were right there. I'm sure they talked to Henry and Walker. Don't think of it as choosing one parent over the other. Think of it as your family growing." Journey shifts and tilts her head to look at me. "Let me ask this. Say Henry is your father, and you just got the most exciting news you've ever had. Who would you call first? Him or Audrey and Sul?" I ask, kissing her shoulder.

"My parents and then Jamie." She says without hesitation.

"See, you have nothing to feel guilty about. They will always be your true family in your heart. Blood doesn't determine that; love does."

Her smile widens when she looks at me. She reaches up and gently strokes my neck. I close my eyes and savor the feel of her touch. "Handsome and insightful. I think I might keep you, Pooh Bear."

I chuckle. "That's good, honey pot, because I definitely plan on keeping you. Do you want to get breakfast? You didn't eat much last night." I don't know why I feel the constant need to make sure she's fed and full.

"Yeah, that sounds good."

By the time we've made love a couple of times and get dressed, the sun is shining, and the world around us is wide awake. I'm not going to lie, I like the idea of having clothes waiting for you when you travel instead of toting suitcases. As we walk to the elevator, a new guard follows behind us. Sul isn't messing around when it comes to keeping Journey safe.

She feels bad about how we left yesterday, but I couldn't give two shits. My only concern was taking care of her and getting her away. I know Baxter will take care of Anna, and Baylor will watch Winter and the kids. Gary seemed uninterested in Walker. His torture likely came from Walker trying to take Journey from Gary while they were growing up. That thought alone makes me sick to my stomach. Hopefully, that means he'll shift his focus to me since I now have what he wants.

As we cross the threshold into the vibrant restaurant, the aroma of sizzling dishes fills the air, and laughter bubbles from the lively crowd, setting the stage for a morning of delightful flavors and memorable moments.

With Ney's hand in mine, we follow the hostess to the table and place our drink order. I can't help but stare at her in her baby yellow sundress. The color makes her tanned skin look even darker. She put on light makeup today, and I still can't get over how fucking hot she is with her short hair.

"Are you ready for some rollerblading?" she asks with a hint of mischief.

"If it will make you happy to watch me bust my ass, then yes, I'm ready."

"It wouldn't make me happy to watch you hurt yourself, but it would be fun to watch you try."

"Oh, yeah. Do you know how to rollerblade?"

"Ah, duh. I'm pretty good at it."

I chuckle. "Of course you are. You're perfect."

The golden flakes in her eyes twinkle when she looks at me. "Not perfect, but close. I promise no skating, but we will be doing a lot of shopping. Be prepared to spend all your money." She says that, but it's a lie. She never spends the money I have.

I reach over and take her hand. "Sweetness, you can have every dime. All I need is you."

"You know you've wowed me in the best way. Not because you're paying me a grand a night to be with you, but because of how you care for me," she says, lacing our fingers together. I laugh a little at her price cut.

Before we can say anything, the server comes and takes our order. When she walks away, Journey smirks at me.

"I thought we agreed on ten grand?" I lean in, resting my chin on my fist. Journey mimics my movement and holds my gaze.

"Baby, I would have said anything to get you inside me."

With my free hand, I reach over and tuck her hair behind her ear. "Hm, well played, sweetheart, but now I know I need to withhold a little longer to make sure you hold up your end of the agreement."

Journey giggles and wrinkles her cute nose. "That just backfired on me, didn't it?"

"Oh yeah. Tell you what. I'll let it go this time, but you have to promise to let me pay for everything today, and you can't hold back on what you want."

We've been together for a month now, and she's barely let me pay for anything. She orders groceries and other household items at work and refuses to tell me what she likes when we go shopping.

"Damn. But what if you don't have to pay for what I want?" The glint in her eye grows as I feel her foot sliding between my thighs. I stifle a groan, thinking of everything I can to keep Russell from standing. Damn it, she named my dick, and now I'm saying it.

I reach under the table, hold her foot, and massage it, making her eyes roll and close. "Nice try, Sunrise. You have cared for me in every way since we met. Today I'm spoiling you, and if you don't tell me what you want, I'll start buying random shit I think you might like." I tell her, then start massaging her calf.

She doesn't bother hiding her little moan. "Fine, but only if you promise to do more of that later tonight."

I smile at her. "I can agree to that. It's a win-win for me."

Satisfaction fills me when our food arrives at the table, silencing Ney's argument. This is the fanciest breakfast I've ever had. The French-inspired herb-baked eggs with toast were fucking good. Ney ordered Crème Brulé French Toast and put half of it on my plate.

She doesn't eat much at a time. Maybe that's why I feel I need to feed her constantly.

"What did you think of the breakfast?" she asks, sipping her orange juice.

"It was different but excellent. Where do you want to start next?" I ask as we stand and walk out of the restaurant.

"I do believe we have some jewelry to find." She giggles, takes my hand, and starts walking. "There's a shop around the corner I like to go to, but it's a little odd, so don't freak out."

I chuckle and play with the ring on her finger as we stroll along the strip. Inside the shop, I'm convinced the owner is a witch.

There are skulls of every animal you could legally obtain, herbs, and candles. A floor-to-ceiling bookshelf is full of books.

174

Knick-knacks are set out strategically. The front cases display a variety of vintage and handmade jewelry. Behind the counter are deep purple curtains.

A tall, pale woman with long red hair and freckles across her face steps out from behind the curtains. Her bright green eyes meet mine, and she studies me for a moment before speaking in a language I don't understand.

She turns her gaze to Journey, and her eyes soften. She speaks in what I think is Irish for a few minutes before finally switching to a language I understand.

"Antoinette, this is my husband, Briggs," Journey says.

"A perfect match. I know just what you need," Antoinette says, walking away. When she returns, she's holding two silver necklaces. One is thicker, with a larger charm; the other is thinner, with a smaller one. Both share the same design.

"The Celtic love knot is a powerful symbol of an unending, unbreakable bond between two people in love. Your souls have become one, intertwined, as they were always meant to be," she says, then walks from behind the counter.

As she steps forward to Journey, she reaches out, places the necklace around her neck, and speaks in Irish, then does the same for me. This is the oddest experience I've been part of, but I appreciate her words about our love.

I don't bother asking about the price; I hand her my card because her presentation was on point. Journey talks to her a bit more before we say goodbye and leave the shop.

"I told you it was a little odd," she says shyly.

"It's okay. I like what was said, but could you tell me what she said first?" I'm dying to know if I was cursed.

"The crow and his one true love," she says, pursing her lips. I dip my chin quickly and look down to check if my tattoo is showing. It is. Pfft, thank fuck.

Journey bursts out laughing at me when she notices what I just did. "She's intuitive, not a witch. Don't worry, she didn't curse us or anything. Only gave us a blessing when she clasped the necklaces."

Feeling a little sheepish, I narrow my eyes playfully at my wife. The fear of being cursed is real. With my arm draped over her shoulders, I pull her close and kiss the top of her head as she continues to laugh.

After five shops, Ney found the shell necklace and anklet. We don't plan to wear them, but we bought them as souvenirs.

Surprisingly, she picked out a few items she wanted and let me pay for them. We had lunch and walked on the beach before heading back to the resort to change. My phone buzzed multiple times today, but I decided to ignore it until now. When I opened my messages, I saw one from an unknown number.

Unknown:

> Hi, Briggs. It's Henry. I'd like to talk to Journey when you two come back. Do you think she would be willing to meet with

Me:

> I will talk to her and see how she feels. If she isn't ready, give her some time. Her life was twisted upside down yesterday.

I understand. Walker
gave me some insight
into what life was like
for them. I'll wait until
she's ready.

I understand he wants to know if it's true, but I won't push
Ney to make that decision. After I add his number, I change so
we can go to the pool and lounge and have a couple of drinks.

At the pool, Ney picks a hammock in the water, and we both
get in. I have to admit, Miami is great, and it's nice to have this
time together.

"Why do you love me so much, Briggs Banks?" she asks,
locking her gaze on mine. The answer is easy.

"Because you're worth it, Sweetheart. You're worth
everything, Journey Banks," I tell her, taking her foot in my
hand. The smile on her face still takes my breath away.

"So are you, love. Tell me a funny story from when you were a
kid," she says as I rub her feet.

"Hm. Ok. When I was fifteen, we all decided to try cow
tipping. When we ran away, I slid in cow shit, did the splits, and
pulled my groin muscle. I thought I'd broken my dick. Birdie,
Anna, and Astor laughed their asses off and kept running. Baxter
and Beau had to carry me out of the pasture." I say, and she
bursts out laughing so hard she snorts. "It wasn't worth it. We
couldn't get any of the cows to move. All we did was piss one of
them off, and the fucker chased us."

"That's fantastic. I shouldn't laugh, but it's funny. I like that
story."

I chuckle at the memory. I don't know why I picked that one. It's not one I remember often. "It wasn't funny then. When I told my mom what happened, she laughed at me before taking me to the hospital."

"I would have too," she says, wiping the moisture from her eyes.

"You tell me another good one now," I tell her.

She thinks for a minute, then sips her drink. "Okay, about two months after Jamie and I were adopted, I was lying in bed, trying to fall asleep. When I opened my eyes, the night-light made my jacket look like a human." She chuckles.

"I screamed bloody murder. My dad flew into the room, flipped on the light, came up to me to check if I was hurt, and tried to calm me down. I told him the jacket scared me. Seconds later, Jamie came flying into the room, screaming, 'Stay away from his sister,' and unloaded his paintball gun on our dad." She chortles, and I bark out a laugh at the thought of Jamie going Rambo on someone.

"Once he realized it was him, he dropped the gun. Paint was splattered everywhere. Dad made sure I was okay and took the jacket off the closet door. He laughed at Jamie, hugged him, and told him he had done the right thing." She smiles brightly. "If you ask Dad, he'll tell you it was one of the proudest moments of his life."

I chuckle and rub her legs. "I can see Jamie still doing that."

"Oh, for sure. Be glad you're his best friend, or he may have killed you the day we got back from Vegas."

"You know, it still shocks me that he managed to keep you a secret from me."

"Good thing he did, or I may have tricked you into marrying me sooner." She grins and winks at me.

178

"Oh yeah? Do you think you could have convinced me?" I ask playfully.

"Ah, yeah. I mean, come on," she says, gesturing her hand up and down her body, which makes me laugh. She isn't wrong.

"You're right. I would have said yes in a heartbeat."

Journey grins, then leans back and soaks up the sun. "This has been a pretty good adventure so far."

"We have a lifetime of adventures, Sunrise," I tell her, bringing her foot up and kissing the top, making her giggle.

I have managed to kiss nearly every inch of this woman's body, and I'll never tire of it. Looking up at the sky, I let my body relax with hers. We needed this time together.

Eighteen

Journey

A sense of dread knots my stomach as we land back home and drive to the house. Our three days in the afterlife have officially ended, and I hate it. I'm not ready to face people or the reality that Gary, Sheila, and Van could surface at any moment.

Sighing, I watch the traffic on the highway pass us by. I shift in my seat and lean against Briggs' arm.

"We need to plan for a full week or two soon. Maybe we could go to Ireland." I wish we could go now, but we both have responsibilities. Though I love my job and I know he loves his, the thought of traveling the world for a year teases and tempts me.

"I'd like that, Sunrise. Ireland is on my bucket list," he says, gently squeezing my thigh.

"I'll start looking at dates for next year. How does that sound?"

"Sounds good. I love that you're thinking about our future together," he says, taking my hand and kissing my palm. I want everything with this man. "I have to go to the shop for a bit. Make sure you keep the doors locked, or go hang out with Winter and the kids if they're home, until I get back."

"I'll be okay, Hercules. I have some things I need to work on, so I'll be upstairs and make sure the doors are locked." I giggle a little. Briggs is fiercely protective, and now it's multiplied a hundredfold.

He sighs and tightens his grip on the steering wheel. "I hate leaving you. Sul is already arranging bodyguards until this is over."

"I'm going to be okay, hot stuff," I say, winking at him. Briggs gives me a half smile, then kisses my hand again.

I know my dad will hire people without Briggs asking him to. I'm sure the place will be crawling with security guards by tomorrow. Glancing out the window, I see the house come into view. The place is enormous, but I do love it.

After parking in the garage, Briggs grabs the suitcase we had to get because of the random shit we picked up in Miami.

Inside, I expect to see the dogs, but I remember they're still at Winter's and she's not home. Briggs rubs my back, then goes to our room to change before he leaves. Probably not appropriate for him to work in a sleeveless shirt, cargo shorts, and flip-flops.

Once he's done, he gives me all the kisses before heading to work. With a drink in hand, I head upstairs and start working through the multitude of emails.

I sigh when I see an email from the marketing manager. He thinks I should create an ad for my fragrance line featuring a male model alongside me. I've been doing this for ten years and have never modeled with men.

I sent him an email saying I'll do it, but only with my husband. Hell, it's my fucking line, and Briggs could be a model. Besides, the final decision is mine. Hopefully, my husband is okay with it.

Who am I kidding? He won't tell me no. I could ask for his right nut and left pinky toe, and he'd give them to me.

Briggs mentioned that Henry reached out to ask if we could meet to talk, but I haven't committed to anything yet. Briggs made sure Henry thought it was a possibility before I arranged the DNA tests. I had mine done at a Miami lab while we were there, and Henry completed his here, expediting it. We should find out the results soon.

The thought still rocks me that Henry could be my father. Briggs was right. I can't see it as replacing my parents, but my family is growing. Walker texted me a couple of times to check on me, and Jamie texted me over two dozen times. Briggs and I are having Walker and Lea over for dinner this weekend so we can start getting to know each other.

Everything is moving in the slowest motion possible. My life was rocked a few days ago. Anna hasn't responded to any of my texts, but hell, who could blame her?

I open my iPad and pull up the app to work on new designs. I've been focusing more on expanding my design work than anything else.

The doorbell ringing has me standing and walking down the stairs. I peek through the door and frown when I see Anna and Astor. Well, shit, this isn't going to be good.

After I open the door, I look at my two guests. Astor looks nervous. Anna looks like she's about to set the world on fire. Her face is red, her neck blotchy, and her scowl is wicked. I notice her body trembling, still reeling from the prior events.

"Hey, come on in," I tell them, stepping aside.

Once they're inside, I walk to the living room. They both stop but don't sit.

"You shouldn't have tricked Briggs into marrying you. All you've brought him is trouble. He deserves better," Anna snarls.

Guess this is how we're starting. Astor gives Anna a shocked look but keeps her mouth shut.

"You think I don't know that?" I say, raising my voice an octave. "You think I haven't told him? I didn't trick him, and I gave Briggs multiple chances to back out. He won't take it, and believe it or not, we love each other. I had no way of knowing this would happen, but once I did, I warned him." I tell her sternly because I did.

"Briggs has never been in love before. He doesn't know whether this is love or lust. Right now, he's infatuated with you. You're famous and rich. How could anyone refuse to marry you when you're showing off your lavish life?" Anna raises her voice, her face growing redder.

"And you know this how? Do you feel what we feel, or at least what he does?" I ask, crossing my arms over my chest and watching her rage-filled face. Poor Astor looks like she's watching a ping-pong game. I'm not going to let her tear Briggs apart.

"He isn't thinking straight. He doesn't need to be put in danger for someone he thinks he loves after a fucking month, and that's what you're doing. Just like you put me in danger." Anna sneers. I have a feeling this is more about her fucking pride than anything else.

I can't help but laugh at her audacity. She was never in danger. "I had no way of knowing Gary would do that. He didn't hurt you. He didn't force you to sleep with him. He used you to get to me, yes, but he didn't cause you any actual physical harm. I apologized. That's all I can do."

"You have no idea what hurt is. I was humiliated. Just like Briggs should be for marrying a woman who's likely sleeping with her brother or God knows how many others. It's weird how close you are with Jamie. Now you discover that Walker is your brother and Henry is your father. I call bullshit; it's all suspicious. I knew I shouldn't have given you a chance." Anna spits out the words with such disdain.

Anger rips through me at her words.

"You don't know a fucking thing about me. You're pissed because Gary told a few people he fucked you. Get over it. I spent nine fucking years being tortured by Gary, my own mother, and my stepfather." I scream at her and start making hand gestures because apparently, my hands want to argue with her, too.

"He has helped break my bones. He has helped starve me. He has made me bleed. He has brought me to the brink of death and laughed the entire time. The only thing that kept him from touching me was that I was a fucking child. Don't you dare tell me I don't know what hurt is. All I knew as a child was fear and pain." The argument has turned into a storm. My shout comes out like thunder, and my admissions crack like lightning. I watch her face falter before she braces herself against the wind of my fury.

"Jamie was the first person in my life willing to do anything to protect me. You're vile for even suggesting I would sleep with him. Walker left me, and I didn't know who my father was. They wouldn't tell anyone, so I was forced into the system." I'm practically screaming at this point.

I feel moisture building behind my eyes as I lay into her. My face feels like it's on fire, and my body starts to tremble with rage.

"Briggs has done nothing but show me what love is. He knows what my childhood was like and chose to love me anyway. Money means nothing to him or me. All that matters to us is that we have each other." I yell.

"If you love him, you need to let him go before you get him killed. He'll fall back into his old ways once you're gone. You can be easily replaced. He doesn't love you. He'll fuck some other twat as soon as you're gone. That's what he's good at." Anna snaps.

Her words slice through me like a double-edged sword. Astor has managed to keep her mouth shut, stunned by horror, her eyes flicking between Anna and me, her mouth open.

"Fuck you. You still think so little of him. Or do you think you could replace me? Is that what this is about? You want my husband?" My laughter grows darker, and I run my hands down my face. "You think he'd fuck you? He's had years to have you and never touched you. Get out of our house." I yell, pointing at the door. "He will never choose you over me."

Anna's fists clench at her sides, and her jaw locks. Oh, that hit her where it hurts. Now I know my assumption was correct.

"Van was found half-dead last night. You know Briggs will be next. Leave him. It's better if Gary kills you than Briggs." Anna grits out.

My horror and fear hit me like an axe to the heart when she told me that. I don't give a shit about Van; I only care about what could happen to Briggs.

Astor gasps. "Anna, no. I didn't come here so you could do this. You just said you wanted to talk to her to make amends. How could you say that?" she says, bringing a hand to her mouth.

"I hope it was worth it, Anna. Because now, whether it's my death, my absence, or my admission, Briggs will never forgive you. He will never want you, either. Get out now," I say as calmly as I can to both of them.

"I'm so sorry, Ny. I didn't know she would do this," Astor croaks.

"Go." I choke back a sob. Astor's eyes fill with salty tears as she walks out the door.

Once they're both out of the house, I clutch my racing heart and walk to the bedroom, wiping away the tears. She's right. I need to let him go to keep him safe. He'll never let me if I keep giving him a choice. It's better to lose his love than his soul.

I grab a quick bag, toss a few things in, and head to the kitchen. I set the bag on the island and let the tears fall as I pull out a pad of paper and a pen. I stare at them, my hand shaking. I can't do it. It's not safer to run. I can't keep running. Will I truly protect him if I leave? Briggs won't give up on finding me if I do. I have to choose, and for the first time in my life, I want to pick him. We can survive this together. I deserve his love, and he deserves mine.

I need Briggs. I promised him I wouldn't run, that he could trust me to stay. I walk back to the room, empty the bag onto the bed, and throw it. Fuck her. I won't let her scare me. He is mine, and I am his.

I hear the doorbell again, and anger and rage ring through me. This fucking bitch has some nerve coming back here. I clench my fists and stalk to the door, ready to tear into this woman.

I fling the door open and am immediately hit in the face with surprise and a fist. Van, fucking Van, is here.

I stumble back and try to regain my balance. I can feel the blood oozing from my nose. Fuck, at least it doesn't feel broken. How is he here? Anna just said he was in the hospital.

"What did I say about the last time you walked away from me, mouse?" he says in a calm voice, closing the door behind him. I let out a whistle to summon the dogs, but I remember they're at Winter's. Panic is creeping into me, but I can't show it.

"Fuck you. Get out now," I scream. I reach behind me for my phone.

Before I can do anything, Van charges at me, grabs me by the throat, and slams me into the wall, lifting me off the ground.

Struggling to catch my breath, I try to calm myself, but my breathing is ragged.

Van's fingers dig into my throat, cutting off more of my oxygen.

"It's amazing how quickly Anna agreed to take the money to come here. She hates you. She did well. I needed you thrown off and not paying attention. You're not so tough without your husband here to protect you." Van smirks.

Shock stuns me at his admission of what Anna did and that he knew Briggs wasn't here. Van brings his other hand up and lands a blow to my cheekbone. I feel it split open, and blood seeps from it.

"You never were much. I don't know why I keep bothering." He laughs.

My blood-soaked teeth clench as I raise my right fist and swing it out, landing a blow to the side of his head. At the same time, I kick him in the kneecap, breaking his grip.

He strikes out when I go to run again, landing another blow to my mouth, busting my lip, then another to my ribs. God, he's going to kill me.

I stumble backward and try to remember all the moves my dad taught me. Once I regain my balance, I kick his ribs and use that moment to kick the same knee again. Van groans and staggers back. I step forward and punch out, landing right on his nose. When I hear the crunch, I'm sure it's broken. I throw another blow to his jaw with my right, then punch out with my left, landing a couple of blows to the side of his head and face.

"You bitch," he grounds out.

When he moves to catch his balance, I sprint to the back door, but it's short-lived before he tackles me to the ground.

"Get off me," I scream, and the sound echoes through the house as I scramble out from under him.

Van grabs me by the back of the hair and slams my face into the tile floor. My vision darkens and blurs as the warm liquid pools down my face.

"You don't get to be happy, Ny. Everything you have will be mine. Tell me. Did you fuck him?" He snarls, rolls me onto my back, and straddles me. Van sits up and hits my temple and ribs again. I gasp, trying to catch my breath. "Ah, of course you did. I should have known you'd be a little whore."

I suck in a breath and stare at the blurry man holding me down. "Fuck." I exhale and inhale again. "You," I say in a strangled voice, bringing my fist up and landing a hit on his jaw.

"You should know better." He growls, grabs my hair again, slams the back of my head into the ground, and wraps his hands around my throat.

I claw at him and try to get his hand off me as I kick and squirm. My vision blurs further, and pure horror floods me. "You know I like it when you fight back."

With my vision darkening, he finally releases me. I greedily suck in a breath. "I won't kill you yet. I'll let Gary have his fun before I take you." Please, don't let it end like this. I try to lift my limb, to fight, but I have nothing left.

"Gary doesn't like broken toys." I hear the gritty voice from somewhere, then a warm liquid floods my face like a damn waterfall. I squeeze my eyes shut and clamp my mouth shut. Fuck, he's closer than he sounded.

I listen to the gurgling sound as the heavy body holding me down falls forward on top of me.

Fuck. Oh God, Gary just killed him, and he's on me. Screaming, I try to push Van off me, but it doesn't work. I'm too tired, too weak.

"Save your energy, Lila," Gary tells me, then speaks to someone else. "Yes, I just killed a man at 7869 Bauman Hill Rd.

188

No, I won't be here when the police come. You'll need an ambulance for the woman he tried to kill, though. Better hurry. She doesn't look so good." I can hear Gary, but I can't see anything through the blood in my eyes and my blurred vision.

"Do not mistake this for saving you, Lila. I meant it when I said I don't like broken toys. I'll be back for you." He laughs evilly and whispers his fingers down my face like a silent veil. A scream rips through my throat at his touch, and I thrash my head. "Eventually." I listen to his boots on the ground, then there's silence.

Stay awake. I have to stay awake. I'm not sure how long I struggle to get Van's limp body off me. Then relief floods me when I hear a new, deep voice.

"CCPD." A man calls out.

"Here," I scream. Boots stamping on the ground grow closer. "I can't get him off." My voice cracks.

"Journey, it's Beau, Briggs' brother." His deep voice says. Thank fuck. I forgot he was a cop.

"Please, get him off me," I sobbed breathlessly. Seconds later, I felt the weight of Van lifted off me, and a new sob broke free as I drew a deep breath. Rolling to my side, I brought my hand up and pressed it to the bleeding wound on my forehead.

"Briggs. I need Briggs."

"I'm calling him now. Noah, check the back of her head. The ambulance should be here soon."

"Got it. I'm sorry." Noah tells me before he touches the back of my head, and I wince. "There's another wound. I need to apply pressure to slow the bleeding." More sirens sound, and the world spins a little. Minutes feel like hours as we wait.

"Where is she?" I hear my husband's husky voice. I sob harder, knowing he's here.

Nineteen

Briggs

As soon as I step through the door, Terry asks, "How's she doing?"

"Better. Not a hundred percent, but she'll get there. How's Henry?" I ask, feeling for Henry.

"A fucking wreck, man. After what Walker told us." Terry shakes his head. "Henry took a leave of absence from the station for a few weeks. The guilt is eating him alive."

"It's not his fault. He didn't know, right?" I ask as I make my way to my booth. The scent of alcohol and earthy ink fills my senses. It's a smell I will never tire of.

"No. Of course not. That cunt Sheila told him her name was Jennifer. She told him she was pregnant, then two months later, she told him she had a miscarriage and moved out of town." Terry says, sighing. His own agony is etched on his face.

"See? Not his fault," I clarify. While everyone tends to blame themselves, only Sheila and Gary are truly responsible.

"Sheila is thoroughly fucked in the head, and Gary is worse," Jamie says from his booth.

"Agreed. How are you doing?" I ask Jamie, then start setting up my station. I have a client coming in for a three-hour session, and then I can go back home to Ney.

Jamie doesn't look up from what he's doing as he answers. "I'm good. Walker explained everything. I'm not worried about him replacing me. I'll always be Tiny's number one brother. I'll be there to support her through all this, and so will our parents."

His response is relieving. Ney's been beating herself up about all of this. "Good. She's felt guilty since it all came out. She's terrified of hurting you or your parents."

Jamie snorts. "Tiny could never hurt us, especially over this. I never told her, but I found my birthparents years ago."

"Oh yeah." That shocks the shit out of me. I'm starting to think Jamie has a lot of secrets I don't know about.

"Yeah. My biological father is a drug addict, and my biological mother lives in Florida. She had an addiction, but went into recovery a few years before I found her. We talk on holidays and birthdays." Jamie shrugs as the front door opens, signaling it's time to get to work.

While I start my only appointment today, I think while I work on my human canvas.

Journey planning for a future vacation is nice, but I can't shake the fear that she'll bolt at a moment's notice. I'm hoping for a twenty-four-hour watch on her, so I know if she does. The thought of GPSTagging everything she owns has crossed my mind.

When we left Miami, it was surprisingly hard. If I didn't have this appointment today, I would have stayed longer. Making love and hanging out on the beach were fucking amazing. We weren't looking over our shoulders or worrying about who would come next. It was just her and me.

Halfway through the tattoo, I check on the guy in my chair, who's laughing at videos on his phone. An easy client.

Journey has tried to reach out to Anna, who has completely ignored her. I'm disappointed in how Anna has handled everything. On the first day she met Journey, she acted like an ass, but I thought Ney was winning her over. The Gary thing definitely didn't help the situation, but it isn't fair to blame Ney for it. She didn't force Anna to bang the guy right after they met.

It's all a mess. I will put Journey first. It doesn't matter how long I've known anyone. My wife is my top priority and always will be.

As I add the finishing touches to the tattoo, I think about the space left on me to get Ney's name tattooed. I know where to get it, and only she'll know it's there. Not on my dick, but close to it. I'm in deep. At least I can do it myself.

After cleaning the area on the man's arm, I wrap it and walk him to the front just as a red-faced, bloodshot-eyed Astor walks in. This can't be good. Astor would never show up like this if it were bad.

"Astor, are you okay?" I ask as I walk up to her. She shakes her head and looks, sniffling.

Before she says anything, she wipes her face with the sleeve of her shirt. "Anna did something. I didn't know she would do it."

Fear sinks in, and my heart picks up. Definitely not going to be good. "What did she do?" I rub Astor's biceps and wait for her to wipe away the tears again.

"I went with her to see Journey. She told me she wanted to make amends. But..." she trails off.

I take a deep breath and refrain from shouting or shaking the information out of her. "But what? Astor, what did she do?"

"She said some awful things, Briggs. Terrible things to Journey." Her voice cracks.

"What did she say to her?" Jamie asks behind me. Ignoring him, I keep my focus on her.

I can hear my pulse thumping in my ears now. I look back at my friend and control my voice. "Astor, I need you to tell us."

"She said that you don't love her and that Gary should kill her instead of you, and that if she loved you, she would leave." Astor goes on to tell more of what Anna said to Ney.

I release her and rub my sternum; this will push Ney over the edge. She's going to leave. I'm not sure my love for her will outweigh her terror.

"Are you fucking kidding me? If anything happens to my sister because of that bitch," Jamie barks, making Astor flinch. I turn to look at him and see him grabbing his shit. I agree with him all the way.

"How long ago?" I ask her, but she doesn't answer. "Astor, how long ago did this happen?" I snap, making her flinch. I will never forgive Anna for this. After twenty-one years, she is nothing to me.

"About twenty minutes. I rode with Anna and couldn't get here until now. Briggs. She looked so broken afterward. Ny loves you. I could see the pain on her face. I didn't know Anna could be so mean." Astor sobs.

Looking at the time, I see it's almost eight. "Because what Anna said fractured her, Astor. She was barely holding it together. Where's Anna?" I raise my voice unintentionally. I run my hands down my face, trying to control the rage.

"At your parents' house with Baxter. I'm sorry," she whispers.

"It's not your fault. Go home. Thank you for telling me."

Without wasting any time, I rush to gather my shit, run out the door, and jump in the car with Jamie. As we peel out of the parking lot, Beau's name comes up on my phone, and I answer.

"I don't have time, Beau," I tell him.

"You need to get home. Now, Briggs. Van attacked Journey. The fucker was dead on top of her, his throat slit. She needs you here. Fuck, she's beat to hell," Beau says, and all the blood rushes from my face.

"I'm on my way." My voice boomed as I hung up. "House. Van got to her." I shout, punching the dashboard.

"Fuck, this is that bitch's fault," Jamie growls.

"I know. I'll deal with her once we make sure Ney is okay," I tell him, grinding my teeth just thinking about Anna. Our friendship is gone in one fucking night. She hated Journey that much.

Jamie and I stop at the house, jump out, and run inside. Beau's waiting for me at the front door, hands on his hips, pacing.

"Where is she?" I bark, looking at Beau's big ass.

"In here."

I follow Beau and see Ney on the floor, on her side, covered in blood. In a split second, my heart split and splintered. I thought I knew pain and heartache, but I didn't know a fucking thing until this moment. My wife, my love, is holding something to her forehead, and Noah is holding something to the back of her head. How the hell did we beat the ambulance?

I rush past Beau and fall to my knees when I reach her. "I'm right here, baby. You're going to be okay," I tell her.

I take her free hand and check the rest of her body. With my other hand, I press a compress to her forehead so she can rest the arm that's been holding it.

"I didn't run. Anna wanted me to, but I chose us," she says weakly, tears in her eyes and a pitiful smile. She's so proud of herself, and shit, I'm proud of her, too. "I love you," she says, her eyes rolling and her speech slurring.

My eyes sting with tears that threaten to fall. I can't let her see me weep. She needs my strength. "I love you, my heart. I'm so sorry. She shouldn't have done what she did. I won't leave your side again. I need you to keep your eyes open, baby."

"Who did what?" Noah asks.

I don't take my eyes off Ney as I answer him. "Anna came here and said some shit. You should check on Astor. Anna brought her along to do it. She was pretty upset when she came and told me what happened."

"Fuck." Noah huffs.

Panic takes hold as Ney's close again. "Journey, sweetheart. Keep your eyes open," I tell her just as the paramedics come in and move me aside. I step back with Jamie while they check on Ney. Jamie squeezes my shoulder as we watch them, and moisture gathers before it runs down my face.

When they move her onto the gurney, she groans. "Hercules." The paramedics exchange a glance, and I step forward. "That's what she calls me. Can I ride with her?" I ask, wiping my face.

"You can, but they may not let you stay with her right away," Angel, the paramedic, tells me.

"I need to be with her as long as I can," I tell her, taking Journey's hand.

"I'll meet you there. I have to call our parents," Jamie tells me, and I nod.

Once they get her into the ambulance, I get in and take her hand. The sirens ring in my ears as we speed through town.

She's trying to keep her eyes open and on mine. When I stroke her blood-soaked hair, she offers me another weak smile.

"You're going to be okay, Sunrise," I whisper to her. Journey reaches up with her other hand and drags it along my cheek. "I'm okay," she whispers back.

My eyes don't leave hers the entire ride. I stay out of Angel's way while she does what she needs to.

At the hospital, I get out and watch as they unload Ney and rush her back.

"I'm sorry, Mr. Banks, you can't go back. I promise we'll come get you as soon as we can," the nurse, doctor, or whoever the woman is, tells me. I stare as they roll her through the double doors.

A man in scrubs steps up beside me. "Sir, if you follow me, I'll take you to a private waiting area. I'll make sure to direct the rest of the family there." When I don't move, he places a hand on my shoulder. "They'll take good care of her."

Reluctantly, I follow the man to the waiting area. It's not long before Jamie flies in with Henry, Terry, and Tink.

"Mom and Dad are on their way. I thought Henry and Terry should be here, too. I called Walker. He's taking Lea to Birdie, and he'll be here," Jamie tells me.

"Jamie, I need you to take me to my parents. Henry, will you call if they come out? It won't take us long. I need Anna to know what she's fucking done."

"Of course," he says before Jamie and I step out of the room.

We're silent as we drive to my parents' house. I'm so pissed. I wish I could bring Van back from the dead and kill the bastard myself. I don't even want to be near Anna, but I'm going to make sure she knows exactly how I fucking feel. The closer we get, the harder my heart pounds and the more rage-fueled adrenaline courses through me.

As we come to a stop, Jamie and I stride up to the house, and I fling the door open. I see Anna on the couch next to Baxter,

196

laughing. It instantly pisses me the fuck off. How the hell can she sit here and act like she hasn't done anything? Her eyes meet mine, and shame fills them, but it only sets me off more. I don't feel sorry for her.

"You had no fucking right, Anna. Because of you, he got to her. Why? Because you couldn't handle the fact that you fucked a psycho. Or are you that jealous that the one person you seem to think so little of found someone before you?" I raise my voice.

"Now, Briggs," Dad starts.

"Oh my God, honey, is that blood?" My mother asks and jumps up, staring at the red staining me.

Baxter stands and squares up. "You need to calm down."

"No." I don't look away from Anna. "I've been there for you through everything in your shitty life. I've supported you, comforted you, lied for you, helped you with the bakery, dropped everything for you, and I've never asked for a fucking thing in return." I shout.

"Briggs, what are you talking about? Briggs, whose blood is this?" Mom asks as she inspects me for injuries.

"Anna thought it was appropriate to call my wife a whore, tell her I didn't love her, and say she should be the one Gary kills. Well, Anna, it wasn't Gary who went to her first. It was Van. When I got home, my wife was bleeding on the floor. Gary slit Van's throat while he was still on top of her. I'm covered in my wife's blood." I roar. Mom gasps and whips her head toward Anna.

"Oh, God. You didn't, Anna? Is Journey okay?" Mom asks frantically. Anna doesn't say anything; she gives me a blank stare.

"She is the only person I've ever cared about, and you tore her down. Journey lives with guilt she has no right to carry, and you fucking used it to break her. Her life had been hard enough. She didn't choose that family, and she got away from Van as soon as she figured out who he really was. I am the good she needs. I am healing her. I am the only man she has ever trusted enough to get close to her. The only one, and it's my decision who I die for," I yell. "And to make it worse, you made Astor an unknowing participant."

Tears stream freely down my face. I look at Anna with no emotion. "This is your fault." I point at the now-crying Anna. "I will blame you for the rest of my life. She is the only person I have ever loved, or ever will. The only fucking person, Anna." I yell, making her flinch and Baxter shift his stance. "Did he pay you?" I wait, but she doesn't answer. "Did he fucking pay you to go there?" I insist again. Anna twitches and looks away. My face falls, and the air leaves my lungs. "He did. You took his money and went there so her guard would be down. You hated her so much that you let him attack her. We're done. I never want to see you again. I will never forgive you, and I will tell the detectives to look into you for helping him."

I slam into Baxter's shoulder, then walk past him. I've known that fucker has been in love with Anna since she was eighteen. She's not the same person I used to know.

"Briggs, where are you going?" Dad asks.

"Back to the hospital. Van was able to beat the hell out of her because of Annabelle."

"I'm right behind you," he says, grabbing his keys.

I nod to my dad. Jamie and I step out of the house and drive back to the hospital. As I enter the private waiting room, I glance at Henry. "Anything?" I ask, leaning against the wall.

"No. You were only gone for thirty minutes. I assume it may be a few more hours, depending on the severity of the wounds," he tells me. He would know, being a fire captain with EMT training. Dad comes over and stands with me while my mom takes my hand.

It's not long before Winter comes flying into the room with swollen eyes. I'm guessing Baylor stayed with the twins.

"Is she ok? Briggs, is she ok? Your brother wouldn't tell me anything when we got home and saw all the police cars," Winter says, sobbing.

"She was conscious when we got here. I don't know all the details yet," I tell her, since it's only speculation that Gary slit the Vans' throat.

When Audrey and Sul rush in, Audrey heads straight to me and hugs me tightly. I explain what I know to everyone, so they stop asking one at a time.

I sit and start shaking my leg while we wait. Time moves like a crippled snail when you're waiting for news like this. It's agonizing and painful. It's fear-fueled exhaustion. But you can't sleep. You can't think. You can't do anything except wait.

Twenty

Briggs

Three hours later, the door opens, and everyone stands. A short woman in scrubs enters and looks around. "Briggs Banks?"

I jump to my feet and stand in front of her. "That's me,"

"I'm Dr. Atkins."

"Is my wife okay?" I ask, shifting on my feet.

"Your wife suffered a concussion, multiple large lacerations, and defensive wounds. She has extensive bruising and multiple stitches and staples on the back of her head. There are no broken bones, and the skull wasn't fractured. There are no signs of a brain bleed or any other internal bleeding. We'll keep her for observation. She'll be in pain, but she'll make a full recovery."

When I hear she'll be okay, my knees almost buckle. I wipe my face and compose myself. "Can I see her?"

"The nurse will be out as soon as we have her in a room," she says gently. As soon as she leaves, two detectives walk in.

"Mr. Banks. I'm Detective Harper. I won't take up much of your time, and we'll be out of your way," the older detective says.

Son of a bitch. I just want my wife. "Ok."

Harper pulls a pad and pen from his pocket before he starts. "We know there was a second man in the house. He called 911 after murdering Mr. Wallen and confessed. Can you think of anyone else who would want to hurt your wife?"

"Gary Thompson," I growled. I know it's that motherfucker.

"Okay. Do you know why he would want to hurt her?"

"Look up the neglect case in Amber Falls, Kentucky, from seventeen years ago," Audrey says, so I don't have to. "Van paid Gary and Sheila to harass her again. He didn't know what kind of psychopath Gary was. Van miscalculated, getting him involved. Gary has been obsessed with Journey since she was a child, and now that Van has fixed him on her again, he won't stop until he gets her."

"Why would Van want to harass her? Was there a history of violence?" he asks Audrey, and she snorts.

"Yes, but Journey was too scared to report it. She doesn't trust people easily," she answers.

"Ok. Do you know how often it occurred and why she didn't leave sooner?" Anger shifts in half the people in the room.

Audrey narrows her eyes at the detective and lifts a lip in a snarl. "That was a stupid-ass question. I won't answer that in front of all these people. You can ask her when it's more private. I mean no offense when I say this, but none of these people need to know what she's already suffered unless she decides to tell them. And I'll be damned if anyone else here who does know opens their fucking mouth." Audrey scolds the detective, daring him to try her. Huh, I now know never to piss her off. When I glance at Sul, I see him smile down at his wife. Shifting my gaze, I see Jamie grinning. She is a fierce Mama bear.

"Okay. Back to Gary. If he was the one who killed Van, why would he leave her? He said the victim needed an ambulance. Why call for help? I'm not asking to sound insensitive; I'm trying to understand the situation." He asks her, and she snorts.

"Because Gary prefers to get to her after she's healed. When she's *'fresh'*, he wants her to be scared, not marked, when he comes for her. He would throw a fit when we were younger if Sheila got to her before or without him." Walker says, crossing his arms over his chest.

Fuck me. It keeps getting worse.

"And you are?" Harper asks him.

"Craig Walker Franklin. I'm Journey's half-brother. Check into Sheila Brown as well. Gary was always her special child. There's a high probability she'll help him or is helping him. Additionally, check the name "Dean Adams". He used it as an alias and said he lived a couple of towns over." Walker states the facts.

"I think that's all I need for now. We'll look into each of them. You have my word. If you have any additional information, please let us know. Given the high-profile nature of this case, I'll have officers posted at the residence once Mrs. Banks returns home. The media has already caught wind of this and is camping out." He says, handing me a card. I should tell him about Anna, but I need her to explain it first. I need to know whether I was right or if she was just scared and didn't answer.

"I'll be hiring private security. No offense to your officers, but we need more than two people at the end of the drive. You can have them there, but I'll have ten or so of my own guys watching the house around the clock." Sul tells the detectives.

The two detectives nod and leave just as a nurse enters.

"She's resting. The doctor asks that no more than two go back at a time for now," she says, and I push forward with Audrey behind me.

As I follow the nurse, my heart sinks to the floor. Audrey sobs as we step into the room and see Journey. Bruises and bandages cover her beautiful face. IVs hang from her arm, and an oxygen mask covers her mouth and nose.

My sweet Sunrise looks so small and fragile. I walk to the bed and stop myself from letting the tears break free again. I bend down, brush my lips gently against her temple, and take her left hand. When I look at her fingers, I see bruises on both. My girl fought back. Audrey pulls a chair up behind me.

"Sit, Briggs. All we can do now is wait."

"Yeah. I'm sorry, Audrey. Someone I called a friend caused this," I say, then sit. I move Ney's fragile fingers in mine, then bring them to my lips.

"We can't be held accountable for other people's actions. Anna took it upon herself to be bitter about this situation. She lashed out because she was hurt." Audrey says, pulling up a chair on the other side. "I'm not saying it was right. I'm only saying don't apologize for her. Everyone in that room can see how much you love my girl."

"I do. I love her more than anything in this life. I didn't need time to tell me that." I tell her, and tears fall.

I wish it were me in that bed instead of her. I would gladly take her place. I wish I had listened to my gut and never left the house earlier.

"You listen to your heart. I knew you two were meant for each other the day we met, and I saw how protective you were of her already."

"I'll spend the rest of my life protecting and taking care of her," I vow to Audrey, but I don't look away from my Sunrise.

"I know you will. I'm going to switch with Sully." She sniffles and rises.

Nodding, I cradle Ney's hand. When Audrey leaves, I lean in. "I'll never leave your side again. I need you, baby. My heart and soul... they can't survive without their other half." I bring her hand to my lips again and stop myself from breaking down completely. "I love you, my heart. I love you so much."

A hand on my shoulder makes me glance back to see Sul's red-rimmed eyes. He doesn't say anything; he stands there, lending his strength for a few moments, then squeezes my shoulder, moves to the other side, and kisses her head. "Dad loves you, babycake," he whispers to her.

The rest of the night turns into a blur as the rest of the family comes and goes. The nurses keep coming in and out to check on her.

The longer I stare at Ney, the more I need to be closer to her. I stand, move to the edge of the bed, and lie on my side, facing her. My heart and brain don't want to sleep, but my eyes eventually win the war. I rest my head on her shoulder, wrap my arm around her stomach, and drift off.

The sound of a giggle and a light touch on my lips have me peeling my eyelids open. Once my vision focused, my eyes met the burning amber irises staring back at me. One of her eyes is swollen and half-open, but she has a tiny smile. God, her face looks worse today. It breaks my heart to see her like this and to know I wasn't there to stop it.

"Hi, baby." She whispers, scooting a little closer to me. She moves her hand, her thumb brushing just under my jawline. Closing my eyes, I relish the feel of her delicate touch.

I bring my arm gently around her and rub her side. "Hi, sweetheart. I'm sorry I wasn't there."

"It's okay. I'll heal. I was going to leave," she admits, and my heart speeds up. "But when I went to write you a note, I couldn't. I need you."

"I need you too. You know I would have found you if you left, right?" I try to keep the mood light, and she gives another half-smile.

"I know. You're my haunt," she jokes. Tilting her head slightly, she brushes her lips to mine and winces. I stop her before she can try to keep going.

"That's right. Even more so now. I don't plan to leave you alone again until this is over," I tell her.

"I didn't think you would." Sighing, she starts playing with my hair. "How bad does my face look? Is my modeling career over?" To me, she's still beautiful.

"No, baby. You're still gorgeous," I tell her, stroking her hair while being careful to avoid the wound.

"Liar. It's okay. I want to focus more on being a designer anyway. I think I'll open an office here instead of in Nashville." She tells me, and I fucking love the idea of her always being close to me.

"I like that idea," I tell her, kissing her cute little nose. "We might have to stay with my parents until the house is released and cleaned."

"I don't care where we are as long as I'm with you."

Those words are music to my ears. My Sunrise chose us over running. She didn't let Anna or what Van did break her this time. I help keep her strong.

A knock at the door makes Ney shift. The detective walks in and sits in the chair closest to her. "Hi, Mrs. Banks, I'm Detective Harper. I'm going to ask you a few questions, and if at any point you need to stop, we will stop."

"Ok," she says, and I help her sit up.

"Can you tell me what happened when you were attacked?"

She inhales a shaky breath. "I was at home, and some friends had just left. I thought maybe they'd forgotten something when the doorbell rang." When she pauses, I look down at her and furrow my brows. Why is she covering for Anna? "I didn't think about it when I opened the door. Van was there. He hit me just as I realized it was him. I tried to get my phone, but he got to me first."

Anger continues to escalate as she recounts what happened. I'm glad the son of a bitch is dead. I just wish I were the one who killed him. My teeth grind throughout the story.

"When he had me pinned to the floor, he." She takes another breath and wipes her face. "He told me he was going to let Gary have fun first." She says, clearing her throat. She's trying so hard to stay strong. "I heard Gary's voice after that. He said he doesn't like playing with broken toys. Then I felt warm liquid pour onto my face." Her voice cracks. I take her hand and start playing with her slender fingers.

Ney shifts and sniffles. I reach over, grab some tissues, and hand them to her. Her shaky hands take them, and she wipes her nose. "Gary told me not to mistake him killing Van for saving me. He said he meant what he said about toys and that he'll be back for me eventually."

Harper leans forward, nodding as he listens. "And you're positive it was him?"

"Yes. He said his name, but he also…" She stops again. "He called me Lila. Gary and Joseph were the only two who ever called me that."

"Your mother mentioned there was a history of physical altercations with Mr. Wallen."

Journey stiffens as a tear slips from the corner of her eye. "I know I should have reported it. I was ashamed and scared. When it comes to my career, I'm confident and can handle it, but in relationships, I'm not as skilled. My parents and Jamie are the only people who have ever loved me." She sniffles and hangs her head. I place her hand on my heart, lending her the strength she needs. She lifts her head, and her eyes meet mine. I mouth 'I love you' to her, and she mouths it back before continuing.

"Van was the only person I'd dated before. At first, he was nice, but after I agreed to go out with him, he started chipping away at the progress I'd made. He would do things to watch me have anxiety or panic attacks. Then he would make me feel like I was the crazy one."

She's starting to play with my fingers now. "Growing up, I was told I deserved everything that happened to me because I was nothing. When he hit me the first time, it was because I forgot to put a lime in his drink. He would get into my head, and I thought I deserved it."

Fucking hell. He knew what he was doing to her. He mentally tortured her.

"That happened a few times. Each time, it got worse. Eventually, I snapped out of it. The night I left him." She whimpers. "It was worse than this. He. He tried to." She takes a shaky breath and shakes her head.

"You don't have to say it, baby," I tell her, bringing my arms around her. The detective and I both know what he tried to do.

"He was too drunk to do it and passed out on top of me instead. He said he was going to take everything from me. I should have reported it, but I was broken. I was so tired of being hurt. I gave up." She sobs. I can't take it anymore. I wipe my face and hold her as gently as I can.

"I'm sorry that happened, Mrs. Banks. I've read the reports from when you were nine and the one from when you were twelve," he says remorsefully.

I keep hearing about her foster family, but she hasn't shared that story with me yet.

"Yeah, I'm starting to feel like I owe death a hell of a debt," she sniffles, leaning into me.

The detective chuckled. "We already issued a warrant for Gary's arrest and have officers following up on every lead. If you can think of any other details, please let me know." Harper stands, then looks back at Journey. "You put up one hell of a fight, Mrs. Banks."

Journey gives him a weak smile before he leaves the room.

"You protected Anna. Why?" I ask her.

"She was hurt and upset. She needed someone to lash out at. I want to give her a chance to explain. It sucks. Until all of this, I thought we were getting along. I lashed back at her, so I'm guilty, too." She lifts a shoulder.

Damn it. This woman's heart is too fucking big. She protected the person who helped set up her attack. How the hell does she do this? I can't stand the thought of forgiving what Anna did.

"Oh, sweet girl, your heart is too pure. There's no excuse for what she's done. You're guilty of nothing." My mother's voice shifts quickly from gentle to harsh. She's clearly pissed off at Anna, too. "She acted out of jealousy and disappointment in herself." When I look up, I see Mom and Audrey standing in the doorway. When the hell did they get here?

"We waited until the detective left. Sorry you didn't hear us come in," Audrey says, walking to Journey's side. "I talked to the doctor. They're going to do a lookover before they discharge you. The house has been released, and we have cleaners there now. Dad has Whitlock security coming to install a system for you and Winter. The security guards around the house will be here today, too."

Damn, that man works fast.

"You guys didn't have to do all that. We would have taken care of it," Ney tells her mom.

"Please, you know how your dad gets. He's not taking any chances." Audrey takes Ney's hand. "Henry is waiting outside. The results came in today, and he hasn't opened the email. I think he wants to see you, though. Is it okay if he comes in?"

Journey sighs and looks at her mom through her puffy eyes. "Are you sure this isn't bothering you or Dad? I don't want to upset you."

"Honeycomb, Henry seems like a good man. If he were a piece of shit, I wouldn't let him near you. That man has spent years thinking he lost the only child he's ever fathered. If he is your dad, you both deserve to know each other. Dad and I know he'll never replace us. We want this for you." Audrey reassures her.

"I still feel bad for even wanting it." Ney sniffles.

"Sunrise, look at me." When she does, I see the turbulence rolling through her. "You're allowed to be happy, excited, or feel anything else about finding him. Remember, this is your family growing, not replacing anyone. When we start adopting our kids, we'll face the same possibilities. Would you want them to feel bad? Or would it change anything for you?" I ask in a soft, low tone. I know the others can hear me, but I keep my focus on her.

She gives her head a slight shake. "No. Never. They'll always be our children," she whispers.

"That's right. And it's the same for Audrey and Sul. Just like Jamie will always be your favorite brother, even though you have Walker again."

She snorts, grins, and winces. "He is my favorite."

"Damn, I'm glad you two decided to stay together." Audrey beams at me.

"Me too. I've never seen two people better for each other." Mom joins in.

"Okay, he can come in." Journey reaches over, takes my hand, and starts playing with my finger.

"We'll step out and give you some time," Audrey tells her, then kisses the side of her head.

Henry walks in as Mom and Audrey leave the room. He moves a little closer and stands nervously.

"You can move closer. I can't move fast enough to bite you," she jokes, and he chuckles. He takes the seat beside her, inhales, and lets out a shaky breath.

"Mom said we got the results?" Ney says.

Henry scoots a little closer and meets her gaze, nodding. "I got the email this morning. I didn't want to overwhelm you. Journey, even if I'm not your father, I'd still like to get to know you. I'm so sorry for everything you've been through. No child should endure that pain or fear. If I am your father, I want to be there for you in any way I can. I've already missed so much time."

Journey reaches over and takes his hand. "I want that too, but please know I'll have three parents. It's important to me that you all get along."

"Of course. I would never try to replace them. Do you want me to check now? We can wait." Henry takes her hand, opens his phone, and waits.

Ney holds his hand back and steadies herself. "Now is okay."

He nods, then swipes a few times, then moves closer, holding the phone so we can all see it, and clicks. Journey's hand tightens, and she chokes back a sob as the results appear. He's definitely her dad. Ney releases my hand and hugs a sobbing Henry.

He cradles the side of her head and holds her gently as they both release twenty-six years of pain. I can't imagine what they're feeling right now.

I rise to my feet and bend down to kiss her head.
"I'll send Audrey back in and give you three some time," I tell her, and she nods. As soon as I step out, I see the security guards Sul hired standing on either side of the door.

Audrey steps towards the door before her brown eye meets mine in a silent question. "He's her father. I told them I would give you three some time," I confirm, and she smiles before walking into the room.

Mom and I walk the halls in silence until we reach the cafeteria and sit. "So, adoption?" Mom asks.

"Journey can't have kids, and I never wanted my own. We both agreed to adopt or foster when we're ready. Audrey, Sul, and Jamie are the best family Journey has ever had. We want to be that for children already in this world," I tell her, then lean back, waiting for any judgment she might have. I've never told anyone I don't want kids.

"I think that's wonderful, Briggs. You'll both be amazing parents," Mom says, taking my hand.

"Hey, Mom, how would you and Audrey feel about helping Journey plan her wedding?" Sunrise deserves the fairytale wedding of her dreams, and if she has it, maybe she'll finally see that she's my forever.

Mom spits out her drink, covering me. I laugh and wipe my face. "Yes, yes. Oh, honey. She's going to be so excited."

"I'll talk to Journey about it, but I want her to have whatever she wants. If she wants a fucking unicorn and a leprechaun, there better be one," I half-joke, and Mom chuckles. More pride swells in my father's eyes as he looks at me and smiles.

"Of course. It's her day," Mom laughs.

Twenty-One

Journey

I sigh as we drive past the reporters camped out in front of our house. I guess the attack on two famous people would be big news. Thank fuck the windows are heavily tinted, and the police are keeping them at the end of the drive. Briggs squeezes my hand, then kisses my palm. I hate that I've allowed my life to be so public.

After a night in the hospital and another at Briggs' parents', we're now pulling past all the media at our house. Dad has a guard driving us in an armored car, which I think is ridiculous. Gary won't use a gun when he comes. He likes torture, not quick and easy.

Ivey and Briggs have tried to reach Anna for an explanation of what happened, but she has been avoiding their calls and texts. I don't want to believe she would set me up, but we won't know until she talks to us. She didn't deny wanting Briggs, so maybe she did it on purpose.

Last night, Winter, Astor, and Birdie came over and spent time with me. Poor Astor was heartbroken over the situation and kept apologizing.

Briggs helps me out of the vehicle ever so gently, then assists me in adjusting my sweatpants and t-shirt. He has been so attentive and overly clingy. I love it, but he wouldn't even let my mom help me in the bathroom because, according to him, taking care of me is his job, and he wants to do it. You know the whole 'In sickness and in health' vow. He likes to point that out.

Briggs holds me and gives me a soft, sweet kiss. Our tongues brush and caress each other slowly. I wish I could take him right here. It hurts a little, but I want more.

He chuckles into my mouth as I try to deepen it, then draws back—pressing his forehead to mine, he breathes in.

"I want nothing more than to ravish you right here and now, but you need to heal. We're going inside, eating unhealthy food, and getting comfortable. Your dad also has this place guarded like Fort Knox, and no one gets to see your gorgeous, breathtaking body except me." He whispers in my ear, sending a shiver down my spine.

Damn it, he's right. There are guards literally everywhere. When I pout my lip, Briggs nips it and laughs, then brings his arm around my back and helps me walk inside. I freeze when we cross the threshold, and memories flood me. I don't feel an ounce of remorse about Van's death, but the fear from the attack makes me pause.

Briggs rubs my back. "Take your time. If it's too much, we can go back to my parents."

I shake my head as we walk deeper into the house, and my two favorite girls come running. Seeing them pushes the bad thoughts away and fills my heart with joy. I hate that I can't bend to pet them. Briggs whistles, and they follow us to the couch. Once I'm sitting, I take off my glasses. Charm and Ebony both get halfway onto the couch with me, and I give them all the love they want. Briggs laughs and stops them from jumping. Leaning back, I hold my ribs, rest my head on the cushion, and close my eyes.

When the doorbell rings, Briggs goes to answer. Now that the girls have settled down, they both lie with their heads in my lap. They always made me feel safe.

The scent of pizza hits my nostrils, and my mouth waters.

"You have visitors. They have blankets, so I don't think they're leaving." Briggs chuckles. Before I can look back, long arms wrap around my shoulders, and I smile. I reach up and pat Daniel's arm.

"Are you boys still worried about me? I'll be okay, but I have to admit I do enjoy your company."

"We always worry about you, Aunt Ny," Dylan says, then hugs me before following Briggs into the kitchen to help.

I can't help but chuckle. "You're good kids."

"Yeah, Mom, listen to Aunt Ny. We're good kids," Daniel tells her, then moves the coffee table. Once he gets it where he wants it, he spreads his blanket on the floor and sits.

"How are you feeling? Want me to get you a blanket or anything?" she asks, then starts digging through her bag and hands me a stack of bridal magazines.

With a giggle, I take them from her. "I'm good. What are these for? Are you getting married? Guess Baylor kept a better eye on you than I thought." I wiggle my eyebrows at her, and she rolls her eyes, but she's blushing. Oh shit. I need the dirt there once the boys aren't around.

"They're for you, sweetheart," Briggs says, then whistles for the dogs to get down. Sitting next to me, he hands me a plate with pizza and a little salad.

I stare at him, questioning. "Um, did we get divorced, and I just don't know it yet? Last I remember, we're already married." I furrow my brows when he gives me a broad smile.

"We're still married, but we didn't go about it the traditional way. You missed out on the announcements, an engagement party, a bachelorette party, and the wedding of your dreams." Briggs' bright Caribbean eyes meet mine, and he tucks my hair behind my ear. "I want to give you the real experience because you deserve it, baby. I want you to plan a real wedding. I want you to make it everything you ever dreamed of, and I want a real honeymoon. Maybe Ireland?" He grins at me, and I giggle. "I'm not going anywhere, Sunrise. I think I proved that. And you're done trying to run from me." We both chuckle as I gaze at him in awe. I am the luckiest woman.

"I am. Why do you love me so much, Briggs Wilder?"

"Because you're worth it, Journey Leann. You're worth everything to me. I love you, my heart."

Giggling, I brush his hair from his face. "I love you, fuzzybutt." Winter and the boys crack up.

Briggs smiles and shakes his head. "You realize you just told them I have a hairy ass, right?" We both laugh.

"It's only a little hairy. That's why I said fuzzybutt." I giggle and take a bite of my pizza. Fuck, it's good. Briggs snuck me some food in the hospital, but the doctor was adamant about what she wanted me to eat and keep it down.

"Uh-huh. Anyway, back to the wedding. I already asked Mom and Audrey to help you plan it," Briggs says, shoving his mouth full, then turning to give me a full-cheeked grin that makes me chuckle. Of course, he already talked to everyone.

"Well, I already know who my maid of honor is." I smile at Winter, who beams at me.

"You'll be limited in how many groomsmen you can have, Hercules. I haven't made the greatest of friends since I've been here."

"I know, baby, and I'm sorry about that," he says, running his fingers through my hair.

"I don't know, Ny. Birdie and Astor seem to really like you," Winter says, taking a bite.

"I guess that's true, but I feel like I caused the rift in the friend group. Anna would still be part of it if it weren't for my marrying Briggs."

"You didn't cause anything, Sunrise. She did. Anna did this to herself. We," he says, pointing between us, "didn't do anything to her. She got ass hurt and jealous. It shouldn't have happened. She didn't even try to apologize or answer our questions, which, by the way, screams guilty. We're done with her," Briggs says adamantly.

I'm not sure he'll ever forgive his friend. I would if she genuinely wanted to make amends. I've learned that life is too short for petty grudges, and I feel bad that Anna ruined twenty-one years of friendship. I won't be able to change his mind, though. It's something he'll have to do on his own.

"I'm thinking of strippers for the bachelorette party," Winter says with a mischievous grin.

"The fuck you are. I like you, Winter. Don't ruin it." Briggs narrows his eyes playfully and points his fork at her. I love my overprotective god.

"Ah, come on, Bigs." She laughs and gives each dog a piece of crust from her pizza.

"You've been spending too much time with Baylor."

"Bay is awesome. We stayed up all night playing video games together while Mom was at the hospital. Then he took us to Taco Bell at two in the morning for gaming fuel. We stayed up until

217

six in the morning," Daniel says with a huge smile. I glance at Winter, who flushes, and her features soften. Uh-oh. She's crushing.

"I like Baylor. He was the first one to make me feel welcome," I say.

"Yeah, I won't tell the others, but he's my favorite brother," Briggs half-jokes.

When the doorbell rings, Briggs gets up to answer it. A few moments later, we all hear his growl. "The fuck are you doing here? You have a lot of nerve."

"Dylan, help me up." Dylan jumps to his feet and gently helps me to mine. "Thank you." Shuffling past him, I walk to the front door.

My heart drops a little when I see Anna standing there. My eyes meet hers for a brief moment before I look at a red-faced Briggs. "I'm not leaving him," I tell her.

When I stop beside Briggs, he brings his arm behind my back and pulls me into him protectively.

Anna shakes her head. "That's not why I'm here. I want to apologize before I leave town. I should never have done what I did. I was out of line and let my misery take hold. I met Van at the bar. I was still pissed and hurt. He filled my head with everything I should be thinking and saying. He said he could talk you into leaving once I said what I needed to. I didn't know he would do what he did." She says one thing, but her features say something different. It's as if she doesn't mean the explanation and half-assed apology. Or maybe I'm more upset with her than I thought, and that's what I want to see.

"Yeah, he was good at getting into vulnerable minds," I say, and Briggs huffs. He's not as forgiving as I am.

"That's a shit excuse, Anna. You don't expect to say sorry and have everything be fine, do you? Because it won't be." Nope, he's definitely not forgiving her right now.

She swipes away the tears from her face and looks at both of us. "I know, and I don't expect you to forgive me. I'm selling the bakery and moving to New York. You two weren't the only ones I hurt that day. I need to get away."

"Baxter?" Briggs asks, working his jaw. I can feel the anger rolling off him. Huh, why would she hurt Baxter? He seems like a nice guy, like all the Banks brothers.

Anna meets his glare. "He told me he loved me after we slept together and that he would choose me over you. Instead of explaining calmly that I didn't feel that way, I freaked out. I broke him down and hurt him. This isn't me, or maybe it is, and I'm just figuring it out. All I know is I can't stay here. I hope you two have a long and happy life together. I truly am sorry for what I did." She sniffles, turns, and rushes away.

"Anna," I call out, and she turns to look at me. "I hope you find what you're looking for and that you can mend your broken spirit."

She nods, gets in her car, and backs out of the driveway. It breaks my heart because I know what it's like to feel that lost, not knowing who you are inside.

"I like that you have such a big heart, Sunrise," he says, closing the front door.

"I like that you get all growly for me," I tell him, cupping his chiseled jaw.

"Always, baby," he says, kissing quickly.

Briggs guides me back to the living room, where Winter is flipping through magazines and ignoring the boys arguing over which movie to put on. I smile at the scene.

"How about I pick the movie?" Briggs interjects, flopping onto the couch next to me. Leaning forward, he swipes the remote from Dylan's outstretched hand and laughs when Dylan gives him a look and a smile.

"Did you tell that bitch to go eat ass?" Winter asks without looking up from the book.

I chuckle and take one of the magazines from her. "No. You know I don't like to be mean. I do hope she finds what she needs. You should text your brother, Hercules."

"Yeah. I'm sure he's all fucked up right now." He sighs, flicks through TV channels, and lands on the first movie I was in. I give him a 'really' look, and he grins. He digs out his phone, clicks a few times, and sets it back down. Twirling around, he rests his head on my lap while I look through magazines.

"I wonder if Tilly would design a dress for me? I don't want white. I want something nontraditional. Blue, maybe?" I say to no one in particular, scrunching my nose at some of the dresses in the magazine.

"I'm sure she will, sweetheart. Want me to text her?"

"Yeah. Could you text her my number?"

"On it." He types a few times, then sets the phone back down. "Done."

"I need one like him." Winter chuckles.

"Mm hm." I hum at her and give her a knowing grin. She clamps her mouth shut and looks away. I need to figure out how to get these boys out of here so we can have a one-on-one.

As I flip through, I imagine what I want my wedding to look like. I don't want hundreds of people, just the important ones. I want a winter wedding and a baby-blue dress like Cinderella's. I like white roses, crystal icicles, and twinkling lights. Yup, I want a fairy-tale wedding.

Setting the book aside, I run my fingers through Briggs' hair while we watch the movie. I want everything with him.

Twenty-Two

Briggs

"Baby," Journey's whisper has my eyes flying open. My gaze meets the burning amber eyes staring down at me. God, I love this woman. I smirk at her and let my eyes roam her silk, tanned, naked body. Biting my lip, I lock my lust-filled gaze onto hers.

"You need my touches, sweetheart?" I ask in a gruff voice.

Ney shakes her head and kisses my jaw, then takes my mouth in a slow, pleading kiss, begging me to let her take what she needs. I bring one hand up and cup the nape of her neck—my tongue twirls and dances with hers.

I reach out, my other hand gripping the thigh straddling me. I fucking love that she wakes me up whenever she wants. I wish she would allow herself more healing, but I won't complain if she's feeling up to it.

She parts my mouth from hers, then kisses and nips down my neck and collarbone, then back up before shifting her hips and taking me in, down to the hilt with a swift roll. Her warm pussy is already drenched for me. We both moan at the feel of connecting. Fuck, I missed being inside her.

Sitting up, I take her breast into my mouth and twirl my warm tongue around her taut nipple as she rocks her hips and twines her fingers through my hair.

"You feel so good, Hercules." She moans and moves faster. Shit, I'm about to cum already.

I let out a guttural groan when she snaps her hips hard and fast. I knead her ass while I switch between teasing her breasts. "Take what you need, baby. I'm yours," I murmur into her breast.

I swear, when her eyes meet mine, I can feel the desire-fueled heat radiating from them. Journey pops and rolls her ass as she moves up and down my hard cock. God, I love this woman.

My hips thrust faster to keep up with her movements. When her walls clench around me, my own orgasm begins to take over. Pure dopamine floods me with the pleasure of being inside my wife.

Fuck, I can't hold it off. "Baby," Before I can finish, she takes my mouth, sucking my tongue, then cries out as her pussy clamps around me and pulses. Thank fuck, one last dip of her hips, and I dig my fingers into her ass, holding her in place as my body jerks and spasms. I release inside her with a groan. Spots form behind my eyes, and pure bliss rolls through me with my climax.

We both take a moment to steady our breathing and heart rate. Ney presses her forehead to mine. "I'm sorry. I needed to feel our connection. I wake you up a lot."

I chuckle and rub her damp back. "Never, and I mean never, apologize for that, Sunrise. I fucking love it." I tell her, then give her several open kisses. "I love you, my heart,"

She smiles, tucking my hair behind my ear. "I love you, my strength."

Gently holding Ney, I roll us so she's on her back, then slip off her. Standing, I walk to the bathroom and take a warm cloth. As I lie beside her, I kiss her and gently clean her.

The doorbell chiming and the dogs barking have us stopping the start of round two. Whoever it is, it had better be important. Drawing back, I groan and look at Ney's beautiful face. I wish her bruises would heal faster. I hate what she went through. I hate that I wasn't here to protect her.

"I'll get it, baby." I peck her nose, get to my feet, and walk to the dresser. I slip on black joggers and put on a white t-shirt. I kiss her again, then head to the front door. The dogs jump off the couch when they see me coming and follow me to the door.

When I open it, I see a short, curvy woman with gray hair and bright blue eyes. Her gaze meets mine, and she tilts the corner of her mouth.

She jumps when she notices the silent dogs, then corrects herself. "You must be Mr. Banks. I've seen photos of you and Journey online," she says, eyeing the dogs. My entire being goes on alert when she says my name. Please don't let this be another crazy fucking relative or the media.

"Uh, huh, and you are? They won't bite unless I tell them to," I say in a clipped tone. I lean on the door frame, cross my arms over my chest, and wait. Glancing at the guard, I give him a *'What the fuck'* look. He hunches his shoulders in a *'Don't know'* shrug.

Idiot.

"My, you are a protective one. Just like Jamie." I arch a brow at her, and she shakes her head. "Right. Sorry. I was expecting Journey to answer."

"Mrs. Courtright?" Journey's surprised, raspy, feminine voice comes from behind me. When I look back at my wife, a smile tugs at my lips at how adorable she is in her sweatpants, one of my shirts that is way too big for her, and her short, gorgeous locks pinned back. "What are you doing here? It's been what? Fourteen years." Ney walks up and wraps her arm around my back. I gently bring my arm behind her and rest my palm at the base of her neck.

"Just Sherry is fine. It's been a long time, Ny. I was hoping to talk with you. May I come in?" she asks.

"Oh, of course. I'll make us some coffee," Journey tells her, moving me aside.

Sherry enters the house and follows Ney to the kitchen. I stay on their heels the whole way. Ney seems to know her and isn't threatened, but that doesn't mean shit.

Journey gestures toward the kitchen table, and the woman sits.

"I'll start the coffee," I tell her, then kiss her temple. I walk twenty feet to the coffee pot and listen while I make it.

"He seems like a good man. You've done well for yourself, honey. I heard about your attack. I'm sorry you went through that."

"Thank you. I'm sorry, but I have to admit I'm a bit confused about why you're here. I haven't seen you since my parents adopted Jamie and me," Journey says politely.

Okay, so she's someone from Journey's childhood. Grabbing three mugs, I set up the tray with everything, carry it over to the table, and scoot my seat closer to Ney. They both make a cup and sit there for a moment.

"Gary's home was raided last night," Sherry says. I watch Ney's body stiffen at the mention of his name. I reach over, my palm circling her back.

"Okay, but that doesn't explain why you're here." Ney lifts her coffee, takes a sip, and watches the women.

Sherry inhales deeply, then sets the drink down and clasps her hands. "They found his three children but not Gary."

225

All the air leaves Journey's lungs before she takes a deep breath. "Oh God," Ney whispers. "How bad?"

"Not as bad as you, but not good," Sherry says, pursing her lips. Okay, I got it now. She was Journey's caseworker.

"Where's the mother? Why were those children even allowed near him?"

"Their mother passed away two years ago. Gary had been living a straight life, or so we thought, and the judge agreed to grant him custody since they're his children." She gives a sad shrug.

"Ok, ok. You can take them now, right? He won't be able to get them again. He already went to jail for child abuse and neglect. This is like a repeat offender situation, isn't it? And he's wanted for murder." Ney says, half-frantically.

"Yes. He'll never be able to get the children back. The reason I'm here is that you're the next of kin, and it's customary to contact you first," Sherry says. Ney sucks in a sharp breath.

"Oh, God. Oh, God. You want me to take his kids? Fuck, fuck." Ney says hysterically, jumps to her feet, clutches her ribs, and begins to hyperventilate.

I quickly gather her into my arms. "Breathe, baby. You need to breathe." I extend my hand and gently rub her sternum as her tears fall. "Big breath in. Little breath out." I tell her calmly. She locks her amber gaze on me and does as instructed. Her breathing begins to even out, but she doesn't look away.

"Good job. You did well. Let's sit back down and listen to what she has to say, okay?" I tell her gently. She shakes her head, then sits back down.

"I know this is a lot," Sherry says, reaching into her purse and pulling something out. "I'd like to show you their pictures. If you want to stop at any time, we will. We'll take our time." She speaks to Journey in a soft, even tone.

"Okay," Ney replies with a shaky breath, wiping her face.

Sherry waits a moment before handing us the first picture. Journey takes it with a shaky hand and whimpers when she sees the little boy. He has dark brown hair and green eyes, and he looks underweight. He wears a small, defeated smile, but you can tell he's trying.

"That's Oxford, but he likes to be called Ox because he's strong and protects his brother and sister from Gary. Ox is eight," Sherry explains.

A painful noise escapes Ney as her fingers trace the child's face in the photo. I feel a sting behind my eyes as I look at the image. How could anyone do this?

Sherry pulls out the following photo and hands it to us. This one shows a younger boy with lighter brown hair and hazel eyes. There's a small mark just under his eye, but it looks mostly healed; he is also underweight—journey hiccups and cokes on her sob. Moving closer, I rub her back and kiss her temple. "It's okay, sweetheart," I whisper to her.

"That's Lux. He's six and a half. He loves Spider-Man because he's a hero," she tells us. Fuck, this is breaking my heart. These poor children. They don't deserve this. No one does.

She takes out the last photo and hands it to us, and the dam holding back the water breaks. My own tear slips from the duct that's been caging it. It's a little girl with dark brown hair and dark green eyes. She's so fucking tiny. She's holding a stuffed pig and smiling at it like it's the first toy she's ever seen. That's the tipping point for Journey, and she completely breaks down in a full, uncontrollable sob.

I wipe my face and pull her close. She buries her face in my neck and lets out that painful cry again. "I got you, baby. I got you." I choke on my whisper. Cradling her head, I rub her back until she calms.

Once she's composed herself, she looks back at Sherry and nods.

"That's Tulip. She just turned three. She only had her brothers teaching her, but they did a good job. She talks well, and they potty-trained her as best they could."

"Gary said I'm not his biological sister," Journey chokes out. Shit, I didn't think about that.

Sherry gives her a small smile. "He's not. That's a whole situation, but legally you're still considered the next of kin."

"If not me, foster care?" Ney asks, then picks up the photos again. Sherry nods slightly. "I don't know what to do." She turns to me for answers. I cup her neck and turn her chair so we're face-to-face.

"I will support you. No matter what you decide, sweetheart. But look at those kids. If anyone can connect with them and understand what they're going through, it's you." I tell her, then place my hand on her heart, trying to convince her it's big enough to do this. I'll do whatever she wants, but I'm hoping she chooses to help them.

"What if I can't? What if all I see when I look at them is everything he ever did to me? What if I can't love them? What if my face scares them?" she asks, then sniffs.

"Oh, honey, your bruises won't scare them. Would you be willing to meet them? If you decide you can't do it, that's okay; this is up to you. No one will think any differently of you if you decide it's too much." Sherry reassures her.

Journey squeezes her eyes shut and stifles a whimper. "If I agree, what happens?"

"You'll both become their legal guardians. If you decide at any point to adopt them, that will be an option. All parental rights have been terminated. Once they find Gary, he will be in jail indefinitely."

"When do you want us to meet them?" she whispers. I am positive this has to be one of the hardest things she has ever done, but my baby is strong. I do not doubt that she will love these children. Her heart is too big not to.

"Would you be able to meet at the hospital at 5 pm today? They'll be getting discharged around then."

"We'll be there," I tell her, not giving Journey a choice. "These clothes. Is that all they have?" I ask, pointing to the pictures. Each child wears a sweatshirt and sweatpants that are far too big.

"Yes," she says.

I rise, walk to the kitchen, and grab a pen and paper. "What are their sizes? I can guess, but if you know, it'll be easier." I write down the sizes for clothes and shoes as she rattles them off.

After finishing the conversation, we walked her to the door. "Thank you for considering this, Journey."

"You're welcome. We'll see you at 5," Journey says, her eyes puffy, then shuts the door behind Sherry. "Get dressed, honey muffin. We have shit to buy. Do three-year-olds need cribs, one of those little beds, bunk beds, or separate rooms? Fuck. Who do we call for help? Do we tell our parents now? Briggs, baby, I need you to tell me who to call." She weeps.

I wrap my arms around her and inhale. She needs me to make this choice. I don't know which is right. "Call our parents. They'll know what kids need." Fuck, I hope this is the right answer.

"Okay, I'll call Mom. Should I call Henry?"

"Do you want him here for all the big things?"

"I do," she whispers.

"Then call him, Sunrise. He's your dad, too. You can have more than one, sweetheart."

"Okay, I'll go call them," she says, walking to the bedroom.

Digging my phone out, I gulp before I click my mother's name. It rings twice before she answers.

"Hey, everything okay?" she asks.

I close my eyes and work the tension out of my neck. "Ah, not really. We're okay, but we got thrown a curveball. Can you and Dad come over, like, nowish?"

"We're on our way," she says, then hangs up.

I put my phone back in my pocket and head to the bedroom. Journey already has ten different outfits laid out on the bed, and she's gazing at them with tears in her eyes.

"I don't know what to wear. I don't want them to be scared when they meet us." She sucks in a breath and meets my gaze. "How do I do this, Briggs? How do I look these babies in the eyes and not see their father?" She sobs.

I frown and rush over to her when she starts to break down again. I hold her in my arms, trying to comfort her. She wraps her arms around my waist and squeezes. Her slender body shakes and trembles as she sobs.

"You won't, sweetheart. You'll see what I see. You'll see small children who need people like us. You'll see what Audrey and Sul saw when they came for you and Jamie. You'll see wanting to love and heal them. You'll see wanting to show them that life doesn't have to be scary and painful." I say, pressing my lips to her forehead and holding her to me.

"Pick the blue dress with flowers. It's a soothing color." I tell her, urging her to pull herself back from the sadness and fear threatening her. "I'll wear blue with you. Come on, baby. We have shopping to do."

She giggles, then pulls back and looks at me. I smile, and my mouth takes hers in a slow, loving kiss. Journey strokes my cheek and deepens our kiss for a few minutes, making me groan before she breaks it.

"Thank you for being my hero, Hercules," she whispers, tracing my tattoo.

"I will always be your hero, sweetheart. I love you, my heart."

"I love you, my strength."

She exhales, grabs the blue dress, and walks to the bathroom. I grab a pair of dark jeans and a light blue shirt. In the bathroom, I get ready while she showers. After I brush my teeth, I pull my hair into a top knot and rush out to answer the door.

Opening it abruptly, I see the people we selected to guide us through this.

"What's going on? Journey just asked me to come here," Henry asks.

"Same," Audrey says, Sul behind her. They haven't left town since the attack, and I'm not sure they plan to.

"Come on in. It's a lot." I tell them.

I walk behind them, and we all stop in the living room. A few minutes later, my tanned goddess saunters in. She looks like she's glowing in her light-colored, mid-calf-length dress, her short black hair clipped back. She wears makeup to cover the bruises. Journey will always look stunning to me.

She walks past me and hugs both our moms at once. I watch as they hug her back. Glancing at the men, I see them give me questioning looks. All I can do is shake my head.

"Honey, what's going on? What's wrong?" Audrey asks. Journey releases them, swipes away the tears, and walks back to me, taking my hand.

"We need help, but I don't want anyone to get their hopes up or be disappointed."

"Babycake, you know you can tell us anything," Sul says calmly.

Journey inhales a shaky breath and looks at her two parents. "Mrs. Courtright came to see us this morning," she starts, and

Audrey lets out a low breath. "We're going to meet Gary's kids. They're eight, six, and three. If we take them, Briggs and I will gain custody and become their legal guardians. I'm scared. I'm scared I won't be able to see past him, and I don't want any of you to be upset if I can't. We need to be prepared in case they come home with us." Journey places a hand on her stomach and takes another shaky breath.

"They look so broken. I want to give them a home and the love they deserve. I know that if I can look past Gary, we can provide that for them. Between all of us, every one of those babies will know only love and safety."

"Oh, you sweet child. How do you exist?" my mom asks, tears in her eyes. "I think that when you meet those babies, all you'll see is love."

"What do you need us to do? Whatever it is. We'll do it," my dad says with a smile, patting my shoulder. Fucker's excited to possibly have more kids running around.

Sul comes up and takes Journey into his arms. "You do whatever your heart tells you. We won't be disappointed if you decide it's too much, but I want you to look inside those kids before you make a choice. Not their faces, because that's where you'll see him, but their little hearts. Okay," he whispers to her, and she shakes her head, holding him tightly before they release each other.

"You give the order, honeycomb, and we'll do whatever you want," Audrey says to her with a sniffle.

"Could Mom and Ivey come with us in a truck while the dads start moving the furniture upstairs?"

Henry's face lights up the room when she includes him among the dads.

"The eight-year-old should be comfortable with the full-size bed, but we'll need a smaller bed for the little girl and a twin for the little boy. We have to meet Mrs. Courtright at the hospital at five, and I have no idea how to shop for children. We'd like all of you to be here when we get back."

"Consider it done. Hell, we have a few hours, fast-drying paint, and paint guns," Dad beams.

"Oh, I like that idea. Text us the colors you pick so we can get the bedding to match," Mom says next.

"We're on it. You guys go start shopping, and we'll start on the rooms," Henry says now.

My body finally relaxes when Journey laughs. I'm glad I made the right decision to call in the cavalry. Now we have to shop for a few hours.

Twenty-Three

Journey

As I load the last of what we can into Bryce's truck, I stare at all the shit we've got. The dads painted the rooms blue, pink, and orange, so we got bedding to match. God, I hope I can do this. Briggs and I weren't ready for kids yet, especially not my tormentors' kids, but how can I deny their tiny, sweet faces?

My heart broke with each photo and story. I can do this. I can love these kids. If I struggle, I have Briggs, and he's patient. I've tested that.

Mom and Ivey come up and stand next to me. "You're doing the right thing. You have such a big heart," Ivey tells me. "She's right. You can do this, Ny. I know my baby girl. I know what's in your heart," Mom says next.

"Thank you all for being here for us. I have no clue what I'm doing." I sigh.

"You will, honey. The instinct is there. Not having a uterus anymore doesn't change that." My mother jokes, and we all laugh.

"Okay, wish us luck."

"Good luck, honey. We'll make sure to get this done before you get back," Ivey tells me with a smile.

I hug them both and take Briggs' hand as we walk to our car. As I get into the passenger seat, I try to calm my nerves. Briggs takes my hand and presses my palm to his lips.

"Are we doing the right thing? Are you certain you want to do this with me? I've turned your life upside down." I sat nervously.

"Sunrise, you have changed my life in all the best ways. I'm positive we should do this. However, if we arrive and it's too much, I will support whatever decision you make. Okay, baby?" he asks, glancing over at me.

"Okay, we can do this," I say on a shaky breath.

How did Mom and Dad do this? Was it this hard, or is it only this hard because of the circumstances? Fuck, I don't know anymore.

We were quiet during the ride as I sorted the clothes and a couple of toys into bags. I don't know what they like to play with, but if it's like when I was a kid, any toy will do.

I hope they don't think Briggs' tattoos are scary. Hell, I hope they don't think I'm scary. I'm a giant next to a child, and my face is covered in bruises. I'm overthinking this again. We'll meet them and get a sense of each other. If they don't want to come with us, I won't make them.

What if I meet them and fall in love, only for them not to like us? When my heart starts racing again, I take Briggs' hand and play with his fingers for a minute. Okay, that's better. He squeezes my thigh when I let him go. He knew what I needed. He always seems to know what I need.

As the hospital comes into view, I retake his hand. This past month has been nothing but anxiety for me, half the time. Gary's really going to be gunning for me if I have his kids. Glancing in the rearview mirror, I see the black SUV following us. That eases some of the anxiety and might make the kids feel safer, knowing their father can't get to them.

After we park, Briggs opens my door and grabs two of the bags with one hand. His large hand rubs my bicep, and he gives me a gentle smile. I can't help but stare at his bulging biceps in his tight shirt. "We got this," he whispers.

"We got this. Let's go, maybe become parents," I tell him, and he chuckles.

He takes my hand and leads us into the hospital. I glance over my shoulder, and one of the guards gives me a grin and a thumbs-up. Fucker must have been listening to us in the stores. But I appreciate the support. I nod and look ahead again.

As we step into the elevator and press the third-floor button, my heart soars. I take deep breaths to calm my anxiety, and Briggs soothes me by rubbing my back.

When we exit and round the corner, I see Sherry waiting outside the room. Her face lights up when she sees us coming. God, I want to fucking barf. Shit, I'm going to have to watch my language.

When we stop, I peek into the room. I see all three kids huddled on the bed, and my heart breaks all over again. Tears sting the backs of my eyes, but I don't let them fall.

"They know someone is coming to meet them. I told them you were a nice couple. Ox is a little skittish, but he adapts easily as long as you don't yell or move toward him too quickly." Sherry says, looking into the room with me.

I nod, remembering how I was when I got out of that same situation. "Can we go in?" I ask, shifting the bag in my hand.

"Of course. Follow me," Sherry says, opening the door. My grip on Briggs's hand tightens, but he doesn't complain.

"Kids, remember that couple I told you about? I'd like you to meet Journey and Briggs Banks."

All three kids look at us, then Lux and Tulip smile. Ox studies us a little longer. The poor child's face is a mix of fresh and old marks.

"We brought you some gifts. Is it okay if we come closer?" I ask Ox. He nibbles his lip, then nods.

Briggs follows my movements. We sit on the floor in front of the bed, and I set the bags down. "We'll wait right here. When you're comfortable, you can come to us, okay?" I ask him gently.

"Okay," he says in a small, weak voice.

"Bubby, I want down," Tulip says, reaching for her brother. Ox gets up and helps his sister down. She isn't shy. Tulip goes straight to Briggs and giggles. "Bubby, look how pretty," she says, pointing to the colorful tattoos on his arms. Briggs chuckles and waits patiently.

She turns to look at me, then walks over. "Ah, you has boo boo?" she asks, gently touching my face. Her tiny fingers feel like feathers.

"I had an accident, but I'm getting better," I tell her. She studies me a moment longer, then hugs me. I gently wrap my arms around her tiny body and hug her back. Then she goes back to Briggs and sits in his lap. "Hi," she tee-hees at him.

"Hi, Tulip. Do you want to see what you got?" he asks her in a soft tone. She shakes her head and waits for him to get the bag from me. When he pulls out the stuffed doll, she stares at it, then takes it from him. "This for me?" she asks him. "Yeah, that's for you. Do you like it?" he answers.

"Yeah," she squeals, hugging the toy, which makes us chuckle.

Tulip looks back at the boys. Lux scrambles off the bed and comes up to me. "Um, are we going home with you?" he asks, twisting his body.

"Only if you want to. I won't make you if you don't want to. Would you like to look in your bag?"

"Yes, um, can I keep it?" he asks, big hazel eyes wide.

"Of course, sweetie. Everything in there is yours to keep."

I hand him the bag. He digs through it and lets out a war cry when he pulls out a Spider-Man toy.

"Yes, Ox, look, I get to keep it. Thank you. I've not had one before."

Lux drops the bag and flings himself into my arms. They smell like cheap shampoo, which is good because it means they've had a chance to bathe since they got here.

"You are very welcome," I tell him. Letting go, he moves over to Briggs and shows him what the toy does. Briggs looks shocked and listens to Lux while holding Tulip.

My eyes meet Ox's hesitant gaze. "May I come up there with you, Ox?"

"Um, sure," he says, shifting. I grab the bag, stand, and walk over to the bed. I raise a knee to sit facing him, placing the bag between us.

"Can I tell you a story?"

"Ok,"

"I was nine when I was rescued from my mother. I was scared all the time, afraid I would never be safe or loved. But then I met someone I now call my brother. He protected me until we met two people I now call Mom and Dad. They rescued my brother and me. They showed me what safety meant and what it felt like to be loved. Do you want to see pictures?" I ask the child, who's now sitting closer to me.

He shakes his head and waits for me to pull out my phone. On my phone, I pull up a photo of Jamie and me. "That's my brother. We don't share blood, but he's the best brother ever." He smiles as he looks at the photo. I swipe to find a picture of me with my parents. "That's my mom now, and that's my dad now," I tell him.

"You look different," he says, taking the phone.

"We do. You see, calling someone 'Mom' or 'Dad' can be just words. When you feel it in your heart, that's what makes it real. When you're safe, happy, and loved, that's what makes them your mom, your dad, or your family. I can't promise we won't make mistakes, because even the best people do. But I can promise you will always be safe with us, and I promise we will take care of you, your brother, and your sister." He reaches over, starts playing with the hem of my dress, and chews on his bottom lip. "Can I hold your hand?" I hold mine out and wait for him.

He places his hand in mine and looks at me. "Can you protect us from Gary?" he asks, then starts crying.

My heart shatters. "Oh, sweet boy. Yes, we can. We won't let him hurt you again."

As soon as I finish speaking, he moves to my lap, wraps his arms around my neck, and cries. His trembling body feels fragile for an eight-year-old. I lift my hand, stroke his hair, and rock him.

"You've been brave for so long, Ox. We'll be brave for you now." I kiss the top of his head and hold him. Glancing at Briggs, I see him give me a soft smile. Tulip and Lux are happily seated in his lap. How could I doubt I wouldn't love these babies? I'm pretty sure I fucking do already.

I don't rush Ox. I let him hold me as long as he needs. When he finally lets go, I gently wipe away his tears. "Does that feel better?"

He shakes his head and smiles. "Can I open my bag?"

"Absolutely. Even though I know what you got, I'm still excited to see what's inside." I tell him, and he giggles.

He gasps as he pulls up the handheld gaming console and games. "A Nintendo." Then he scrambles to pull out everything else. "Nikes and Legos." He gasps again and pulls out the clothes. "Jeans. Socks. Lux, we have socks."

"Socks," Lux says, digging through his bags again. "Ox, look." Lux holds up the Spider-Man undies to his brother.

I swipe the tear away before he sees it. He gets more excited about the fucking socks and jeans than anything else. I will make sure the kids have everything from this moment on.

"Mrs. Courtright, can we change? Please?" he asks her.

"Absolutely, boys. Right through that door." I giggle as they grab their things and run to the bathroom. I sit on the floor next to Briggs, and Tulip comes to me. "Me too. I change?"

"You want to change? Okay, let's see what you've got. You can pick." She pulls out her clothes and picks the pink dress. "This one."

"This one. It is beautiful." Briggs stands and sits on the bed. I listen to the boys laugh in the bathroom. "Arms up," I tell her, lifting my arms so she knows what to do. She lifts her arms, giggles, and tickles her own belly when her shirt is off. I can't help but laugh.

By the time she's dressed, the boys come out in their new clothes. "You boys look like little gentlemen," Briggs tells them, and they both grin at him.

"Bubby." Tulip pulls on Ox's shirt. "Is it pretty?" she asks, holding the dress out to the sides. "It is pretty, Tulip. Do you like it?" he asks. I can tell the boy has been taking care of her for most of her life. She shakes her head and runs back to Briggs. He chuckles and lifts her.

"Kids, how do you feel about going home with Ny and Briggs?" Sherry asks, and my heart halts as I wait for their answers.

"Me. I want to," Tulip says.

"Ox, can we?" Lux asks his big brother.

"Yes, we want to," Ox says confidently.

"Do you boys like dogs?" Briggs asks them.

"Yes. Do you have a dog?" Ox asks in awe.

"We have two." I pull my phone out again and show them a picture. "Wow, they're big. Are they nice?" Ox asks.

"They are, and they'll help protect you," I tell them, then get to my feet. "Do you want to stop for Happy Meals?"

Both of their jaws drop. "We do. Can we have a milkshake?" Ox asks, his eyes widening as if he's pushed his luck by asking for more. Smiling, I help them gather their things.

"You have whatever you want, and however much you want. I can't have a hamburger without a shake."

"Thank you. Thank you so much." Ox hugs me again, then runs over to Briggs and hugs him.

Briggs places a gentle hand on Ox's shoulder and offers him a warm smile. "You're welcome, but you don't have to thank us for taking care of you. We want to do it because you kids deserve it. Are you ready to go home?" Briggs is the most incredible man I have ever met, and he's mine. MINE.

"Yes," Lux yells, then starts moving his toy arms.

While Briggs talks to the kids, Sherry goes over everything with me. We'll have to go to court and undergo random home visits, but I'm not concerned. I can work from home until I open an office in Cedar Creek. These kids will be well cared for.

"Okay, everyone, when we walk out the doors, you'll see two men following, but it's for our protection. They're going to help keep us all safe." I tell them to prevent panic when we leave the room.

"From Gary?" Lux asks, putting on his shoes.

"That's right. From Gary or anyone else who makes us feel scared."

"I like that," Ox says, taking my hand. Lux bounces over and takes my other hand. Briggs carries Tulip and the bags as we all walk to the car.

I'm glad we brought our moms shopping earlier. I had no clue what car seats to get. After we strap everyone in, we head to McDonald's for these babies' happy meals.

Briggs takes my hand and squeezes. "We did the right thing, baby," he whispers. Smiling at him, I squeeze his hand back. "We really did."

Twenty-Four

Briggs

I gently unbuckle Tulip while she sleeps. I hold her while Journey assists Lux. The kids were so damn excited for a stupid Happy Meal and milkshakes. Tulip annihilated her nuggets. I was scared she wasn't even chewing, and then she asked for more. The entire thing damn near made me crumble. Ox was on guard when we first went in, but all he needed to hear was that he was safe from Gary.

I've already made up my mind that I'm going to kill the bastard if he comes near Ney or these kids again. Journey has a big family to help her if I end up in prison. Okay, I know I can't do that logically, but I want to.

Ox seems most comfortable with Ney right now. There's no doubt they share an unseen bond. Lux keeps bouncing between us, and Tulip barely lets me put her down.

Watching my beautiful wife with them is a sight to behold. She's patient and gentle. She knows how to approach them and gives each the option to engage with us on their own terms. I knew she would fall in love with these kids. To Ney, blood never mattered. I knew she wouldn't let Gary win and deny them a better life.

"We have our moms and dads inside. They're nice people who helped set up your rooms. If you feel uncomfortable, you don't have to say anything to them. You can stay with us the whole time, okay?" Journey tells them before we walk inside.

They both shake their heads. Lux takes my hand, and Ox takes Journey's. We enter through the mudroom and walk through the kitchen. Both boys look around in awe. I did the same when I first moved in. The house is pristine and massive.

We don't get far before the dogs come flying in. Lux's hand tightens on mine as he sees them running at us. I let out a low whistle, and they sit.

"Do you want to pet them?" I look down at Lux. He beams up at me and shakes his head vigorously. Chuckling, we walk the boys up, and they start petting the dogs, which lie on the ground and roll onto their backs for belly rubs.

"Can they sleep with us?" Ox asks.

"Sure, if they want to," Ney says, watching them.

Tulip stirs in my arms and looks at the dogs. She gasps, then squeals, "Puppy." Laughing, I kneel and set her on her feet.

She has no fear. Tulip lies on the floor and hugs Charm, who starts licking her face. Tulip tickles the dog, and it squirms on her back. It's cute as hell. "Puppy, puppy," she keeps saying in her tiny voice. The little girl is bright, and the boys did a good job teaching her, considering they were still learning themselves.

All the parents are waiting in the living room. We asked them to wait for us so we wouldn't startle the kids. We're in no rush. Ney and I wait while the kids soak up all the love from the dogs. I have a feeling they won't be in the bed with us much longer.

Once they've had enough, they come back to us one by one. When Ox takes Ney's hand, Ebony stays beside the kid. In the living room, we stop so the kids can see everyone. They all smile and wait for the kids to make the first move.

Journey squats and starts talking to the kids. "That man is my dad. His name is Sul, and the guy beside him is my other dad. His name is Herny. Henry and I just found each other, and that woman is my mom. Her name is Audrey."

"That's my dad, Bryce, and that's my mom, Ivey. You kids can call them whatever you're comfortable with. If my dad looks like a mummy, you can call him that," I tell them, and they laugh. "Would you like to go meet them?"

Ox nibbles his bottom lip as he decides what to do.

"Down," Tulip says. When I set her on her feet, she walks up to everyone. "Hi. I'm Tulip. Look." She says, holding out her doll. "It's mine."

Dad smiles and squats down. "It's nice to meet you, Tulip. That is a cute doll."

Once Tulip breaks the ice, Lux walks up and puts his arm around her. "I'm Lux, and that's Ox." He looks back at his brother. "He's strong," Lux tells everyone, making them chuckle. "Are you our grandpas and grandmas?" Lux asks innocently.

"I believe you. He seems super strong," Dad tells Lux.

"We are if you want us to be," Sul answers Lux.

"Okay, can I name you?" he asks, then waits. I cover my mouth to hide my smile.

"Sure, we'd like that very much," Audrey says. Lux stares at them and goes down the line. "You look like a Mimi," he tells Audrey. "And you look like a Nana," he tells my mom. They are all so patient as he continues. "And you look like a Papaw," he tells Sul. "You look like a Papa because you're big," he tells my dad. "And you look like a Pops," he finishes with Henry. Well, that was easy, I guess.

"Wonderful names. We are so honored to have them," my mom tells them. I can tell she's fighting back tears.

When I look down at Ox, I watch the turmoil roll through him. I take a small step closer and squat with Ney. "Would you like to meet everyone if I walk with you? Do you like the names?"

"Yes, to both," he whispers. I have no doubt this boy is brave, but right now, he's more scared of everyone because he doesn't know what to expect. I stand and hold out my hand, waiting for him.

He takes it, and we stroll toward everyone. When we stop, the room waits for him.

"I'm Oxford, but I like Ox," he says in a strong voice now.

"Strong name for a strong young man," Henry says, slowly squatting. "How old are you, Ox?" he asks. They all know, but he's trying to earn their trust.

"Eight, but I'll be nine in November."

"I three." Tulip cuts in, then walks to my dad to be picked up. He doesn't waste any time taking the little girl into his arms.

Henry chuckles. "Eight is a big number. You are a young man. Have you ever gone fishing?"

Ox shakes his head and squeezes my hand. When he looks at me, I give him an encouraging nod. "No, but the kids at school talk about going with their dads or grandpas."

"I'll tell you what. Once you're ready, we'll plan a day for all of us to go fishing. How does that sound?" Henry asks.

"Can I come?" Lux says, making us all chuckle.

"I come. Ah, Pop, I come," Tulip says, moving her hair from her face with her tiny hands. She doesn't give him time to answer. "Papaw, Papa. I come." Everyone chuckles and giggles.

"Of course, you can come too, little flower," my dad tells her.

"Yay, bubby, I come too," she tells Ox, and he smiles at her.

"I'd like that. Thank you. Can I shake your hand?" he asks Henry, holding out his hand.

"You bet." Henry takes his slowly and gives it a light shake. "Whoa, that's one heck of a grip you got there. Now I know why they call you Ox." When he lets go, Henry shakes his hand as if it hurts, then smiles, making Ox laugh. He shakes the other two's hands, and they emphasize how strong he is.

Henry moves slowly past the kids and me toward Journey. When I glance back, I see her wiping her face. Henry hugs her and whispers something that makes her giggle. I love how well they're adapting to each other. He releases her and rubs her biceps. Audrey and Sul both smile at the pair before turning their attention back to the kids.

"Do you want to see your rooms?" I ask them.

"We get our own?" Ox pinches his brows together and looks at me.

"You do. Unless you want to share with your brother, in which case we can arrange that." I watch as Tulip reaches up to Sul now. He smiles and picks her up. It has to be the tattoos. Lux and Ox take my hands as we walk up the stairs.

"I like these. I like to draw, too." Ox stops and stares at the drawings.

"You do? I drew these, but I bet we can get Ny to add your drawings, too. We'll go tomorrow and get whatever you want to draw with."

He gives me a bright look and starts walking again. At the top of the stairs, I unlatch the kiddy gate and step into the first room. "This is your room, Ox," I tell him, flipping on the light. We left the full-sized bed, which now has a bright, gaming-themed comforter.

The dads painted the walls orange, mounted a TV, and added a shelf to hold the Nintendo. There's a table in the corner for building with Legos or drawing, plus additional shelves for storing items. We made sure there were clothes in every dresser and closet. It sounds like a lot, but it's pretty much basic shit you need for a kid, except maybe the TV and Nintendo.

Ox enters the room and looks through everything. When he lies on the bed, a breath of relief escapes him, and he starts to cry. Fuck, have they ever had beds? I glance at Journey, and she shakes her head no before walking past everyone. Squatting again, she takes his hand and brushes his cheek. "Are you okay, honey?"

"This can't be real." His voice starts to crack.

"It is, Ox. We're going to take good care of each of you. I promise." She whispers to him.

"Thank you." He hugs her for a few minutes before we go into Lux's room. We went all out on Spider-Man stuff for him and installed a twin-size bed instead of a full. He now has blue walls and a TV, but we decided not to get a gaming system for a six-year-old. He has a night-light and a trunk of toys.

"Oh my god. Look, Ox." He tells his brother and starts pulling out all the toys. Ox walks over and looks at them with his brother.

I rub Ny's back as we wait for them to put everything back, then we go into Tulip's room. She has no idea what's going on, but she screams with joy when she sees the stuffed animals. "Down, Papaw. Please." She tells Sul, who quickly obeys. She runs over, gathers each of them, and hugs them. "Bubby," she says, shaking the toys. She walks to her bed, gets in, and pats it. Charm doesn't waste any time and gets in with her. "Puppy."

Today has been the most humbling thing I've ever witnessed. I grew up with socks and a bed of my own. I knew what it was like to have clean clothes and toys. I grew up eating whatever I wanted, whenever I wanted. I knew what it was like to have loving parents. But Journey and these kids didn't.

I know myself, and I will spoil them all. We gather everyone back together and head downstairs. The kids settle onto the couch with a cartoon while we thank everyone and say goodbye. We wouldn't have been able to pull it off without them. We asked them not to say anything to anyone else yet. We want the kids to get used to the seven of us first.

Journey and I stand there, staring at the three kids. Turning, I gather her into my arms. Her slender frame fits mine. Resting her head on my shoulder, she lifts her hand and runs her fingers through my hair. Her sweet scent hits me, and I inhale deeply. Fuck, she always smells good.

"What are you thinking about, sweetheart?" I ask, kissing her shoulder.

"I wonder if this is how my parents felt when they got Jamie and me," she whispers.

"And how do you feel?"

"I love them already. How is that possible?"

My lips tilt up. "I knew you would, Sunrise. Your heart is too big not to love them. I'm sure that's exactly how your parents felt. The protective side of me looks at those three kids, and all I want to do is kill the man who hurt all of you. My logical side is holding me back, but damn, I'm struggling. You're not the only one who already loves them. You've shown me everything my heart is capable of, Ney. Let's sleep out here with them tonight. It's a new place, and they need to know they're safe."

"I think you're right. Go shower and change. I'll sit with them." Journey kisses my cheek, then sits with the kids.

I rush to take a shower and get dressed. I leave my hair down, then brush it back. Stepping into our bedroom, I see the blanket is missing and smile. Damn, that woman works fast.

In the living room, I see the large bed they've made on the floor. At the foot of the bed, the dogs are sleeping, and food and drinks sit on the coffee table. My heart flutters as I take it all in. Journey lies in the middle of the bed, with the kids surrounding her in pajamas. It's the best thing I've ever seen. I pull out my phone and snap a photo of them. She's a natural at motherhood. I move closer, then stop and sit on the edge of the couch.

"Go change, sweetheart. I got them." Her face practically glows as she looks at the kids, and she rises to her feet. As soon as she's out of the room, I grin at them.

"I'm taking her spot. What movie are we watching?" They all giggle as I wiggle into Journey's warm space.

"Spy Cats," Lux tells me. Tulip wastes no time curling up against my side and armpit.

"Do you want some? It's good," Ox asks, handing me the popcorn.

"Heck, yeah," I tell him, grabbing a handful. "You know, during the winter, my mom puts on funny Christmas movies, makes popcorn, and we drink hot cocoa."

"Can we do that too?"

"For sure, young man. It's a family tradition, and you are all our family now," I tell Ox.

"I like that, but I like everything about you, Ny, and being here. I'm okay now. I don't feel so scared, and I like our new grandparents. We haven't had any before." My heart skips a beat when his smile shows how happy he is. God, I can't wait for his bruises to heal. I love these kids already, too. I started to worry I wasn't capable of loving anyone until I met Ny.

"That's great, Ox. That's how you should always feel. And when you don't, let us know. Ny and I will help you, no matter what. You can always come to us."

When Journey comes back, she dims the lights and lies down next to us. I shift Tulip so all three kids are between us. It's music to my ears to hear them laugh at the movie.

As I gaze at each of the now-sleeping faces, I can't believe how much my life has changed. Tomorrow, I'll text everyone and ask for a family gathering. We also need a railing around the pool.

Journey put video baby monitors in each room so we can check on the kids at night once they're upstairs. Honestly, she and our moms bought everything they could think of.

Now, to find and stop Gary. With Van out of the picture, I hope we don't hear from Sheila. We're going to file for a restraining order to protect the kids. Journey's scared Sheila might try to get to them. We have a lot to figure out, but we'll do it.

On my side, I hold Tulip, who seems glued to me. I brush my hand over each kid's head and land on Journey's forearm. My eyes close, and I allow sleep to consume me.

Twenty-Five

Journey

Tonight is our family dinner night at our house. We were specific that everyone show up at precisely 6 pm. The kids and I hatched a little plan: they'll wait upstairs with Dylan and Daniel until everyone arrives. Then Briggs and I will announce them. I'm trying to make it fun for Ox, since he struggles the most with new people.

It's been almost a month since we picked them up. Our parents visit us daily to get to know their new grandkids, and our moms help me plan the wedding. We're going to have the wedding at the distillery event room in January.

We've barely left the house since the attack and since gaining custody of the kids. I don't want to risk people taking photos of us. I'm not sure who's still lingering in town, and I don't want to risk Sheila or Gary seeing us in public.

Winter and the boys obviously met them because they live next door and saw us playing outside. Dylan and Daniel have been great at helping Ox build his confidence. They each now sleep comfortably in their own rooms, and we have a good schedule. Every day I wake up, I fall more in love with these babies I now claim as mine, and I'll be damned if anyone takes them from us.

I called my realtor and attorney. The realtor is exploring spaces for me to relocate my business here, and the attorney has filed a restraining order against Sheila and Gary. He will also assist with any custody issues that may arise and, hopefully, with an adoption one day.

Until Gary is caught, the security around the house will remain unchanged. Ox loves it and asks the guards all kinds of questions. They answer each one easily. He's really come a long way in the past few weeks.

"Who wants to help me set up the snack table?" I ask the three smiling faces as I walk into the kitchen.

"Me. I can help," Tulip says, bouncing up to me. Briggs French braided her hair into pigtails today, and she is so damn cute. He is definitely her favorite.

"Um, Ny. We wanted to ask you and Briggs something," Ox says, standing with his siblings. Briggs sets the BBQ plate of meat down and walks over to me.

I grip Briggs as my mind races. What if they tell us they're not happy here? I love them so much and can't imagine my life without them anymore. I start to spiral, but Briggs' touch steadies me. The kids need to know they can always come to us. "You can ask us anything," I tell him, and Briggs squeezes my hand.

"You haven't known us long, but you said we would feel it in our hearts when we love someone. Um, Gary was never a dad, and we don't remember our mom." My heart picks up, and tears prickle my eyes. I squeeze Briggs's hand tighter. Ox straightens his shoulders and holds his head high. "We love you in here," he says, pointing to his little heart. "You and Briggs feel like our mom and dad. Is it okay if we call you that?"

"Yeah. Mommy and Daddy," Tulip says, twirling her dress.

I can't stop the tears. "Oh, my sweet babies. Of course you can," I tell them, dropping to my knees. Briggs follows suit, and we gather them into our arms. I pepper each of their faces with kisses, making them giggle. "We love you all very much. We are so proud to call you our kids."

"We're honored to be your parents," Briggs says beside me, wrapping his arms around all of us.

"Daddy, I help," Tulip says between us, making us laugh. "Bubby, help Mommy."

"I can always use the help, Nugget. Come on, everyone will be here soon," Briggs says, standing. Tulip takes his hand and walks with him.

"You boys want to help me?" I ask, wiping my face. I get to my feet and hug them one more time.

"I'll get the dip," Lux says, then runs to the fridge while Ox and I set out the chips, drinks, and buns.

Ox and I fall into a routine of talking and adding things to the table. I let the kids pick what they wanted to serve today, and even though it's way too much, they enjoyed choosing it all.

When I notice red and blue lights reflecting off water bottles, I peer out the window. My heart races when I see two police cars outside.

"Ox, Lux, go out back with Dad," I tell them. Ox looks out the window, then the two take off outside. I force myself to walk to the front door and swing it open. I see officers talking to an irate Sheila. Pure fucking joy strikes me as I watch them struggle with her.

Stupid cunt.

As soon as I step out the door, she starts fighting with the officers.

"Let me go, you dumb motherfuckers. Those are my grandkids in there. Mine." She growls, then slugs the officer in the face.

Oh, this just got better. I feel pretty smug right now. "I'm pretty sure you're going back to jail, Sheila. Parole violation, restraining order violation, assaulting an officer, and resisting arrest."

"You think you're better than me, you bitch? You think Gary won't kill you? Oh, he will, and I can't wait to hear about it. Those are his kids. They'll never be yours." She snarls, kicking and screaming as the officers pin her to the ground.

"They're already *OUR* kids. Mine and Briggs'. Gary is a piece of shit like you." I hissed at her. "I'm not scared of him anymore because I have them to protect. I hope you rot in prison, Sheila. I hope it eats at you that they'll never even know your name. But they will know Audrey, Sullivan, Henry Ivey, and Bryce as their true grandparents." I smirk at her. Burning-hot hatred clings to her face as she keeps yelling. With a laugh, I turn my back on her.

Briggs is in the doorway, a big, sexy grin on his face. His hair is down in waves, and he's wearing a tight white shirt with blue jeans—looking ever so fucking yummy. Wetness pools between my thighs. Oh, he's mine tonight. It's been a month, and I need it. The butterflies take flight in my stomach, and my heart picks up pace.

I amble up to him, grab him by the nape of the neck, and crush his lips to mine in an urgent, desperate kiss. Our tongues wrestle and tangle. Briggs buries his fingers in my hair, grips a handful of my ass, and pulls me into him. I'm aware we have an audience, but I don't care.

When our lips part, he presses his forehead to mine. "I'm so fucking proud of you, baby. You did it."

I lick my lips and smile. "You were healing, but those babies in there. They finished it. I will do everything in my power to protect them. I love you all with everything I am, Hercules."

"We love you, too, sweetheart. So very much," Briggs tells me, kissing my forehead.

"Yeah, Mommy, love you," Tulip says behind Briggs.

We both chuckle, and he steps aside so I can see their beautiful faces.

I gasp and clutch my heart. "You do. Oh my gosh, I am the luckiest Mommy in the world." She giggles as I pick her up and twirl her. "Okay, everyone should be here soon. Are you all ready to meet the rest of your family?"

"Yes. Can we change into our special clothes now?" Lux asks, standing at the gate at the bottom of the stairs.

"I'll help them so you can change, baby." Briggs wraps his arms around me, and I lean in to whisper, "You're mine tonight, big guy."

He groans and bites his lip. "Can't wait." He whispers back and releases me. Hmm, he needs it as much as I do.

Briggs opens the gate and heads upstairs with the kids. In our room, I put on a plain white T-shirt and jeans. We decided to wear matching outfits as a little family.

When I check the time, it's 5:55 pm, and everyone should be waiting outside. Rushing out of the room, I see Briggs and Winter waiting in the living room.

"You got this, Mama. Everyone may be shocked at first, but they'll all love those kids," Winter says, hugging me. "Dyl and Dan are upstairs with them. Daniels is at the top, so he can hear when they need to bring them down."

"We got this, Sunrise. The most important people already know," Briggs says, holding out his hand. Taking it, we walk to the front door and open it together. Everyone is outside, on time, and waiting. They shuffle past us one by one and head to the living room, where we direct them.

Briggs and I stand facing them all. My heart starts to beat so fucking fast I can hear it thudding in my ears. Briggs squeezes my hand, giving me the strength I need.

"We asked everyone to come here tonight because Briggs and I have an announcement. As you all know, nothing about us has been traditional, and life really likes to throw shit at us. There's a reason you haven't seen much of us lately." Taking a shaky breath, I glance at my handsome husband, who offers me an encouraging smile.

I release my breath and look back at everyone. "A month ago, Briggs and I had a special visitor, and we made a big decision. It was easy for us. I need each of you to stay calm. Don't get too loud or make sudden movements." I tell them because Ox still flinches if we do either.

I look at all the grandparents, who are in pure bliss right now, smiling. Mom and Ivey have their phones out for pictures or videos—typical grandma move.

"We had you all come here to introduce you to three amazing people." I look at Winter. She nods, and I hear the shuffling on the stairs. Everyone watches as Dylan and Daniel walk into the room with the three kids.

"Daddy," Tulip squeals, bouncing to Briggs. He catches her and holds her while Lux hugs my waist and Ox takes my hand. Everyone sits there, mouths agape and eyes wide, stunned.

"After Gary's home was raided, they didn't find him, but they found these beautiful kids. Briggs and I now have custody of them and are proud to call them ours. We promised them we

257

would keep them safe. Briggs is holding Tulip, and little Miss Nugget just turned three." I tell them, then tickle her belly. "Mommy." She laughs and tosses her head back. Briggs chuckles and stops her from flinging herself to the ground.

I rub Lux's back, smiling down at him. "This handsome little man is Lux, and he's six years old."

"And a half, Mom," he tells everyone.

"My apologies. Six and a half." I wrap my arm around Ox's shoulder and pull him close. "And this brave boy is Oxford. He's eight and likes to be called Ox because he's super strong. They would like to meet all of you. All of our parents have been spending as much time as possible with them over the past month. We felt it was important to introduce everyone to them a little at a time."

I glance at our mothers and see happy tears in their eyes. Bryce, Dad, and Henry are all smiling brightly.

"Kids, that's my brother Jamie and his girlfriend Tink. That's my brother Walker, his daughter Lea, and my Uncle Terry," I tell them.

"That's my brother Beau, his wife Birdie, and their kids, Harley and Blue. That's my brother Baxter and my brother Baylor. Those two people beside them are very important friends who feel like family. That's Noah and Astor."

"Are they our aunts and uncles?" Lux asks.

"Heck, yes, we are," Jamie calls out with excitement, making everyone laugh.

Ox straightens his shoulders and walks up to everyone. "It's nice to meet you. Our Mom and Dad saved us, and we love them here." Ox points to his heart again. "So we can call them that because they're the best. Like our grandparents, we love them here, too. Mom also said Uncle Jamie is her favorite." When he says that, I snort a laugh and shake my head. I don't know why he included that, but what the hell.

"Hell, yeah, I am. Sorry, not sorry, Walker," Jamie says, and Ox laughs. Walker chuckles, narrowing his eyes at Jamie. "It's okay. For now."

I watch as Harley and Lea push their way through and introduce themselves. "I'm Harley." "I'm Lea." They tell the other kids. Then Harley looks back at her mom. "Mommy, what family do I call them?"

Birdie chuckles. "They're your cousins and Lea's cousins, squirt."

Harley gasps. "Lea, we're all family now." Briggs and I laugh because that's not how it works, but they think it is.

Once they're done talking to everyone, Tulip and Lux ask if Harley and Lea want to see their rooms.

"We'll watch them, Aunt Ny. Ox, do you want to play Mario Kart?" Dylan asks.

"Yeah, Uncle Jamie, do you want to play?" he asks my overenthusiastic brother.

"Hell yeah. Lead the way, Hulk," he tells him. "I'll help the boys keep an eye on them." He winks at Briggs and me, then goes upstairs with the kids.

Once it's just the adults, questions start flying. "Damn, Ny. His kids?" Walker asks, scratching his face. I knew this question was coming.

"Once we met them, we didn't hesitate. I thought I would, but I fell in love as soon as I saw them. How could anyone not? They're amazing, and Briggs was right. If anyone could help them, it was us." Briggs wraps his arm around me, rubs my back, then kisses my head. "I'll understand if you have a harder time, Walker."

"No, I'm okay. I was shocked. That's all. I already know what they've been through. They need loving parents. I'd like to go up and spend some time with them if that's okay."

"It is." As soon as I say he can, Walker takes off up the stairs.

"Well, I'll be honest, I thought you two were going to tell us she was pregnant. Not that you already have three kids." Birdie laughs, making the baby in her arms flinch.

"Adoption or fostering was our only option. It came faster than we thought, but we're happy it did." I smile at her, then look at Briggs. He lifts his lips in a smile and winks at me.

"Oh, shit. I'm sorry. They're beautiful children. I think it's commendable that you can look past him and focus only on those kids." She comes up and hugs us both. "I look forward to playdates."

"I'd like that. Tulip loves meeting people."

Beau, Baylor, and Baxter come up and hug their brother, then pat my shoulder. I like that they don't hug me. It's too uncomfortable. I watch as Baxter takes Briggs aside to talk. That's good. They needed it after the Anna thing.

The rest of the night goes off without a hitch. The kids can't wait to start staying the night with family. I want Gary caught before I let them out of my sight. I love how easily everyone has adapted to them. Tulip seems to be the fondest of Baxter.

It's amazing how I went from only having my parents and Jamie to having the huge-ass family I always wanted.

Twenty-Six

Briggs

"The night went better than I expected. How are you feeling about our new titles?" Journey asks, running the brush through her hair.

I smile as I lean against the bathroom door frame and watch her. "I knew tonight would be great. I didn't think I could be any happier, but when the kids asked if they could call us Mom and Dad, my heart felt so full. They're amazing, and they're ours. Let's reach out to Mrs. Courtright and the attorney about adopting them. I want them to have our last name."

Journey turns to me, her eyes bright. "Yeah? I think they would love that. Can you believe this is our life? Within a couple of months, we've gotten married and now have three kids."

Chuckling, I walk up behind her and trail my fingers down her spine, making her shudder. Journey leans back, melting into me. "I can, and I love it, sweetheart. I like that it didn't take us years to get here. This is the best life I could have asked for, Sunrise."

"Me too, Hercules. I finally have the big family I always wanted."

I stroke her cheek lightly. "Good."

Ney's body arches into mine, pressing that ass of hers against me as I kiss her neck, below her ear, and down to her shoulder. My dick is already hard.

Gently slipping my hand down her stomach, I lower her panties, and she kicks them aside as they hit the floor. I then take off my boxer briefs, keeping her turned away from me as I explore and tease her smooth skin.

She is stunning in every way. Just looking at her gets me ready and on the edge.

Adjusting my position slightly, I notice her watching me intently in the full-length mirror. A smirk forms on my face. I bring my lips to the curve of her neck, biting and leaving a mark, then drag my teeth over it. She responds with a quiet gasp, her lips parting.

Ney rolls her hips and grinds her glorious ass against my hard-as-fuck shaft. Russel is up and ready to play. My hand roams her body and lands on her teardrop breast. I twist and tug her nipple between my fingers, making her inhale sharply and moan. Then I tease and caress it more gently.

My eyes meet her fiery irises in the mirror. Burning desire is etched on her face. I lean in, pressing my lips to her ear. "You like watching, sweetness?" My large hand covers her flat, taut stomach and moves down to the sweet, wet spot between her gapped thighs.

"Yes," she says breathlessly as her stomach and chest rise heavily.

Ney tilts her head back, and I capture her soft, succulent lips in a hot, wet kiss. I release her and give her a devilish grin. "Mm, keep watching, baby. I want you to see how beautiful you are when you cum for me," I whisper, sucking on her lobe.

Ney spreads for me, and I slip my fingers through her folds. Fuck, she's already soaked. "Always so ready for me." I rub her sensitive clit between my fingers.

"Always." Journey moans, tilts her head back, and shifts as her arm comes around my neck, pulling my lips to hers again. Our breaths mix as our tongues taste and explore.

Gently parting our lips, I tilt her head back so I can watch as I insert my fingers and circle her swollen bud with my thumb. When her eyes begin to close, I nip her neck. "Eyes on me, baby," I command, and she meets my reflection's gaze in the mirror.

I move my hips, grinding my cock against her ass as I massage her sweet pussy. "Briggs." Her tight walls begin to clamp around my finger. My thumb picks up the pace. I want to feel her unravel while my fingers are inside her. "Let go, Sunrise," I tell her, biting her neck again.

I bite my lip, not taking my gaze from hers, and twist her nipples between my fingers, sending another wave of pleasure through her. "Fuck, I'm, I'm." She doesn't get the words out before her stomach tightens and her pussy sucks and pulses around my thick digits. Ney lets out a low, closed-lipped cry as her orgasm hits.

Her glowing eyes meet mine again. "Fuck me, Hercules. I need to feel you inside me."

That's all I need to hear. I pump my fingers slowly a few more times, then slip them from her and bring them to my lips. She watches as I suck her sweet juices from them.

My arm snakes around her, and I rest my forearm between her breasts. My other hand digs into her hip as I line up and slam into her. She sucks in a sharp breath at my intrusion, and her head falls back against my shoulder.

My hips move slowly in and out of her tight pussy. "Briggs," she moans.

I let out a groan at the feel of her and the sound of my name. Sex with Ney gets better every time. It's like being on ecstasy.

Ney's arm comes up, and she sinks her fingers into my hair and pulls. Fuck, I love when she pulls my hair. I plunge in and out of her a little faster, and her breathing quickens. She moans with each pump, meeting my every thrust. My own breathing becomes ragged as my heart picks up pace. The sound of our bodies joining pushes me over the edge.

"Fuck, baby. I'm going to cum." My hand moves down her body, finding her swollen clit and circling it as my pace quickens. "Oh god, Briggs, love." With those words, I know she's as close as I am.

"Watch while you cum with me, baby." Her hooded gaze meets mine in the mirror. Holy hell, watching myself claim her is more than I expected. It's dominant and exhilarating.

I pinch her clit, slamming into her hard and fast. She cries out my name again, and when I feel her pussy tighten, my own orgasm hits as I pound into her one last time, holding her hip tightly. I groan her name as I release my seed inside her. I twirl my hips as we ride the waves of pleasure and bliss.

Our breathing comes fast. I lean my forehead against her shoulder for a moment. Holding her tightly to my chest, I tilt her face to mine and kiss her softly. Pulling back, I gaze into her eyes. "I love you so fucking much, Journey Banks," I tell her.

"I love you more, Briggs Banks. You were right," she says breathlessly.

I chuckle lightly and kiss her shoulder. "Right about what, sweetheart?"

"It gets better every time. I like that you never gave up on me," she whispers. Her radiant gaze burns into my soul, touching me in a way only she can.

"It does, baby. I'll never give up on you. I like that you chose us. I'm yours, and you're mine, Journey Leann. Now it's your turn."

Ney gives me her breathtaking smile. "I'm yours, and you're mine, Briggs Wilder."

I capture her lips and seal our promise. "That's right, my heart. Don't move," I tell her, then gently slip my cock from the warm blanket of her pussy. In the bathroom, I warm a cloth and walk back to clean her.

We both put on our pajamas before getting into bed. We've learned that sleeping naked is no longer an option. The kids wake us up in the morning. I love that they come straight to us when they wake up, smiling.

Journey curls into my arms and twines her legs with mine. I inhale her sweet scent, run my finger through her hair, and press my lips to her forehead. Closing my eyes, I let sleep take me.

I shift on my feet and watch Journey, Mom, and Audrey teach the kids to swim. I'm a nervous fucking wreck. Every time one of the boys goes under, I have to fight every instinct not to dive in and save them.

These kids are my pride and joy. The thought of anything happening to them makes my chest tighten, and my heart ache. My eyes flick to Tulip, wearing her life vest, running and jumping toward Audrey in the pool. The laughter of the kids and the women with them is like a lullaby.

Journey has Ox, and Mom has Lux. Mom holds Lux under her arms as he learns the doggie paddle. Journey shows Ox how to stroke his arms. Both my boys can't stop grinning and laughing. My own smile hurts my cheeks. I love my instant family. It's the best family anyone could ask for.

A hand clamps onto my shoulder, pulling my gaze away. Henry stands beside me, his face full of pride.

"They're doing well. You have a beautiful family, Briggs. I have somewhere I'd like to take you. I called Baxter and Baylor. They're going to stay here with the girls and the kids. It's important," he tells me. Glancing around, I see Baylor and Baxter walking out the door in their trunks. I'm glad Bax and I were able to sort out the Anna thing. He did what I would have done if the roles were reversed, but it sucks that she shredded his heart after he chose her.

Fuck her.

"Unk Bagser." Tulip squeals. "Unk BayBay." She squeals again with excitement and takes flight toward them. She hugs both my brothers' legs and beams up at them, making them laugh. "You swim wit me?" she asks. She is so damn cute.

Baxter is a total sucker for kids. He chuckles and picks her up when she reaches for him. "Of course we will, little flower," he tells her, then walks to the pool. Baylor grins at me and joins the others. Minutes later, Dyl and Dan come running out and tackle Baylor into the deep end of the pool. I bark out a laugh when Baylor screams, "Oh shit." Winter walks out the back door, shaking her head at the shenanigans. I don't miss the look in her eyes when she looks at my little brother.

Oh, damn, okay.

Before I can tell Henry yes, Ox calls me. I turn my attention back to my boy.

"Dad, watch us," he says, with the biggest grin and a twinkle in his eyes.

I step closer and watch Ox and Lux. Journey and Mom back up a bit and nod. Both boys push off the wall and start kicking their legs and moving their arms. Pure pride runs through me, and I take another step as I watch them swim to the woman in front of them without help. Feelings I never thought possible exploded inside my chest. My heart is so damn full of love for my wife and kids.

When they make their way to Mom and Ny, my hands fly in the air in victory. "Hell, yes, those are my boys. Look at my kids swimming," I tell anyone who will listen. Everyone around us erupts in applause. I clap, whistle, and jump in. I grab them both, and they giggle. "You both did great." When they hug me back, triumph takes over. These are mine and Ny's kids. Ours. Fuck Gary or anyone else who tries to take or hurt them.

"Are you proud of us?" Ox asks. He waits, big green eyes fixed on me, his brown hair stuck to his forehead, a smile on his face. He told me he wants his hair to grow like mine.

"I am so damn proud of you. Every day, everything each of you does makes me proud. Mom and I are so lucky to have you all. We love you, each of you, so much." I praise them because they deserve to know how much we love them and how proud we are to be their parents.

Their faces light up. "We love you, too. You're the best dad ever," Ox says, hugging me. "The best of the best," Lux says next, hugging me, which makes me chuckle. I kiss the tops of both their heads, then walk to where they can touch the bottom of the pool and set them down.

"What am I? Shark bait. I taught you two goof monsters," Ney jokes behind me. Both boys toss their heads back, laughing with complete amusement.

"You're the best, best Mom," Ox says, hugging her. He's a mama's boy, and that extra 'best' shouldn't count, but I'll let it. "Best of the best." Lux hugs her next. The smile on Journey's face makes my heart jolt, and my lungs stutter. No matter what we're doing, she always steals my breath.

"Yeah, Mommy. You bes, bes, Ah, bes." Tulip says. Damn, the pool is full of traitors. I take that back when Tulip reaches for me. "Daddddyyy." She drawls out the name, making me laugh. I take her from Bax and kiss her little head. Yup, she's a daddy's girl, and Lux is obsessed with both of us. He can't seem to pick a favorite. Most days, he bounces between us like a basketball.

I bring my arm around Ney and kiss her temple. "I'm going to go with your Pops for a few minutes. Bax and Bay will be here, along with the small army guarding the place."

"Okay, Hunky Monkey. Be careful. We're going to keep working on our technique. I love you."

"I love you, too, my heart." I kiss her, then hand her Tulip.

I get out, dry off, and let Henry know I'm changing.

Once I'm in jeans and a T-shirt, I slip on my boots and walk out the front door. When I open the passenger door, I'm shocked to find Sul, Jamie, and my dad in the back seat.

Shit, I hope they're not planning a bachelor party right now. I don't want to leave my family while Gary is still at large.

"Ah, what's up with the entourage?" I ask, buckling up.

"You'll see. Sul, Bryce, and I have been working on something. Jamie's here because he's your best friend and Ny's brother," Henry says.

"Um, okay, but I have to be honest. I don't want to be away from my family for too long. I know they're safe, but I still don't like leaving them." I tell them, then tap my finger on the door handle.

"Baxter and Baylor will be their shadow," Dad says.

"They're safe. We would never jeopardize that," Sul says. Logically, I know that, but every time I leave Ney, she ends up hurt. Now with the kids? My heart can't handle anything happening to any of them.

"Ok, you guys missed it. My boys swam on their own. I'm so fucking proud of how far they've come." I'm ecstatic and can't help but feel content.

"Damn it. Do you think they'll do it again when we get back? Oh, I forgot to ask you. Ox wants to spend the night with Tink and me once this is over. We're going to make one of the guest rooms theirs at our place for when they stay with us," Jamie says. He is one happy man to have the kids as his niece and nephews.

"Lux asked me to show him the firehouse once this is over, and then he asked Beau and Noah to show him the police cars. I think he's going to be a firefighter or a cop when he grows up," Henry grins. I wouldn't mind that at all. I want each of them to follow their dreams.

"Ox wants to learn to fight with Dylan and Daniel. Audrey and I are getting a place here so we can be closer. I'd like to train him if you and Ny are okay with it. I taught her and Jamie when we adopted them," Sul chimes in.

"I'm sure that will be fine. Tulip asked to spend the night with everyone before bed last night," I chuckle. "She started holding up fingers, saying 'I stay' before each name. She's so damn adorable."

"They all are. They've adjusted so well to you and Ny. You're a good man and father, Briggs," Dad says with pride.

"That was mostly Ney. She's amazing with them. I follow her lead. She's their rock, and I'm hers," I tell him because it's the truth. She deserves the credit.

"Are we going to cry like a bunch of bitches now?" Jamie jokes, making us laugh. "Put your tampons in and soak it up, ladies. It's go time."

I pinch my brows together as we pull up to the old, abandoned house. A house I know. A house that gives my wife nightmares.

Terry is waiting outside, leaning against his truck, with a couple of other men.

Once we've parked, we all get out and meet the others.

"You guys ready?" Terry asks.

Each of them nods, and we start walking toward the house. use.

Twenty-Seven

Journey

I can't even begin to explain the feeling inside me when Ox and Lux swam on their own. They were thrilled to show their dad, and damn it, he praised them to the highest power when they did it. He truly loves these babies.

"Mommy, hold me." I glance over and see Tulip reaching for me. I smile and take her from Baxter. I push her wet hair from her face. Her little legs wrap around me. I hold her close as she plays with my necklace. She is the most adorable little girl. My smile widens as I look into her big, sleepy green eyes.

"Are you tired, baby nugget?"

"No, ah, yeah. I hired." She says, then lays her head on my chest. "Love you, Mommy," she tells me in the cutest little voice. I kiss her little temple and breathe her in. I can smell her bubble gum soap through the chlorine. It's one of the best smells.

"We'll keep an eye on the other honeybees. Go sit with her," Mom tells me, then goes back to helping the boys.

"I can take her. Winter looks like she needs to talk to you," Baxter tells me.

"Are you sure?" I ask him.

"Absolutely. Can you help me get this off, though?" he asks as I pass her back to him.

"Yup," I tell him, and we work together to get the safety vest off her. By the time we get it off, Tulip is already half asleep. "Thank you," I whisper to him.

"You're welcome," he whispers back, then gets out of the pool, holding her.

I'm glad things aren't super weird between us. I like all the Banks brothers. It breaks my heart that Anna hurt Baxter. I can get past what she did to me, but not what she did to them.

As we step out of the pool, Winter brings each of us a towel. Baxter wraps it around Tulip, then sits and starts rocking her. Smiling, I follow Winter and lie back in a lounge chair.

When I glance over at Winter, I see her face flush with bashfulness. I follow her gaze and see Baylor wink at her. Holy shit. Hell, yes, she needs a Banks brother. I knew she was crushing on him.

"You should ask him out," I whisper to her.

"Wha, no, what? I, no." She rolls her eyes and shakes her head in protest. I chuckle at how flustered she is.

"Why not?"

"He doesn't want a single mom hanging on his arm." She sighs and leans back.

I chuckle. "You don't know that. Single men date single moms all the time, Winter. And the boys like him."

"That's another reason. The boys like Bay, and if it didn't work out, it would hurt them. They love having all the guys around. They've never had a father figure, but with all the men in this family, they have that now. I want them to know what real

272

men are like. They see it all around them here. Briggs and his brothers took to them as if it were totally natural."

I exhale and look back at Baylor. His eyes are still on Winter. There's a flame I know all too well burning in his lake-green eyes. Briggs gets the same look when he looks at me. I frown a little because Winter will be hard to crack. Hopefully, if he wants her, he's just as determined as his brother was with me.

"I think it's natural for the Banks' men. Maybe don't discount Bay yet. Get to know him better, and if you decide to try it one day, talk to the boys. They're great kids, Winter, and they want you to be happy, too." I reach over and take her hand, holding it.

"I've only been with one person my entire life. I'm definitely less experienced than he is." She groans and leans back.

"Let me tell you about being inexperienced. Briggs has shown me, um, a lot. It's exciting." I shrug, smirk at her, and lean closer. "Last night, I watched him in the mirror as he fucked me from behind," I whisper. "It was fire. I also tend to wake the poor man up a lot for it."

Winter bursts out laughing. "I always knew you'd be a freak in the sheets. Good for you, hot tits."

I twirl my hand in the air and bow my head to her with a cheeky grin. Briggs makes me brave enough to do anything. He praises me even when I think I'm not doing it well or the right way.

"Anyway, enough about me dating the man-child. I have something I want to ask you. You can say no. There will be no hard feelings." She squeezes my hand and sits up. When I look at her, I can tell she's nervous.

"You can ask me anything. You know that."

"The owner of Lore Labyrinth is going to sell the place. I want to buy it, but because of Troy, I need a co-signer for the business loan." She stops and gnaws her lip.

"Done. But I could loan you the money instead. If you get the loan from me, there won't be any interest, and your payments will be lower. Hell, I don't care if you pay me back. Is that what you want to do? Will it make you happy?" Hell, I'd buy her anything she wanted and never ask her to pay it back. Winter has struggled for years. She needs a reprieve.

"It's a lot of money, Ny. I can't let you do that. A co-signer is fine. And yes, I would love to own a bookstore. I want to host readings for the kids and have adult reading nights. I could invite local authors for book signings. With Troy out of the picture, I finally feel free. I'm finally finding my happy." Winter swipes at her eyes.

"Babe, the money is yours. If you want to pay it back, fine. We'll come up with a lower payment plan that works for you, but you don't have to. When do you need it by?" I ask her. Winter is the only family member I have who needs help, and I want to help her.

Winter's face lights up. "The end of this month, but I expect you to come up with a legitimate payment plan. You're a fucking genius, so I think you should crunch those numbers."

"What if I make you a different deal?" I ask her.

"Like what?" she arches a brow at me.

"I'll give you the money for the bookstore, and you can use what you would have gotten approved for to buy you and the boys a house here? I don't want you to leave. That's not why I'm saying this." I nod toward the kids. "They're so happy here, and it's time you didn't have to carry the weight of the world on your own. Let me do this for you. Or we'll take out the business loan, and I'll buy you a house." I shrug. "Your choice, sweet cheeks."

"That's too much, Ny," she argues quietly.

"It's not. I'm not bragging when I say this, but what's the point of having millions of dollars if you never spend them? I can and want to help. It would make me incredibly happy if you let me. You're my sister, Winter. Those kids are my nephews, and family helps family." I smile brightly at her. "I'll be cashing in babysitting hours if that helps at all."

She giggles with a sniffle. "You're too much, Ny. I would love to babysit these kids. You're my sister, too, hot tits."

"I'll buy the bookstore for you. Start house hunting. They'll be excited about it. And consider asking the man-child out. That's a stipulation." We both crack up when I tell her that. "I love you, bestie."

"I love you too, bestie," she says, then lies back in her chair. "I think I'll go swim with the boys."

"Yeah, you will. Go show off that rockin' bod, babes. Give Bay a little sneak peek." I wiggle my eyebrows and wink at her.

"Shut up, you asshole." We both laugh, and she shakes her head.

I can't help but watch as Winter walks over and sits on the edge of the pool. Baylor swims up beside her, crosses his forearms on the ledge, and they start talking.

When I look over, I see Tulip lying on Baxter. Briggs put her hair in pigtails this morning. I love that he helps with her hair. Glancing at the boys, my heart swells every time I look at one of them.

I shift my gaze and keep my eyes on Ox and Lux. The joy on their faces is priceless as they run and jump in. My heart sinks, and I fling myself forward. Fear and panic seep into my bones. They can't swim well enough for that. I rise, my heart racing. I watch as they paddle up and break the surface. They both laugh and stay afloat. I choke on a happy sob, overwhelmed with pride in them.

"Yes, you did it," I shout, not thinking, and wake my precious three-year-old. Tulip stirs in Baxter's arms and sits up. He holds her until she regains her bearings. Both my boys look at me with the biggest smiles.

"Unk Bagster, I swim," she says sleepily, making me laugh.

"You just woke up, little flower," he chuckles, rubbing her head.

"Please," she pouts.

"I got her," Ivey says, coming to them. She really is a gorgeous woman.

"Nana, I swim?" Tulip asks, then goes straight to Ivey.

"You can swim. Let's go hang out with Uncle Baxter in the pool."

"Yay," she squeals, clapping her hands. Ivey tosses her head back with a laugh, then meets my gaze. Ivey walks over and pats my arm lightly.

"I am so proud of you and Briggs, honey. You are amazing parents. It brings me joy to know I'm your mother-in-law and that these are my grandbabies. I do love you, Ny. Never doubt that. And Bryce? Girl, he is over the moon to have you all. He's trying to plan all these trips with all these kids. He even wants to make sure Dyl and Dan tag along. We are so happy. We always wanted an army of grandkids." Ivey giggles and wipes my tears away.

"Thank you. I love you all so much. I love having this huge family." I hug her again, and then she pats me once more before walking back to the pool with Tulip and Baxter.

The thought of her being happy to have me as part of her family is almost too much to bear. I've closed myself off to the possibility of people truly loving me for so long that I don't know how to handle the emotion moving through me.

"She's right, you know." I turn my head and meet Baylor's gaze. "You're like one of the daughters now. They always wanted at least one girl, but Mom had complications after me, so they couldn't have any more kids."

I frown and look back at Ivey. It's sad because she's such a good mother. "It doesn't seem fair sometimes," I tell him.

"No, it doesn't, but she's had Birdie, Astor, and Anna since they were seven. Well, she had Anna. You're one of hers now. I heard you say adoption or fostering was your only option." He says it without asking the question.

"Yeah. I had tumors. It didn't bother me to make the choice I did. I never wanted to give someone else Sheila's DNA. I also wanted to help kids like them. The older you get, the harder it is to be adopted. I got lucky that Briggs didn't want his own kids." I shrug.

"I can understand that. Briggs never told anyone he didn't want kids, but I could see it."

I look at him and frown again. Worry swirls inside me. "Do you think he was lying? I would never want to stop him from having that."

Baylor's eyes widen, and he starts to panic a little. "No. Not at all. Briggs wouldn't lie about that or anything, really. He prefers to be honest. Sometimes his honesty makes him look like an asshole. Watching him with the kids, I can tell you. Those three are his in his heart. I've never seen his face light up the way it did when the boys called him dad and showed him they could swim now."

A broad smile spreads across my face at his explanation because they are my kids in my heart, too.

"Thank you, Lamb Chop. That actually made me feel better."

Baylor barks out a laugh at the nickname. "No problem, tater-tot."

I giggle when I look at him, and he smiles. "You get me, Bro fries. I think we just became besties. You were the first person to make me feel welcome. I guess I could call in a model friend for you now." I joke to get his reaction.

Baylor shifts uncomfortably, rubs the back of his neck, then looks at Winter and the boys. I knew it. "Nah, you don't have to do all that."

I grin to myself when he doesn't take his eyes off her.

"Are you a quitter, Bay?"

"What? Hell, no. I just don't." He flusters, and I chuckle, waving my hand at him.

"Don't quit on her. And don't ever hurt my boys. I will punch you in the dick and laugh once I'm done, chili-cheese."

"Damn, okay. You don't need to threaten Captain Mushroom Head. I wasn't planning on quitting. Are we sticking with food names?" He chuckles.

"Eh, I think it's our thing now, bestie."

"Guess it is, Corndog."

"Har, Har. Roast Beef. How's Baxter been since everything?" I ask, then head into the house to grab a snack for the kids. Baylor follows to help.

"He's hurt. He thinks Anna was the love of his life, and he lost her."

"You don't think she was?" I ask, opening the fridge. I pull out the lunch meat and cheese while Bay sets out the bread.

"I think, like the rest of us, Bax is a protector and caregiver. Anna always seemed to need something. If Briggs wasn't dropping what he was doing to help her, then Baxter was."

My cheeks burn with jealousy. I know it's irrational, but it's there. We start making the sandwiches.

Baylor laughs when he notices my death grip on the knife. "Don't worry, little ham. It was never like that for Briggs. I don't think Baxter truly loved her. I think he had a crush and a strong need to protect. He's confusing that need with love. It doesn't make it hurt any less, though. Or I could just be blowing smoke out of my ass because I don't know shit about love."

"I don't know. I actually agree with your assessment. But then again, I've only loved one person, so I don't really know shit, either."

"And that, my dear little sis-burger, is why we're besties now." We both laugh when he bumps my shoulder.

"You know you're only a few months older than me, right, bro steak?" I say, then start stacking the cut sandwiches on a tray.

"A few months still count."

"Fine. I'll let you have this one."

I grab the tray while he grabs the box of snacks and drinks. When we step outside, the boys come running toward us. I can't help but laugh. I let them eat as much and as often as they want. They finally have a normal weight, and we keep healthier snacks in the house.

"Thank you, Mom. I love your sandwiches," Ox tells me, fist-bumps Baylor, then jumps to high-five a laughing Baxter.

"Thank you, Mama. I love you," Lux says, grabbing a couple before he sits down.

"I love you," I call out to them, and they give me full-cheeked smiles. I take a seat and watch Tulip with Baxter. I love the life Briggs has given me.

Twenty-Eight

Briggs

As I enter the abandoned house, my heart picks up, and joy-powered adrenaline pulses through me when I see Gary tied to a chair. Wee'z about to do some mob shit, and I'm here for it.

"Gary, we haven't officially met. You knew me, but I didn't know a fucking thing about you," Henry says.

Gary throws his head back and laughs. I want to punch the motherfucker, but I have to follow Henry's lead; this is his show.

"What do you want to know, Daddy? Oh, wait. That's right. You didn't get to be one of those." Another dark chuckle slips from Gary. This guy is insane. In the blink of an eye, Henry lands a right hook on Gary's jaw.

"You know, Gary. They say psychopaths struggle with genuine emotion, and it's almost impossible for them to love anyone. It took us some time to find your weakness," Henry tells him. "But before we get to that, I'm going to let Briggs get a few shots in."

"Oh, pretty boy wants to play. I like it rough and dirty. Make it count, daddy-o. That's what my kids call you now. Isn't it? Little bastards." He spat the insult like venom.

When I step forward, I throw two consecutive punches—one to his nose and another to his jaw. Fuck, that felt good.

"They're my kids. They won't remember your name. You won't even be a distant memory to them." I hissed.

When Gary unleashes his cynical laugh, a chill creeps down my spine. I throw a few more punches to his ribs, finally making him groan. It feels good to hurt this man. It should scare me that I want to kill him. I want to feel his blood soak my hands.

"Keep 'em. I never liked them. That cunt Jozie just kept getting pregnant," he says breathlessly. "I took care of that problem, though."

"What the actual fuck is wrong with you? Did you do something to their mother?" Of course he did. We should have known Van wasn't his first victim.

Gary smirks at me with his bloody mouth. Good God, I hope I never come face-to-face with a man like him again—twisted freak.

"I'm not telling you a fucking thing," he says, spitting blood at me. I dodge most of the spittle, but some lands on my arm. Disgusted, I wipe it off with the bottom of my shirt.

"Gary, I'd like to introduce you to my friend Tomahawk," Henry says as a big, burly man steps up, phone in hand. "He has a special gift for you. After my other friends are done."

Sul steps up and hits Gary with a left hook, then Jamie steps up and hits him. Terry comes over, wipes away the blood from Gary's face, and stops the bleeding so he can see. I glance at Dad, who stands with his arms crossed, completely unfazed by what he's seeing. I know it's because he already loves Journey and our kids.

"Tomahawk, you ready?" Henry asks with a grin.

The man brings the phone up. "Nattie, baby, you there?"

"Yeah, sugar, I'm here. Is the husband and father with you?"
He looks at me, then hands me the phone. I glance at the woman
on the screen and see her in orange prison clothes.

"Hello."

"Briggs, are you doing this for your wife?" she asks.

I don't have to think about this answer. "My wife and kids.
This man has tortured all of them for years. I'll do anything to
keep them safe. If killing him is my only option, I'll do it without
a single ounce of remorse."

"You're raising his children now?" she asks. I'm not sure what
her angle is, but it's pissing me off.

"They're mine and my wife's kids," I growl into the phone, and
she smirks.

"And the mother who hurt your wife. What about her?"

"I'd kill that bitch, too," I say without hesitation.

"That's all I needed to hear. I commend you for what you'd do
to protect your family. Let me handle the next part for you. Go
ahead and put Sugar on for me." I get it now. She was testing my
loyalty to my family. Clever, I guess.

"Thank you," I tell her, even though I'm not sure why I'm
thanking her.

"See, Gary. There is one person you care for. One person you
would do anything for," Henry says. Tom holds the phone so we
can all see. Nattie steps aside to reveal a strung-up Sheila in her
prison uniform.

Yes, fuck yes. I'm almost giddy right now.

"No. What are you doing?" Gary practically yells as Nattie hits
Sheila multiple times, breaking her nose. "Stop. Stop hurting
her."

"Why, Gary? I thought you would enjoy it. Isn't this what you did to my daughter and the kids?" Henry asks.

"Fuck you. Stop. Mommy. Stop hurting her." He shouts and fights the restraints as Nattie hits Sheila again and again. Sheila screams and writhes against the restraints. I fucking laugh when he calls her Mommy.

"What do you want?"

"Good boy, Gary. We're going to get you all cleaned up, and then you'll turn yourself in. You're going to admit to everything you haven't been caught for, including what you did to Jozie. When they ask what happened to your face, you'll tell them something creative, or Nattie here will kill Sheila. Right here, right now." Henry says in a calm, scary voice.

"I'm not doing that," Gary growls, keeping his eyes on the screen. Henry shrugs and nods at the man.

"Make her bleed, baby," he tells Nattie, who now has her own evil grin. We all watch as she steps behind Sheila and lifts her shirt. She brings her hand around and slowly pierces Sheila's stomach. Blood begins to leak from the wound. I know I should be disgusted, but I feel nothing.

"Gary, honey, please, my special boy. Please help Mommy." Sheila pleads with Gary. Nausea swirls in my stomach as vomit creeps up my throat. Sick. They're both sick. Sheila screams louder as the object digs deeper, and Nattie starts dragging it.

"Stop. Okay. Stop. Stop. I'll fucking do it." Gary is now crying in the chair like a bitch. "Just stop hurting her. Mommy, it's going to be okay. I'll do it. I'll save you." He tells Sheila.

I have to cover my mouth at this point to keep from upchucking. I choke a little as I struggle to keep my stomach and gag reflex under control. Dad pats my back to help keep the vomit at bay. The way they talk to each other is more disgusting than watching the women get stabbed.

"Stop," Tom tells Nattie, and she pouts her lip, but she listens and yanks the object from Sheila's stomach.

Terry steps aside and pulls out a suture kit.

"Remember, if you don't do everything I said, Nattie will happily take care of your, hm, Mommy." Henry laughs and nods at Dad, who pulls out his phone and steps outside.

Henry squats in front of Gary and tilts his head. "Tomahawk here will be in the vehicle with you while he's on the phone, so he can see whether you do what you agreed to. I have a lot of friends at the police station, so I'll know if you don't tell them everything, if you miss a single word or admission. She dies. Then you will have to live the rest of your life knowing you're responsible for killing the only person you're capable of caring about." Henry waits for Gary's acknowledgment, then stands.

"Briggs, you take good care of your family," Nattie says.

"I will. Thank you."

"No thanks needed. I live for this shit." She laughs. Okay, she's a psycho, but I won't tell her that.

"I'll call you back when he turns himself in. Love you, pudding pie."

"Love you too, Sugar."

They hang up, and the other guy with us starts stitching up Gary's face while Terry holds his head. The smug dickbag isn't so smug anymore.

I can't believe Henry was capable of this, but I'm glad he was. He just won the Father of the Year award in my eyes. Henry checks his watch, then looks at Terry.

"Give us a twenty-minute head start. Hawk, thank you for the assist. Consider your debt paid."

"It was a pleasure, Hen. You're a better man than I am. He doesn't deserve to live," Tom tells Henry.

"No, he doesn't, but my daughter and grandkids need to see him taken away so they can feel safe again. That's the only reason he's breathing."

In that moment, my respect for the man grew even more. He's right. Journey and the kids need to know they're safe from this man. If we killed him, they would always wonder when he would come for them.

Tom gives Henry a nod of respect before shaking his hand. I don't miss it when Sul slides something into the other guy's hand as he shakes it.

"Ready for the next phase?" Henry asks as we all step outside. Dad leans against the truck with a smile on his face. He's the largest of us, so I walk to the back of the truck and get in so he can have the front seat.

Rubbing my raw knuckles, I don't look back as we leave the shack of a house.

"Beau and Noah will be waiting down the drive at your house when they get there with him," Dad tells me. Holy shit, they weren't kidding about Journey and the kids watching the man who tortured them being taken away.

"Thank you. All of you. Not going to lie, that was one hell of a bachelor party." I joke to ease the tense mood, and everyone chuckles.

"Henry's kind of a badass for a fire captain," Jamie says, still laughing.

"It was a group effort. It took us a month, but Sheila eventually led us right to him before she was arrested again. She was sneaky. The cops never caught on to how she was getting to him." Henry says, pulling away from the shackled house.

"I still wonder how the hell she ended up with him," I say. That thought still bugs the hell out of me.

"Oh, Sheila convinced his mother that she could give him a better life. Sheila was seeing a wealthy man at the time, and she convinced him to adopt Gary with her. Six months later, she left him for Joseph and took Gary with her." Sul says, scratching his face.

"They got married, and it was an on-again, off-again thing. Sheila got knocked up with Walker after their first break. She dated that guy until Walker was a couple of months old, then left him to go back to Joseph." Dad says next.

"I was the third victim. She got knocked up during their last break. When Joseph found out she was having a girl, he groveled, and she told me she'd lost the baby. When Journey was born, she left the father blank and gave Ny her last name instead of Joseph's because she was already jealous of her own newborn daughter, my newborn daughter." Henry growls, as if in pain.

"How the hell did you three find all that out before the Detectives?" Jamie asks them, wide-eyed. I'm shocked, too. They should have been PIs or some investigative bullshit.

"We did a deep dive and found the only friend Sheila ever had. Once the woman found out what Sheila had been doing to the kids, she tried to disappear. She said she felt so much shame that she was always too loaded to notice what was happening. She blabbed about everything," Sul says with a smile.

"Damn, I'm glad you three did this. Ney and my kids will be able to fully relax for the first time in a long fucking time," I tell them. My voice comes out thick with admiration for our fathers. Even though this all seems to have just started, I know the thought of Gary being out never left her.

"Son, there isn't a thing we wouldn't do for our children and grandchildren. Even you proved that today. I do not doubt that if we had let you, you would have killed that man," Dad says with a broad grin.

"In a heartbeat."

Leaning back in the seat, I let the thought of my family finally having peace wash over me. I can't wait for them to see Gary being cuffed and placed in the back of a police cruiser.

We drive past Beau and Noah in their cruiser as we make our way up the drive. When we park in front of the house, we all pile out and walk to the back, where everyone is now sitting by the pool, talking and laughing instead of swimming.

Tulip is in Audrey's lap, coloring with Mom on the stone with chalk. Both boys are talking to Baxter about something. Journey and Winter are deep in conversation, and Bay is wrestling with the twins in the grass while the dogs bark at them. It's a beautiful sight.

I stride up to Journey, lift her from the chair so she's standing, and press my lips to hers in a quick kiss. I wrap my arm around her waist and rest my forehead against hers.

"Everything okay?" she asks, her voice concerned.

"Everything is perfect, baby. Did you have a good time?" I ask, tucking her hair behind her ear.

"I did. Wait until you see how well the boys are doing in the pool now." She beams.

"I can't wait." I kiss her again, then look at everyone. "Hey, let's go out front. There's going to be something you all will want to see soon," I tell them.

I look at the dads, and they all nod in approval. Ney pinches her brows, but we all walk out front where we can see Beau and Noah.

"Dad, could you teach Lux and me how to ride a bike? I think Mom can do it, but I don't want to hurt her if we fall," Ox whispers beside me.

I pull him to my side and give his bicep a light squeeze. "Of course, I will, son. We'll start working on that right away." Ox hugs my waist as we wait. Tulip must be getting jealous because she reaches for me from Audrey. I take her into one arm and place a hand on Ox's shoulder. Looking over, I see Journey holding Lux.

It's mostly quiet as we wait. Twenty minutes later, Terry's truck comes into view. Beau and Noah get out of the cruiser and step in front of it.

Terry's truck comes to a stop, and he gets out and opens the back door. Tom steps out, phone in hand. He grabs Gary's arm and pulls him out of the truck. His face is fucked up, and I love it. I'm glad I at least got to do that.

Journey gasps next to me, and Ox's body tenses. I rub his little back in hopes of easing the tension running through him.

Terry and Tom walk Gary to Beau and Noah, who take him from them. They pat him down, and when they put the handcuffs on, our entire crowd erupts in applause and whistles.

The celebration grows louder as they put him in the back seat of the cruiser. Beau and Noah smile and nod at us before they get in and take off to book the murderous psychopath.

"He's gone. He's really gone. He can't hurt anymore. I'm so happy." Ox cries and holds me around the waist as Lux cries with relief into Journey's neck. Her tears pour down her face as she cradles his tiny head.

Audrey takes Ox into her arms, and Mom takes Tulip from me. Tulip is three and has no idea what's happening. Baxter takes Lux and helps comfort him. I turn and wrap my arms around my wife. I hold her tightly as her hands clutch the back of my shirt.

"It's over. It's finally over. How?" She sobs into my neck.

"Doesn't matter how. You and our kids are safe, sweetheart. He'll never get out, and neither will Sheila. The four of you are finally free, Sunrise." I tell her.

Journey draws back with her big, brilliant smile. She lets go of my shirt, cups my cheeks, and gives me a quick kiss.

"I love you, my heart. You're mine, Journey Leann. Always. Now it's your turn," I whisper to her.

"I love you, my strength. You're mine, Briggs Wilder. Always," she whispers.

"That's right, baby. Are you ready for the happy ever after now?"

"Hell yes." She flings her arms around my neck and kisses me with a smile. And now, our lives can fully begin as a family.

Epilogue

Journey

I stare into the mirror and smooth the tight fabric over my stomach. Today, Briggs and I will exchange vows we'll remember. Tilly designed the perfect dress for me. I feel like a princess in it.

The baby blue dress features a romantic sweetheart neckline and detachable tulle bishop sleeves, creating a classic silhouette that cinches at the natural waist. Layers of satin and sparkle tulle are embellished with delicate beading, creating a soft shimmer. I have an elegant silver-and-light-blue crystal tiara to match, because I wanted to be a total princess today.

It's been five months since Gary turned himself in. Turns out he confessed to a shit ton of other charges. He'll die in prison. Two months after Sheila went back to prison, she killed another inmate and will never see the outside world again.

Everything fell into place. The day after everything happened, we took the kids on one of our adventures to Disney World before school started. They loved the airplane ride. We spent four days doing nothing but having fun, with no care in the world.

To say I'm over the sun that Briggs never gave up on me is an understatement. We now have this beautiful life together. The expansion of the tattoo shop looks fantastic, and I now have my business here in Cedar Creek. I get to take the kids to school and pick them up. Mom and Ivey take Tulip most days, but when they don't, she comes to work with me.

Yesterday, Briggs and I had one of the biggest days of our lives. We've kept it secret from everyone except Jamie.

When I hear the knock, I turn to face the door.

"Come in," I call out.

Dad steps in, and his eyes glisten. "You look beautiful, pumpkin." Henry looks every bit the gentleman in his navy-blue tuxedo and white undershirt. All the men are huge, so I told them not to bother with ties.

"Thank you, Dad. I'm so glad you're here for this." I walked over and hugged him tightly. I love him more than I thought possible at the beginning. He's one of the best dads I could have asked for.

"I wouldn't miss it for the world. I'm so proud to be your dad," he tells me, kissing my cheek.

As I walk over to the table, I gently pick up the sparkling tiara. I left my short hair down in curls and pinned the sides back so the crown would nestle neatly on my head. I walk back to Dad and hold it out.

"Would you like to help me?"

"I would." Dad sets down what he's holding, and I sit on the vanity bench. He places the tiara on my head and makes sure it's just right. When he's done, he wipes his eyes. "I love you, pumpkin. So much."

"I love you too." I stand and hug him again.

"I have something for you." He walks over, retrieves the item, and returns.

"This was your great-grandmother's ring." He opens the box, and inside is one of the most beautiful rings I've ever seen. It's a thick silver band with a large opal at its center. I can tell it's old. Dad takes it and slips it onto my right middle finger. I can't take my eyes off it. "It was always meant to be yours, and it can be your something old."

"I love it. It's beautiful. Thank you." I whisper.

"You're welcome. Okay, are you ready to get hitched? Or, well, are you ready to do this properly, I should say?" he jokes, making me laugh.

"Yeah, I am."

He loops his arm through mine as we head to the spot where we wait. My other father comes up on my other side and takes my arm. The ceremony is being held in the distillery's main hall. Briggs and Bryce will be waiting at the bottom of the side stairs. Since we're already married, we ask him to officiate, or whatever you want to call it, for us.

We decided to have the kids up front with us. I watch with a tear in my eye as Ox walks down with Harley, and Lux walks with Lea. Then Jamie and Winter walk down together.

When the music starts, I take a deep breath. I don't know why I'm nervous, but I am. Stepping out with both my dads, we walk to the end of the aisle.

My gaze locks onto Briggs, who has the biggest smile I've ever seen on him. He looks like a god, standing there in his light-blue tux, a white button-down dress shirt, and white Converse.

His hair is down and flipped to the side. Our three beautiful kids smile so big when they see me, and my overzealous three-year-old can't contain herself.

"Mommy," she shouts before she takes off running to me. And that's why I skipped a bouquet.

Letting go of my dad's arms, I bend down and catch her as the entire room laughs. "You pretty, Mommy," she tells me when I stand.

"Thank you, nugget," I tell her, kissing her head. As we continue our walk, Henry takes Tulip when we reach the end of the aisle. It's a proud moment for both men in my life when Bryce asks who gave me away.

As soon as I step in front of Briggs, he grows impatient and pulls me into his arms, then kisses me.

"Not yet, Briggs," Bryce tells him, but my husband doesn't care and waves him off.

"It's fine. We're already married," he murmurs against my lips, making me and everyone else laugh.

Steadying me, Briggs mouths 'I love you' before the nuptials begin. It's beautiful. I'm kind of glad we didn't remember the drunken version of this.

"Now, you may kiss the bride," Bryce says sarcastically.

"Bout time." Briggs pulls me into a dip and gives me one of his heated, passionate kisses. I never thought I'd find a love like ours, and damn, I'm glad we did. He brings me back up, presses his forehead to mine, and we face the small crowd as we walk down the aisle together with our kids.

Two hours later, the pictures are done, and we all sit down to eat before we start dancing.

After every dance under the sun is over, Briggs and I put on the jean jackets. Winter and Tink help the kids put on their jackets while I take off my heels and put on socks.

Briggs takes my hand and grins at me as we see Jamie step onto the dance floor.

"Hello, everyone. I do believe it's customary for the best man to give a speech," he says, and the crowd goes quiet. "I can't think of two people better suited for each other. Except Tink and me," he says, winking at her. "Love you, babe." He smirks, and the audience laughs. "Anyway, that's not why I'm here. I wish Ny and Briggs a long and healthy life. To say they are two of the best people and parents I know is an understatement. Everything today was perfect, but I think it could use a little extra, a little more officialness, you could say." Everyone stays quiet as he continues. "So, to make it the absolute best day for Tiny and Bigsby, it is my great honor to give you all the extras this event needed."

Jamie nods at the DJ, who starts the song 'Happy.'

"Welcome, Briggs Banks." Briggs kisses me, then slides out onto the dance floor, his back to the crowd, wearing a jacket that says Daddy Banks, and starts dancing.

"Next up, Journey Banks." I slide out wearing my Mommy Banks jacket and join Briggs in dancing.

"Oxford Banks," Jamie says next, and the crowd erupts as Ox slides out, dancing in a jacket that reads his new official name. He pops the collar, making me burst into laughter.

"Lux Banks." Lux runs out and slides to the ground on his knees, playing air guitar in his official jacket. More applause and laughter echo through the space.

"Tulip Banks." Tulip runs out, screaming 'Daddy', and goes straight to Briggs.

He swoops her up, laughs, and kisses her forehead as we dance as a family.

"Everyone, give it up for the official Banks family. Now this event is perfect," Jamie says, then drops the mic, claps, and whistles with the crowd. I watch as our mothers beam and swipe at their faces. The pride on our fathers' faces is palpable.

Looking at our children, I find their smiles and laughter the greatest pleasure I have ever had the opportunity to be part of. The adoption was finalized yesterday. They are officially ours.

When the song ends, our parents rush to us to congratulate us and tell us how proud they are. They gush over the kids and say the announcement made the entire day feel special.

As the kids drift to their favorite people, Briggs embraces me and pulls me close for a slow dance. I wrap my arms around his neck and gaze into his beautiful Caribbean irises.

"I like that you have made me the happiest husband and father in the world. Now it's your turn," he says to me.

Smiling at him, I tuck his hair behind his ear. "I like that you see me. I love that you've made me the happiest wife and mother on the planet. You're mine, Briggs Wilder. I love you, my strength. Your turn."

"You're mine, Journey Leann. Always. I love you, my heart." He presses his lips to mine, and we get lost in the magic of the day.

ALWAYS HERE PREVIEW

CHAPTER 1

BAYLOR

Broken branches and crisp leaves crunch under our feet as we stomp through the woods with our gear, heading toward the small cave along the hiking trail. It's astonishing how many people read the big-ass "Do Not Enter" sign and ignore it anyway.

When we come to a stop, Henry points his flashlight inside, sighing and shaking his head.

"Banks and Harris, you're up," he says, tossing a hand out and gesturing toward the cave.

He always picks us because we're the slimmest of the guys here.

The air inside the channel is thin and suffocating, making anyone feel claustrophobic. As we crawl on our elbows and stomachs through the cave, Karson and I make our way through the tight passage to the hiker. The man has gone down a narrow shaft and gotten himself stuck in a crawl space.

"Hey, I wanted to talk to you about something," Karson says.

"Okay, what is it?" I ask, taking a controlled breath.

"I ran into Megan at Hideaway a couple of weeks ago and wanted to know if you'd be cool with me asking her out." He asks slowly, carefully controlling his breathing.

The question makes me want to laugh, but I'll conserve my oxygen for now. Megan is a piece of work, but he can figure that out on his own. I'm not sure why he's asking me this. I haven't talked to Megan in almost a year.

"Go for it, dude," I tell him, then keep crawling. Thankfully, I'm not as broad as my brothers, or I'd be just as stuck as the hiker. Then again, if I were their size, I wouldn't have been selected for the retrieval.

When dirt and small rocks fall from above, we both tuck our chins. We wait a moment after it stops, then resume moving.

"How is she in bed? She's not into any weird shit, right?"

"Depends on what you think is weird."

"Ah, that is not reassuring at all. I'm not going to get a finger in the ass, am I? That's all I need to know. I'm not into that," he says warily.

Chuckling, I decide to mess with him by reaching out and running my hand up the back of his calf. "How do you know you're not into it?"

Karson squirms, sending more dirt around us. "Ahh, stop it, you fucking asshole," he damn near screeches. He huffs out a breath and answers the question. "During a college hookup, the bitch took me by surprise and took my ass-ginity. That shit is not for me. I hated every second of it."

I can't control the burst of laughter that erupts from me. Karson is not impressed and grumbles.

"That's hilarious. I was messing with you, man. I don't know how she is in bed. We didn't get that far, and even if I knew, I wouldn't say. Just a heads-up, Megan is a vulture. She'll chew up man."

"Damn, I was worried you might say something like that," he says. "What about the new girl, Winter?"

Jealousy sparks my rage. Winter is mine, even if she won't admit it yet. This ass eater knows it, too. Without thinking, my fist flies out and connects with Karson's ass cheek.

"Off-limits. Don't even think about it." I snarl, my voice low and threatening.

"Damn, okay. G.I. Joe." He grumbles.

Winter and I have settled into an uncomfortable friend zone. It's a slap in the face every time she says we're just friends. Secretly, I'm biding my time, waiting for the right moment to lay the charm on her.

Winnie is a vision from every dream I've ever had, resembling an angel sent from heaven with her white-blond hair, smooth porcelain skin, and crystal-blue eyes. She has a perfect pear-shaped figure; I've always preferred ass over breasts, and Winnie has a hella ass. The cute softness on her stomach makes her even more desirable, and those thighs. Fuck, I love her thighs.

Damn, I need to stop thinking about her. I'm in the middle of a rescue, getting a damned stiffy.

When we stop, I wait for Karson to slide down the small shaft because he's smaller than I am. I then toss him the harness once he's at the bottom.

"Sir, I'm with Cedar Creek Fire. We're going to get you out of there. Hang tight," Karson tells the man.

I can barely hear the muffled, wheezing man say, "Ok."

"He's losing oxygen," Karson says, moving quickly.

Karson wraps a strap around the guy's legs, tosses me the end, and we work together to hoist and maneuver the man out. When his head emerges, he greedily gulps air. Karson gives the guy a quick exam to see if he can make it out on his own. Thank fuck he can.

As we exit the cave, the guy's kids run up and hug him. Hopefully, he learned a lesson today.

"Thank you both," he tells us.

"No need to thank us. Maybe next time, pay attention to the sign," I say, pointing to the sign with big, bold letters… DO NOT ENTER!

"Noted. I won't make that mistake again."

I shake my head and walk over to the truck to remove the gear we needed. We load it into the fire engine and head back to the firehouse. Today is the fifth time we've had to remove someone from the situation. The park needs to come up with a way to close off the entrance. Obviously, just the sign isn't working.

My dream of becoming a firefighter has been with me since first grade, when our class visited the firehouse. I realized this was my calling. After graduating, I earned a degree in fire science and promptly joined the fire academy. I can't picture my life doing anything else.

Today marked the end of my three-day shift, and I'm ready for it. The past three days have been a chaos of nonstop calls, ranging from stove fires and car accidents to one group of kids jumping off a bridge into a river.

Once I've showered and changed, I grab my gym bag and head out of the building. Right as I walk out the door, Henry stops me.

"Banks, you haven't RSVP'd for the firefighters' ball. I need to know if you have a plus one so I can send this in. It's coming up," Henry shouts as he stalks up to me.

Shit, I forgot about that, but now I have the perfect reason to ask Winter out. "Oh, yeah, ah, put me down as having a plus one."

A broad grin spreads across the man's face as he stops beside me. Henry isn't stupid. He knows I've been pining for Winter for months. I spent four days watching over her and the kids while Ny and Briggs were out of town last summer. That's when I realized I was utterly captivated by the audacious woman.

"I already did. I just wanted to hear you say it," Henry smirks.

Asshole

"Has anyone ever told you you're kind of a dick?" I grumble.

"All the time, kid. I'm just trying to give you the push you need. It's been almost ten months," he says with an amused laugh.

"I'm taking my time. Winter needed a friend, and I didn't want to push her," I say, adjusting the bag on my shoulder.

Henry claps me on the back as we walk. "I get it. You're being a good man, but a word of advice."

"Ok."

"You'd better hurry. Ny told me Winter signed up for the speed dating event with Tink," he says, dropping his hand.

There's that jealous fucking rage again. Speed dating? Really? She'd rather speed date than entertain the idea of going out with me? That has to be a fucking joke. Does she not realize that the chances of her or the boys getting hurt by someone else are higher? I would never hurt them. The boys are my life.

"When? Tink is with Jamie," I ask incredulously. I'm struggling to believe she's actually doing it.

"No one tells Tink what to do. She's forcing Winter to go. Saturday night." He says, rolling his lips, trying not to laugh. He knows I'm seething right now.

"Guess I'm crashing a speed-dating event then," I grumble, then start stomping off.

"Good luck," Henry shouts with a chuckle.

This has to be a joke. It's Wednesday morning, and Friday night, Winter has girls' night at Birdie's. The kids and I will be at Briggs for poker night. I'm already planning how to cockblock the hell out of her. I just need Ny to make my plan work and keep Briggs from killing me for suggesting it.

Now in the car, I start the ignition and head to the school to pick up the kids. It's my routine when I'm off shift. Today we're going to get pizza and go to the arcade.

It helps that we're neighbors. I pick them up, and they hang out as long as they want because they only have to walk 30 feet back home. It was pure luck that the house next to mine went up for sale just as Winter was about to give up. I was ecstatic when I found out, and so were the kids. They come over every time they see me at home.

Sometimes I wonder if Winter picked the room directly across from mine on purpose. I can see her shadow in the window at night, and I know she can see mine. I felt like a creep the first time I noticed, but now I've accepted my creepiness and always search for her shadow before bed. I've also caught the angel looking into mine a few times.

There's a level of comfort in living next door to them because I'm close if they ever need me. The only time I struggle is when I'm on duty for three days straight. Now I'm not so sure. If Winnie meets someone, I'll be forced to see her with him. I'll know when he comes and goes, and when he doesn't leave.

A gag runs up my throat at the thought. I'm definitely going to try to stop that.

I park at the school, get out, and wait for Dylan and Daniel to come outside. When I see Ny walking up to me, carrying a sleeping Tulip, I can't help but smile. She and Briggs took to parenthood so easily.

"Bayrrito, I didn't know you were picking them up today," she says in her raspy voice.

I chuckle at our ongoing nicknames for each other's food. Journey has become my best friend.

"Nychos, good to see you. They wanted to hang out. I'm treating them to an afternoon of fun," I tell her proudly.

"That's how it works. They want to give you the world, but you have to pay for it."

A deep, hearty chuckle slips from my throat, and I nod. "Noted, and I don't mind. I enjoy spending time with them."

Journey shifts Tulip and kisses her head. "I know you do. They love living beside you. Dylan told me they come and go whenever they want."

Satisfaction fills me knowing they talk about me to my family. "They do. Although the first few times they did it, they scared the shit out of Winter, and she yelled at me for being too neighborly."

"That sounds like her."

"Hey, I need your help tomorrow. Briggs might kill us, but you'd be doing me a solid."

Ny gives me a sly sideways grin, as if she already knows what I'm thinking.

"Let me handle Briggs. Does this have to do with a specific event happening?"

"Yup."

"Yes, I can't see what the plan is, and it's about time."

Before I can ask her anything else, we hear the bell ring, meaning Dyl and Dan will fly out that door with Ox, Lux, and Harley any minute.

As if on cue, the little group rushes out together. Dyl and Dan's faces light up when they see me.

"Baylor," they say in unison. They damn near tackle me to the ground when they hug me, making me laugh and steady myself.

"We made these for you in class."

I watch as they both pull out cards they drew for me, with cute pictures and "Best friends" written on them.

"These are awesome. Thank you both. I have a big day planned for us."

"Yes, I love hanging out with you," Dyl says.

"Me too. I enjoy hanging out with Mom, too, but we get to do more manly things with you," Dan says seriously.

My gaze meets Ny's, and we both hold in our laughter at his brief comment.

"I'm glad you enjoy it. Say bye to Aunt Ny, and we'll go."

Both kids run over and hug her, while the other three hug me. They each walk beside me back to my car.

With them buckled in, I start the ignition and drive to the Fun Barn for pizza, arcade games, and a movie, if Winter says it's okay.

"Bay, can we stay overnight with you and play video games?" Dan asks.

When I look in the rearview mirror, I see him watching me with enormous eyes.

"Our dad never played games with us. He stole them," Daniel says. It tugs at my heartstrings to hear that.

The mere mention of the man always starts a raging fire inside. Their father is no man. He chose a harsh life over his family. Winter tried to get him help, but he never stuck with it. Instead, he took off six years ago, leaving them and only reappearing on rare occasions to ask Winter for money.

Then last year, he resurfaced and stole everything she'd worked for. To make it worse, he got her fired from her job. She had virtually nothing left. Had it not been for her friendship with Ny, she would have faced homelessness. What kind of man could allow that to happen to his kids?

The tension in my hand from gripping the steering wheel pulls me from my thoughts. I need to stop thinking about it. I take a calming breath and loosen my grip on the wheel.

"We'll ask your mom, but tomorrow you have school, so no staying up until midnight," I tell them.

That answer satisfies them. I'm pretty sure they would move in with me if they could. I get it. They crave a father figure. Winter is fantastic, but sometimes you need your father. I remember times growing up when I needed my dad. Mom would try, but it wasn't the same. Not everyone is as fortunate as my brothers and I were to have both our parents.

I shouldn't say this, but I'm glad their father will be in prison for at least ten years. That means he can't hurt them anymore while they are still young and impressionable.

I swear, sometimes it feels like I share parenting with Winter.

After parking outside, the kids and I got out and walked into the place. I prefer to come just after school lets out, so there are fewer people and shorter lines for the games.

We ordered our pizza and sat at the table. "How's school going?" I ask.

"Good. I want to play soccer next year," Daniel says, sipping his drink.

"I don't know if I want to fight with Uncle Sul more or play football next year. Uncle Sul said I should try football, then pick the one I like best," Dylan says.

"I don't enjoy fighting, but I like soccer, and my gym teacher says I'm good at it."

"I played soccer in school. I could help Daniel and Baxter play football. If you want help, Dylan," I tell them both.

"That would be awesome," Dyl answers, then leans back when the pizza comes out.

The conversation halts while we eat and play games. The boys don't want to watch a movie because they want to play video games at home, and who am I to argue with 11-year-olds?